More praise for Frederick Busch and *Closing Arguments*

"There is something in this book, in its formal organization of the human relationships and the glimpse of a terrible truth in a jungle, that suggests the work of Joseph Conrad. A more powerful comparison, in terms of the plumbing of the depths of familial transgression and the appalling revisiting of the past upon the present, might be with William Faulkner."

—PATRICK MCGRATH
The New York Times Book Review

"Brilliant . . . A book written at a pitch very close to a scream, which manages, like most works of fiction that are also works of art, to be more than one thing: First, of course, it is a highly sophisticated exploration of character; but it is also a can't-put-it-down murder mystery and courtroom drama; it contains strong elements of domestic tragedy and of social history, and it delivers a shocking portrayal of the lineaments of evil . . . Charged with huge moral and psychological outrage, crafted in subtle yet nervous, evocative prose, it is an astonishing, an audacious performance. . . . A brutal parable about truth, a vision of what lies really cost us. In an age of the big lie, that is brave, wonderful writing indeed."

—RICHARD BAUSCH
The Boston Sunday Globe

"*Closing Arguments* is both a taut courtroom drama and a disturbing examination of the physical and emotional damage that people inflict on others in the name of love. . . . A powerful novel of deceit and betrayal with images as haunting as any of Marcus Brennan's nightmares."

—DON O'BRIANT
The Atlanta Journal & Constitution

"Superbly drawn drama . . . The novel succeeds brilliantly. Busch's prose, as addictive as Estella's embrace, leaves us enthralled, frightened and emotionally spent."

—DAN CRYER
New York Newsday

"Reminiscent of both *Fatal Attraction* and *Presumed Innocent*. . . . Thoroughly gripping . . . Busch's finest novel."

—W. P. KINSELLA
The Vancouver Sun

CLOSING ARGUMENTS

BY FREDERICK BUSCH

FICTION

Don't Tell Anyone • 2000
The Night Inspector • 1999
Girls • 1997
The Children in the Woods • 1994
Long Way from Home • 1993
Closing Arguments • 1991
Harry and Catherine • 1990
War Babies • 1989
Absent Friends • 1989
Sometimes I Live in the Country • 1986
Too Late American Boyhood Blues • 1984
Invisible Mending • 1984
Take This Man • 1981
Rounds • 1979
Hardwater Country • 1979
The Mutual Friend • 1978
Domestic Particulars • 1976
Manual Labor • 1974
Breathing Trouble • 1973
I Wanted a Year Without Fall • 1971

NONFICTION

Letters to a Fiction Writer • 1999
A Dangerous Profession • 1998
When People Publish • 1986
Hawkes • 1973

CLOSING ARGUMENTS

FREDERICK
BUSCH

Ballantine Books • New York

A Ballantine Book
Published by The Ballantine Publishing Group

First published by Ticknor & Fields, Houghton Mifflin Company.
Reprinted by permission of Ticknor & Fields, Houghton Mifflin Company.

www.ballantinebooks.com

Library of Congress Catalog Card Number: 92-90479

ISBN 0-449-90750-3

Manufactured in the United States of America

First Ballantine Books Trade Edition: February 1993

10 9 8 7 6 5 4

To Elaine Markson
and Geri Thoma
with gratitude
and love

For instruction on legal matters I turned gratefully to Edward S. Nelson, Attorney-at-Law, and my brother, Eric Busch, who counsels me on the law and much more. Perversions of jurisprudence, corruptions of statute, and distortions of proper advocacy are mine alone; what's true about the practice of the law is theirs. There is no county seat in New York State called Randall. The courtroom I describe is in another city, and the people in this novel do not live there. They are fictive characters, inhabitants of the imagination, and not of any other place.

CLOSING ARGUMENTS

Opening Argument

Let's say I'm telling you the story of the upstate lawyer, the post-traumatic combat stress, the splendid wife, their solitudes and infidelities, their children, his client with her awkward affinities, the sense of impending recognition by which he is haunted.

You can see me, can't you? You can see me in my office after hours, after dark, after dawn. The bottle of ink, the sharp-nibbed pen, the pad of yellow sheets with their line after line.

Stand and be recognized a sentry was supposed to call to anyone dragging in after dark. Maybe they'd be on the end of a long-range recon. Maybe they'd be sappers with mines. The perimeter people at Da Nang were Marines, and they were disciplined. They almost always shouted something before they tried to kill you: the best defense is a good story.

Haunted is the word to use, though. His story's about his wife, Rochelle, her need to publicly acknowledge his war, the recognition he will suffer if she does, and how she'll suffer worse. The threat to him is real. The deception is real. This is a very cruel story, you know.

If one word is *haunted*, another is *sad.* Use it for his wife and kids. And *betrayed*, because the innocent can never be protected.

And numerous other words that in the course of this testimony you will be asked to consider.

Family

IT WAS February, very cold, lots of snow. It warmed up during the day and rained, then it froze again: glass on top of slush. I slid my way home, it was ten or eleven, and in the kitchen I found Rochelle sitting over a cup of coffee the way people huddle at a fireplace. Jack was leaning back in his chair, sitting across from her, tilting so far back you knew he had to fall. Those big feet were planted in their unlaced moccasins, his socks were pooled beneath his ankle bones at the tops of the shoes. His face was tight. *Tight.* Schelle's was wet with tears. I didn't need filling in. I knew it. He'd been orbiting further and further. She'd been handling the distance. That's what we tell each other. Handle it, we say. Which means you don't take it personally that your kid is insulting you and pushing you and standing in your eyes. Because he needs you taking it personally so he can pop off.

I sat down in my coat. I waited in the silence a little.

"Hello, Dad," I said. "Have a long day?"

"Yeah, Jack," I answered myself. "Pretty tough. But I'm glad to see you, kid."

"Me, too, Dad," I said.

"Don't," she said. "Really. Don't."

"Can I do *some*thing?"

Schelle said, "Jack? Can you think of anything?"

His large, wet, very dark eyes looked over my shoulder at nothing. I said, "Mom spoke to you, Jack."

With no expression, he said, "I didn't hear the question."

"I think we're trying to find out why you're angry. Am I right, Schelle?"

She nodded, reluctantly. I knew how much she wanted me out of this one.

"I can't remember," Jack said.

"Is it about something Mom or I did?"

Rochelle said, "We've pretty much been through this, Mark."

"You could answer me," I said. I was gentle.

"Excuse me?" Jack said.

"Why are you being so evasive, hon?"

"Me?" he said.

"Yes," I said gently.

"What was the question?"

"Are you on drugs?"

"That's a new question," he said.

"Are you?"

Schelle said, "Mark."

"I don't *think* so," Jack said with exaggerated care.

When he was younger, we'd been through one like this, we were homing on the end of it, and he said something mean, what a parent calls "fresh" before he clips the kid. We were standing up, I remember. Upstairs in the hall, I think. I put a four-finger jab, the hand rigid and fingers locked, directly into his solar plexus. He started to double, and I said, Stand up. I remembered that at the table, trying to get him to talk. Stand up, I remembered saying. I must have said it right. Because he stood. He kept wanting to collapse. His face was very white. His eyes got huge. He wobbled. I told him, The breath'll come back. You won't die of it. You'll get your wind back. You stand and mind your manners, I told him.

I was thinking of that while we sat at the table. My face must have showed it. I must have showed whatever I felt. I thought I regretted what happened. I think my face showed something else. Because Schelle said, "Mark."

She said it the way I would tell a dog to heel if I had a dog and trained it.

"Mark."

I said, "Jack." I sounded gentle. "Jack, it doesn't feel like we're functioning here. You know what I mean?"

He looked at me.

"I think you do," I said. "You're a troubled boy. You maybe need some help. Mom and I are willing to find it for you."

"I'm not going to a skull doctor," he said.

"Psychiatrist. Psychologist. Some kind of professional person who can help you," Schelle said.

"I'm—listen to me: I am not going."

Schelle said, "Darling, we don't think you're, you know, crazy. It isn't anything to do with words like that. It's for *help*. It's what you do with a, say an infection. We don't think you're *crazy*."

"No," I said. "Good."

Jack said, "She was talking to *me*."

I said, "What?"

Rochelle said, "Are you all right, Mark?"

I said, "What?"

"Yeah," Jack said. "Oh, *yeah*."

Problem Solving

IT FEELS GOOD. It feels right. My radar intercept officer in back hears me howling when we go in. He calls the numbers off, we let the 500s go, and then we're supposed to orbit, wait for the wing leader, go home to Da Nang. But I came in hard on my wing leader's approach. A little close, but still in the classical mode. Maybe I cut it a little steep. I come in, Bird Dog the spotter is asking if I'm hit, my wing man's heading back up toward 4,000 and he's asking, Who's hit?, and I'm howling. Six

Phantoms in the squadron had the external pod with the 20 mm gun, they even had ammo that week, and I was in one of them. What I'm saying: it's 1968, I'm a Marine Phantom pilot, I'm strafing a flak installation and it feels good. Turn the selector, look through the display, punch the tit. The ground jumps up around them, then they jump up. They explode, frankly, and sometimes you get to see. That's why I was noisy going in and up and out, and everybody's checking off, checking in, checking up, I level us off at 4,500, stable, and I say, "Goblin on an even keel. Goblin is silky, flight leader."

"Tuck your ass in here and come home," Baseball says.

"Roger from Goblin. Tucking in, heading home. Fuel is not an issue. I have you, Baseball. Here I come."

"Baseball is overjoyed."

But nobody chewed me. I killed some, and that was the job. We interdicted the Ho Chi Minh Trail. We flew out of Da Nang, and every now and again when we went out to bomb the berry people, we blew some up with cannon shells. Now here's what I'm saying: you're up there and I mean *homing* on them, running right down your own tracers and you're God, you are winged fucking fury, they explode for you like popcorn.

Of course, I'm a reasonable man now, a sane and reasonable man. I sit at a desk that used to belong to a banker. We bought his whole houseful of antiques when I opened the office in what used to be his very Colonial home. I sit at this desk with a top, it rolls down, all these little drawers and compartments are opened out in front of me. This is organized. I write up my notes on the usual legal pad, black ink, yellow paper, green lines, red-ruled margins.

Bomb runs were good. Shooting off the Sparrows was good—take out a prop job the NVA flew, watch those guys break up. The sky looks yellow and green by the time they're down, it's time to go home and debrief, talk the talk. On the way home, the yellow's out of the sky. It has to do with burning aviation fuel, someone told me. So that was good. The napalm runs were good. We had to mix the stuff ourselves, the first few months we were there. Bad-looking stuff, but it did stick to them. It did fry them. So it was good work, and the main thing is: we got to fly. Am I right? We were flying. There's the slipstream noise coming off the bomb pylons and the gun pod and the radar sticking out of the McDonnell Douglas F-4 Phantom, and this was before they rigged the slats on the outer wing, so there's a bit of stick play going on, but nobody's complaining because in the middle of the roar there is a trimmed aircraft and a very well-adjusted, well-trained airplane pilot, and once in a while I got to ride down howling and make popcorn out of people.

Pop pop pop.

If you have a problem, I've always found, you can solve it with a lined yellow legal pad and a good extra-fine point. Draw it up, write it down, lay it out. You work your way in, steady, steady, and you see it. After a while you see it. Tallyho. You say it really low and slow, because you're a Phantom jock, and yours is bigger than theirs. Goblin has the target. He does.

Footwear

YOU WANT it new and improved? Goblin offers sneakers, for example. But we approach the issue of the foot by way of, well, what you'd get, sometimes: a rat. You were pretty sure his head would pop partway out of your asshole and swivel around. If the rat takes a look and goes back in, forget about an early springtime. If the rat has no hair, sailor beware. If there's a bald rat chewing out your chest from the inside, popping out between your nipples, then you got a lifetime of less than wonderful luck looking up when you look down. That never happened to me. But I considered how it might. While I was strong enough, and they were letting us use the latrine they made us build, the log on a ditch they told us they might bury us in, I did consider what might climb up and into me.

Also, I thought their shoes would be made of tires from some leftover Renault the French once used. But they were Keds. Old-time, high-cut sneakers. They'd kick your ass around with them, and then they'd line up and piss on you. They would laugh. All I saw was piss like rain, and these all-American canvas shoes on foreign feet. The weather was body temperature, I can tell you.

Which makes it tough. Your kids grow up, and you try and tell them. But how can you *tell* them why you will not buy them sneakers? Isn't that half of what a daddy does? This daddy doesn't. This daddy can't.

Not Adidas, New Balance, Endicott Johnson Chucky Taylors, Converse with the Velcro strap. So Mickey, my daughter, who is twenty and lives at the other end of the state, in New York City, used to wear loafers, like the kids in the Archie comics. Good girl, Mickey, I want to tell her. She doesn't want to hear it from me. Jack has to wear four different kinds of sneakers because he's a high school jock. Schelle has to buy them, though, along with extra laces. Jack is complaining that somebody took out five long laces from his smelly lost sizes of sneaker. Why would someone need laces? Answer: to tie things with. "I can't do it, Schelle," I tell her. But she knows, of course. She doesn't know exactly *what* she knows anymore, I think. But she knows. She deals with it. She is a very good woman, and I wish I could have brought home something better for her than a shot-up Phantom pilot with a Navy Cross and carnivorous dreams.

Dr. Micah told her. I was there. It was necessary, she said, for us to see him together. He said, "Old times, they called it shock. Modern days, they said it was battle fatigue, nervous breakdown, if you will. New, improved times: post-traumatic stress syndrome."

So Schelle knows its name.

She spent her last teenage years doing what the other college kids were doing: fighting me. Well, fighting the war. Signing petitions. Marching and getting arrested. Jailbait jailbait is what she was. She ends up marrying me. Marrying *me.*

I have a wife who has worked for three years toward a commemoration of the heroes of the Vietnam War. In our county seat an enormous boulder will be set in the square outside the county courthouse. On a vast polished facing of stone, they will engrave the names of local men who died in the Vietnam War. And I, the lawyer with three-piece suits and European neckties, will stand at the microphone and tell them some stories about the war. She will have arranged it. Schelle. In a world like this, in a world like *this,* she has worked to celebrate her husband back to health.

To call it irony is to understate the sadness. And no one tells her.

Least of all I.

All Warfare Is Based on Deception

SUN TZU, *The Art of War,* number seventeen of his Estimates. The eighteenth I wear on my soul, it's engraved. Goblin reports number eighteen on his soul, as those who have watched his courtroom dogfights will tell you. When the plaintiff's attorney expects an attack, Goblin executes a rapid roll in the opposite direction to his turn. Putting Goblin tight in *behind* him, he then gets to choose: 20 mm into the cockpit, or the very satisfying Sidewinder missile up the tailpipe. Number eighteen: "Therefore, when capable, feign incapacity; when active, inactivity."

Do you love it?

Holding the legal pad up in the air, nice big man in a vested suit, reading notes, saying *writ* and *affidavit, precedent* and *petitioner*, humbly addressing the court. As now: scribbles and scribbles, ink and paper, Your Honor, my honor.

Then I shoot.

So here I am, the small-town upstate New York lawyer, graduate of Binghamton and Columbia, the handsome income, the office shining with refinished antiques in the big Colonial house. It's on Main Street, of course. One block before it crosses, what else, Broad. It's late at night. I am sitting over the legal pad and writing representations. "When near," Sun Tzu instructs, "make it appear that you are far away; when far away, that you are near."

The Cong were the Minh. They studied the Red Chinese. Ho learned from Mao. Though what Ho mostly wanted, Phan Tuy taught me in the camp, was Vietnam running Vietnam, not Frenchified Catholic fascists. Well, sure. But that's what he said. It's some of what I had to recite. Mao to Ho, the hip bone connected to the tarsal bone. Tarsal bone connected to the finger bone. Finger bone connected to the pen.

You feel like all your bones are broken. The primary ejection handle is built right into the top of the seat. You force yourself straight back, then you pull. If that doesn't work, go for the secondary handle, down on the seat, between the legs. But you better sit back once you yank. Because we're talking about terrible g's. The drogue line comes out if you paid your dues up, then the main chute, and that's what takes you up out of the seat you ejected in. You have the seat box with you, and that contains your useless equipment.

It was a part of the story Jack wanted to hear but I didn't tell him. Did you have a gun with you, Daddy? And I would say, Another time, all right? So Ho studied Mao, Mao studied Sun Tzu, and Marcus Brennan, Esq., Attorney-at-Law—Mark to his deceived family, betrayed friends, and benighted clients—is setting down on his monument of inky legal paper what he learned from his elders. I write, "Now, there are five sorts of secret agents to be employed. These are native, inside, doubled, expendable, and living." Sun Tzu to Ho, Ho to me, me to Schelle and the kids and the country.

Every night I collect my pages in a black spring binder that sits on the trestle table behind my desk chair. That's where I also place briefs and applications, documents, lies, mail, paperweight rocks that Schelle collected on trips. My binder sits there, and anyone can see it, black and thick. It looks like one more set of words. I have just now recited into it, I tilt back very wearily. This brain is another country. This brain is a state of siege, a psycho-geographical joke. I am writing in the office late at night.

The Judgment of Conviction Is Reversed, and a New Trial Ordered

I'M STUDYING *People v. Hart.* The judge did not instruct the jury as to what would constitute a partnership. I intend to appeal a case, for a beef farmer in the county, which I've lost. The loss will be sustained, and I know it. But I hate to lose, and so does my client. I'm contemplating the nature of partnerships. I begin to think not of beef cows or bull semen, not of misappropriation of a partnership's funds, but of Schelle. She used to stick her hand out and wait for me to offer mine, then grasp it, hard, and look me in the eye as kids were taught, once, to do when shaking hands, and she'd say, "Put it there, pardner," because that was a favorite line from a John Wayne western.

"How can you love the Duke," I'd asked her in the seventies when she hated the war that Wayne made news by loving, "and despise the generals who run the war? Wayne would *be* one of them if he could."

"Because he was always such a beautiful boy," she said. We were sitting on a bed in the Maui Hilton on the second day of my leave. We were holding hands. I have to say, it was pretty much all I could do. We used to call it Soft Stick. I let her kiss me and stroke me and rub my back. She let me talk. Later, she said I sounded overdosed on adrenaline. "You remember," she asked me, "what he looked like in *The Man Who Shot Liberty Valance*? That big, sad, beautiful boy just becoming a slightly middle-aged man? And puzzled by it?" Yeah. Yeah. Poor Duke.

This is not correct, though. It was the Hotel Syracuse. It was the Bar Association dinner in Syracuse, New York. Obviously, it couldn't have been in Hawaii. I've never *been* to Hawaii. When near, far away, when far away, et cetera.

In a Phantom you are far away, and then your radar intercept officer talks about a vector on the intruder, he's telling you the knots, and then you're *there,* on him, far and then near and then *wham,* the gunsight image on the glare shield sliding onto him, then you lock. You are the weapon. The weapon is armed.

Ruthie, my secretary: "Mr. Brennan, your wife called, and Mr. Moldauer called again to ask if we're closing on his property."

"And you said—"

"To your wife?"

"All right."

"I told her I'd tell you."

"And Moldauer."

"I didn't shout the way *you* would have."

"You never do. That's why I keep you here."

"I said we still haven't got the papers from the seller's attorney, and we can't close without a title search and survey."

"You are not fired. Would you get my wife, please?"

"She didn't leave a number, Mr. Brennan."

"And she isn't at work?"

"It didn't sound like it, the noise didn't sound like her office noise."

"What'd it sound like, Ruthie?"

"A restaurant? A mall?"

"Someplace public. Well, public's better than private, Ruthie. Public's better than pubic."

"Yes, Mr. Brennan."

"I expect she'll call me back."

"Yes, sir."

"Yes."

A nice little country practice, with the living room of an old house for a waiting room. Cherry stands to hold the ashtrays and magazines, narrow settles of waxed and polished pine for the clients to sit on, a varnished antique map of the county on the wall, everything bright and old and brought back. Restored. Like me. Restored. Like order, like the law. Law's the history of decisions. How we interpret history gives us right behavior. The only cheap thing in the waiting room is the rug because the farmers sit there with cow shit on their boots. The room always smells of tobacco and manure. Sometimes a handsome woman or a pretty girl, little children, will sit there, dressed clean and neat, sometimes even stylishly. But they smell to me like barn. Even the school board members. Everyone's got a little shit on their shoes.

And Ruthie and the girls in what used to be the kitchen, the clickety of word processors, and the bang of the electric typewriters we occasionally use. File drawers trundling back and forth, high heels, the click of cigarette lighters, the clearing of throats. It's a little like a doctor's office, strangers waiting next to each other, mostly in silence, to come inside and be naked to me.

Schelle, are you calling me from some hotel? Who are you with, Schelle?

When you see the trees move, Sun Tzu instructs us, the enemy is advancing.

Requisite Denials Checklist

THE PRACTICE is good, my health is almost fine. I almost achieve good health by almost never consulting a doctor about it. Schelle, who got pudgy once, got slim, now moves with confidence again. She's very attractive. We're a good-looking, youthfully middle-aged couple with two bright kids. Schelle and Mickey talk a lot. Jack and Schelle and Mickey talk a lot. I am not a perfect father, but you wouldn't call me out of touch. Hell, I still haul half a *war* in here. I'm pointing at my head. Not drafting a brief tonight the way I said I would. Not researching it in my little law library with its round oak table. I'm at my desk, sitting in the yellow light, inking up the yellow paper. Telling my life it is on the glide slope, sighted by the tower, and cleared to land.

This is Goblin.

This is Goblin calling.

"Mark?"

"Hi, Schelle. You all right?"

"Me? Terrific. Listen: are you, were you going to come home for dinner?"

"Are you waiting there to eat it with me?"

"I can't. That's why I've been calling. You got my messages?"

"Got your messages, Schelle."

"Good. Listen: we found out the state's coming down on us again next month. They didn't like some of what they saw, and I can't imagine why. *Lots* of hospitals have chiropractors running their outpatient clinic."

"You'll be assistant administrator of a non-certified hospital if you guys don't clean it up."

"Would you be good enough to find me some nurses? Some doctors? A few thousand extra *patients*?"

"You should have stuck to nursing, Schelle."

"I should have skipped growing up."

"So where did you say you were this morning?"

The usual pause at this point, me smiling through it.

"Did you ask me?"

"Just now. Yes. I did."

"Why?"

"But why not?"

"Mark, there is no reason why not. Just as there isn't a reason why you should."

"So you're telling me there are no reasons, and you were in no places. Am I right?"

"You're cross-examining me."

Goblin to Rochelle. "Ruthie just remarked that it didn't sound like your office in the background. I don't mean to be sinister. Am I sinister, Schelle?"

"Yes."

"Well, I don't mean to be. You're working late?"

"Just like you. Yes. I already talked to Jack, he's fine, he knows what's going on."

"Oh, does he."

"*That* is sinister," she said.

"Goblin confirms," I told her. Guess who hung up first.

High-Altitude Maneuvers

SEE HER. See her writing to Washington, to Albany, the county seat, the civic groups in Syracuse, Utica, Norwich, Wampsville, Oneida, Rome. Listen to her on the telephone, see her in the Wood Duck Restaurant on Saturday mornings, visiting tables in the steakhouses on Friday nights. She campaigned until the county administrator agreed to raise the money, reserve the morning, and celebrate the installation of the stone. This was a woman fearful for her husband's health. This was a loyal person shaping loyalty to deeds. This was the woman who had made love to me in the shower of the Hotel Syracuse when I was all but impotent with not knowing how to grieve when my mother died, the night I spoke to the convention of the Bar. See her eyes, light blue on pale skin, shadowed by the frame of her nearly black, long hair. See her broad mouth, curving nose, the almost ferocious bright glare that her face radiates unless she is pitying or sexually aroused. It is noble then. There is no other word to use for her at those moments. Say again: noble.

The higher you fly and turn, the more fuel you use up.

I'm using up my time. Not my time to write on yellow pads and thicken the black spring binder, but my time to calculate how to stand before the people, and the honor guard the state will send, the members of the VFW, American Legion, Boy Scouts, Cub Scouts, Future Farmers of America, the whole of the varsity football team. Schelle has waited through twenty years of our life. And she started this movement toward all that she could give. She offers me what of the nation, state, county, village, and town that she can. She'll commemorate a war she hated and worked to halt. She'll give me what's left of her love and the country's. She will tell me their thanks. She will ask me to at last be well. She will ask me to at last be home.

The day of her gift is the name of my deadline. She counts on the day, but I count down to it. I'm fairly certain I won't be there.

Schelle Lies Sleeping

I USUALLY walk to work. That way, they see the confident stride, the high head, the friendly face of their local lawyer. I'm an advertisement for me. Usually, I leave the house with just a cup of coffee in me. Stop at the Quick-Serve for the local papers, a cup to go, sweet roll, et cetera. I'm first in the office. Turn on the lights, jack the air conditioner up if it's hot, ditto the furnace if cold. I walk around. I look at everyone's desk. They know I will. That's why I do it. Not to touch things. Not even to inspect. Just to see what's mine, and keep on walking, back to my office and my chair. Where I sit now, there's the dark room, the drawn drapes, the pool of bright light on the desk. Light in the darkness. A kind of clear space. And I see in the papers what high school kids have scored basketball points, who's dead in case I represent the estate. Though you are called if not summoned when they die. When people die, you know it. Still, I read down the names of the dead. It's like checking through the box scores of the out-of-town games. Then on to the traffic citations, and then the bad news about school board decisions, taxation, what the bozos in Albany have decided to do to my clients and me. Papers from Albany and New York, local towns, nearby little cities, and scalding coffee, generic Danish to soothe my mouth. Ruthie comes in, and then one of the women. MerriLee, always on time. Lou comes later. She drops her kid off at a sitter's out of town. The phones are ringing, the women are typing, Ruthie is in with messages and problems. Here comes the day. Dead people, divorced people, people acquiring, people headed for loss. I'm the driver. I get them there. I don't lift the binder, I don't look at it. Papers get stacked on top of it sometimes. Diet soda got spilled on it once. That's fine. That's life. This is business in the daytime. Schelle lies sleeping when I leave. She likes to get to work a little later, and she needs her rest. When we were very young we would wake up near dawn in the same bed. We would go downstairs and brew coffee and whisper. We stole the hour before the children wakened. We made lists of chores. We talked about that night's dinner. We told each other who we were.

Stew

HOME late at night, and it's Schelle on our telephone, talking to someone far away. I can tell. She shouts a little, because she's thinking of distances. She stands in the long hallway, and I sit in the kitchen, eating leftover steak off the bone. I'm scraping down on cold gristle, Schelle is calling out, "So, yes. This creep takes her up on the roof and, well, he throws her off. Down onto the ground. *That's* why I asked you to be careful."

Mickey, in New York. The brave, wayward daughter who works by modeling shoes. Mickey is famous from the ankle down. She studies acting. We pay, she goes to class. She lives in a reconditioned slum, we do the worrying. Sometimes on weekends she works for a caterer. They do large parties on Long Island and in Westchester. Honor student in high school, national honor society, two years at Skidmore. This qualifies her to carry trays of cream cheese and pickles wrapped in Italian ham stuck on toothpicks.

Schelle sings the next stanza. "How can I say this without

being disgusting, Mick? This monster person cut a girl up and kept her in the basement of the apartment house. In the hot water boiler! Oh, Mickey."

I say, "The special today is stew, folks."

Once in the officers' mess at Da Nang they served Irish stew. A captain named Gullickson knew it was monkey. He walked around to everybody's table with this little brown hard furry thing. In that light, if you're already alerted to monkeyhood, you can maybe think it's a cooked, wet monkey finger. Toe, maybe. Everybody's gagging or pretending to. Gullickson is just back from dunking off Quang Tri, he's drunk enough to say "monkey," but maybe not his own last name. Stuart, who flew wing with me a couple of times, starts complaining because he wants monkey, too. A commander stands up and walks out. Does one of those shooting-you-a-sharp-glance numbers. Gullickson by then is on the floor with his shoe and sock off, trying to compare his toe to the monkey's.

One time, a congressman joined us. He was ex-Navy who didn't fly, didn't sail, almost didn't walk. He talked, was what he did. Ate in the mess because he wanted to see some gyrenes. Marines were big in the papers that month. He said it: gyrenes. Nobody suggested he hitch himself a ride to, say, Khe Sanh. They had Marines there. They had Marines, Seabees, Special Forces guys, all kinds of dead men. That was the night a C-141 Starlifter came in too low. Just a case of tired pilot, maybe tired plane. It happened. He smeared them a couple of hundred yards across the new runway. Somebody came in and told us. Congressman said, "Oh, dear." He cried. Sat there at the table and cried. They kept him in a colonel's tent overnight. Let him go home, talking about terrible carnage but we've made a commitment to the brave et cetera.

Schelle to Mickey: "Are you thinking of a weekend home, sweetheart?"

Then: "Okay. You know, the same. Uh-huh."

Then: "Sure. We'll talk about it. Sure."

So back to the office, right? Just forgot something, don't worry, right back. Because of her face, coming into the kitchen and looking at me. She figuring I'd listened. Knowing I knew Mickey wouldn't come home because I'm—what would you say, *troubled?* Kids don't come when you're troubled. If you don't go to them when *they're* troubled, it's child abuse. Child *neglect,* if you sue on behalf of the kid. Schelle comes in, she's wearing a bathrobe with flowers on it that I don't remember. Long, white, shiny pajamas. Her hair is back in a ponytail. Her eyes are pretty sad.

"I'm still the magnet I used to be, huh, Schelle?"

She sits. She sighs. She tucks one leg under her and sticks the other out, under the table. It's the kind of table you expect to find in a garden or someplace, heavy white metal, shiny black top. I'm always surprised it looks good in the big kitchen with all its white wainscoting and cabinets. That's Schelle. Give her a giant Victorian house plus an auction at a local greenhouse plus a few thousand bucks and there we are, sitting in the kitchen with nothing to say about our daughter and us.

"You all right?" she asks me.

"Great. Yeah. Listen, I left something in the office. I'll walk back over. I'll be home in, you know, ten, fifteen minutes."

She says, "I'll see you in the morning, then."

"You're getting up early tomorrow?"

"Oh," she says, "I forgot." She smiles a little smile. "I'll—I don't know. I'll see you tomorrow night."

I get up and I kiss her on the forehead. She holds on to my vest and pulls, and I go along and she kisses me on the mouth.

"Good night," she says. She's in the hall, heading for the stairs when she calls back, "You can leave the bone here, unless you're really attached to it."

I look down at the steak bone in my hand. After I toss it and wipe my fingers on a dish towel, I walk to the front door and out. I'm whistling, what else, that the tarsal bone's connected to the steak bone, now hear the words of the Lord.

Goblin to Lord.

General, Basic, Average, Everyday Life

RUTHIE was just about running, we got so busy. She wiped her forehead and said, "I may need *gym* shoes, Mr. Brennan."

"Don't take it out of petty cash."

"Oh, I wouldn't," she said.

I didn't look at her. Which made her go away. I swiveled completely around so the desk was behind me. I was looking over the stacking table and out the big window. Half past two, and there goes Jack. Big kid, swaggers a little, walks on his toes the way a lot of athletes do. Maybe somebody would have smiled if they saw their kid mooch by after school. But Jack was supposed to be in the math room, getting help.

"Schelle," I said into the phone when she answered, "I saw Jack outside just now."

"Yes?"

"He was going for tutoring in math, you told me. On account of an interim report of basically F? Remember?"

"I do, Mark."

"So?"

"So what?" she said.

"So there's a discrepancy, Schelle. He's one place when he's supposed to be another."

She blew a lot of air across the phone. It was supposed to sound like a sigh. It was also supposed to say, Back off. I was supposed to listen to it.

"Schelle?"

"I'll ask him."

"When?"

"Mark: what do *you* think he's doing? Is he selling drugs to grade school children? Going to the pizza joint to drop acid along with a calzone? What, Mark?"

"This pisses you off, huh, Schelle?"

"No. Why would I want you to *trust* our child?"

"It isn't that."

"No."

"It isn't," I said.

"What is it, Mark?"

"Things go wrong, Schelle. Things happen to kids. Near them. Around them. In the fucking *neighborhood* of kids, Schelle. It isn't safe."

"Mark, what isn't?"

I closed my eyes. When I opened them, I found that I was looking at the binder on the table.

"Mark?"

"General, basic, average, everyday life is what I have in mind."

"I can't talk like this," she said. She whispered it.

"No."

"I can't *live* like this."

"No." I nearly opened it, but I just put my hand flat on top of it. I felt the pebbly grain. I took my hand away and gestured at the window. "I shouldn't have pestered you with this in the middle of the day," I said.

"Oh, it isn't that. It isn't anything like that. Do you remember when we were happy, Mark? With everything except maybe Lyndon Johnson and Hubert Humphrey and Richard Nixon?"

"I liked Nixon. He always wrote on legal pads. And you're forgetting Agnew and Watergate and Mitchell and Haldeman and Ehrlichman and Liddy and the Plumbers and the CIA and the American Legion and the NRA and, yeah, I remember when you loved the world, Schelle."

"Don't try and make me laugh. You made me feel horrible and I want—"

"To be consistent," I finished.

"Mark," she said. "Please don't give up on Jack."

"I won't. I never give up."

"But on Jack."

"No."

"Promise me."

"I promise."

"And you'll figure out how to be happy with your life."

"Piece of cake," I said.

"I mean this."

"Yes. All right. I will."

"Will what?"

"You know."

"Be glad," she said. "That's what you mean?"

"I promise you. That's what I mean."

The buttons were winking on the phone. Ruthie came in to check.

Schelle said, "Why are you quiet?"

"There are calls coming in, Schelle."

"Me too."

"We better go."

"Thank you for brightening my day," she said. She put a smiling tone into her voice.

"Sorry about doing that to you. I did get scared."

"Me too. But he's *ours.*"

"All ours, Schelle."

"I'll see you tonight," she said. "We'll talk. Unless you're working?"

I said, "Bye, Schelle," and I got the receiver into the cradle on the second try. I missed because I was seeing her shoulder in our house three years ago. In the kitchen alone again, and eating something fast and cold and looking at nothing out the kitchen door. There in the hall at the telephone: Schelle in my T-shirt, a gray workout shirt much too big for her, falling off at the shoulder, almost. Some kind of baggy jeans with big pockets. Another one of her whispering low hisses on the phone. But I could hear it.

She said, "My husband was a hero. My husband was a *prisoner.* That's why!"

Jack and me, pegging a hardball the length of the yard, and we're not talking. It's the best way to be a father: you *do* stuff, you sweat together, and nobody knows what to say but that's all right for a change, because you're sweating in the same rhythms. He was thirteen, maybe. He caught it. *Pop,* it bangs into his mitt. *Catch,* and then let the hand swing back with the impact, then *swing* the left arm the other way, then *pluck* it out of the mitt with the right hand, then *let* the right swing back and cock, then *throw* and follow through and set, then *catch.* We were both of us doing that on the muddy sod of the yard in springtime. It was still cold because it was April. More snow would probably fall. But you had to get out there and peg the hardball because it was baseball season and we were kids or former kids. So there we were, and he caught it, tossed it hard, made me jump a little for it, and he said, "You never told me what kind of gun you carried, Dad."

"I don't talk about that a lot, Jack."

"Yeah. I thought maybe you would, though."

"Did you."

His face began to close.

I said, "On the airplane or on my person?"

"When you, you know. On the ground."

"Nothing. Usually nothing. We were on the base at Da Nang,

there were Marines all over the place guarding the planes. I had a Kabar knife. I also had one of those folding knives with the big blade. My radar guy carried a Swiss Army knife with about thirty-two gadgets on it. Corkscrew, everything. And I had a thirty-eight. A revolver. Hey, they even issued us a little *saw.*"

"Did you carry extra ammunition?"

"Some of the guys carried fast loaders. You could slide them into the chambers fast. I had shells on sticky tape rolled in one of my vest pockets. I couldn't hit anything fast *or* slow, I figured."

"Ever shoot it off?"

"I shot rockets. I shot a twenty-millimeter gun on the airplane." He threw it back just as hard. *Pop.* "But I never fired the pistol, no."

"Oh."

"Okay?"

Big, handsome kid with Schelle's wonderful nose. His eyes are brown, like mine. He's big, like me. But when I see him, I see Schelle's face. Mickey's got mine. Which is why she's doomed as an actress, I told her. That was the last time she kissed me, probably. Jack doesn't kiss me anymore. He hugs his mother. Sometimes he comes up behind me and hugs me. Sometimes he used to. He doesn't anymore. We don't touch now except long distance.

Ruthie said, "I've been buzzing you, Mr. Brennan, but you didn't answer. Are you all right?"

I swiveled in the chair to face exactly front. The lawyer on his guard. Alert to all the greeds and affronts requiring his advocacy.

"I was thinking," I said. "But you can put the calls through now. I'll stop."

His Compassion

FOR EXAMPLE, standing any winter in the back yard snow with a fifty-pound sack of sunflower seeds to fill the feeders. Chickadees sitting on the low limbs, unfrightened. The Northeastern Parrots, I call the bright green and yellow or soft taupe evening grosbeaks gathered in a frightened huddle in the fir across the yard. Reaching to ladle out handfuls of the stuff, jamming the feeders, seeding it across the snow of the yard, boots unlaced and suit trousers pushed inside them, a stained parka undone over the jacket and vest and tie. It's kind of moving to see a man in touch with animals like that, maybe. Maybe they'd remember that sometime and say, one of them to one of the others, "He wasn't all bad, you know. Remember him with the birds? The way he worried about them in the winter?"

The pattern of the seed across the snow, the leading motion of the dispensing hand—accurate placement. You put the little black objects where you want them, predicting in your head the way the computers and the radar predicted where the projectile, launched from a moving craft, would land. Trigonometry, nothing more. You can do it while feeding the birds.

Lists

To keep our promises.
To build.
To defend.
Not to dishonor.
Not to be unforgivably wrong.
To strengthen world order.

To strengthen world confidence in us.
To not appease the appetite of aggression.
To say, "Hitherto shalt thou come, but no farther."
Responsibility.
Defense of freedom.
To achieve independence for South Vietnam.
To do everything necessary.
To do only what is necessary.
To increase response to increased attacks.
To therefore make attacks by air.
In light of which we were equipped with
  Prophylactics
  Halazone tablets for purifying water
  Signal whistle
  Signal mirror
  Thin, strong climbing rope
  Signal flares
  Flashlight
  Maps
  Code books
  Knives
  Saw
  Emergency transmitter
  Emergency transponder
  Rice
  Fish hooks
  Fish lures
  Fishing line
  Morphine
  Krugerrands
  Matches
  Shark repellent
  Insect repellent

Sewing kit
.38
Booklet on how to survive.

Pro Bono Publico

RUTHIE SAID, "Mr. Bevelaqua from the County Bar? He says it's urgent."

"I'm in the middle of a *call*, Ruthie. Somebody in Hancock would like me to collect a three-thousand-dollar debt. Hire me some knee-breakers and let me get on with this high finance."

"Mr. Bevelaqua says—"

"It's urgent. It always is whenever he calls. Just ask him. *He's* urgent."

"Murder," she said.

"That means he wants me on a *pro bono*. Murder."

"Yes, sir."

"Get on the line, Ruthie, and tell this computer-supply mogul that Mr. Brennan doesn't do bill collecting, will you?"

"Yes, sir."

"And I'll talk to Mr. Urgent."

"Yes, sir."

"Michael," I crooned into Bevelaqua's ear. "Hey," I said.

"You'll get the call tomorrow," he said, after we'd told a few lies. "You'll get it from Jake at the D.A.'s and from the public defender's office. They just talked to me."

"And they can't find a kid out of Cornell two weeks ago to kill three months of his time for nothing to lose, defending a—what've we got, Michael? The kid raped his sister's six-month-old, and she stabbed him? Some guy blew away his wife and her tootsie roll in their trailer last night? Michael, why me?"

"Because we all take a turn. Because it's your turn."

"That's a cheap excuse for making me keep my word," I said.

"Hey," he said, "I'm a very cheap guy."

"Yes, you are," I said. "Who's the client? What'd he do?"

"She. I hear she's a tasty tidbit."

"Did I hear you say that right? Tasty tidbit? Michael."

"I'm gonna have to stoop to your level pretty soon, Mark. I hate when I do that. I have to take a shower after I get down there."

"You're a very bad man, Michael. But your wife must tell you that all the time."

He sighed at me. "I don't know the charge yet, except it isn't manslaughter and it wasn't self-defense."

"Murder?"

"I hear it's possible."

"Shit, Michael. That means somebody has some goods on your tidbit. *Four* months of work."

"It was pretty ingenious. It's your kind of deal, Mark. This is not only a tasty one. She's a *savage* tidbit."

"That sounds like an hors d'oeuvre that attacks from the toothpick. Did you and your wife ever consider having sex, Michael? It'd relax you."

"We talked about it once," he said. "Your client's in the Randall jail. Her name's Estrella."

"First or last?"

"You'll have to find out."

"She'll be all right overnight, do you think? Nobody's questioning her?"

"In *our* county, bimbos aren't broken without benefit of counsel, counselor."

"I'll go down in the morning."

"Your check's in the mail, Mark. Thank you. A grateful public thanks you. Hell, Lyndon Johnson thanked you, what do you need *me* for?"

"Thank you, Lyndon. Thank you, Michael."

"Over and out," Michael said.

Beloved by his family. Held in great affection and esteem by his colleagues and his community.

Thin-Skinned Aircraft

WE WERE on a patrol protecting the Navy. We were watchdogs. The ships were on station in the Gulf of Tonkin, off Haiphong Harbor. We were supposed to hang around in the air and keep them clean. The flight was a couple of hours plus change from Da Nang. We refueled en route, which is always a trick, with the fuel boom coming down at you, the tanker guys bitching at you, your RIO for Radar Intercept Officer at the air-to-air system talking altitudes and attitudes and speeds, and you're telling him, "I *got* it, kid, we're good, we're good." We had fuel for an hour and a half on station, a lot less, maybe 40 percent of that, in a combat mode. Nobody came.

It was on the way home. My wing man went inland over Dong Hoi. I didn't see him. I was working at staying awake. Billy, behind me, says, "Wing turning right."

There he was, bouncing a little. Turbulence, I thought. But we experienced nothing. I called him. I said, "Goblin to Anteater. Anteater."

He said nothing. He'd been in the air with us for a week. He always talked a lot. Black man from Peabody, Massachusetts, who sounded exactly like Kennedy.

"Anteater," I said, "Goblin wonders what in hell you're doing."

He slipped down fast, always going right. When he was below us, I saw the smoke.

"Yeah," I said, before Billy got hysterical. "Tallyho one

bagged aircraft, heavy smoke. Do we have chutes, Billy?" I called our base. "Old Yeller, Old Yeller, this is Goblin reporting a Mayday."

Da Nang came back fast: "Get onto Guard frequency, tell them your story, Goblin."

"Goblin roger," I said. I was trying to follow Anteater down, I was watching for flak monsters and SAMs, so was Billy. I was looking for caution lights, saw none, turned to Guard, which they monitor for distress calls.

"No chutes," Billy said.

"Goblin calling a—" All I had a chance to say.

"Flames!" Billy shouted.

I told the Guard monitors, "Shit, goddammit, he's burning. Goblin reporting a burning aircraft at—"

"No chutes!"

"Goblin."

"They blew," the kid said. Billy said, "No chutes."

I didn't talk to him anymore. I told Guard where they'd come apart. Then I was turning left and heading for water. Left, then south, then safe. I was checking for warning lights, monitoring oil pressure and temperatures. I listened to the air howl over us. "Sounding good," I told the kid. "Keep watching our ass."

"They fried, didn't they?"

"Deep-fried Marines. Roger."

Fliegerabwehrkanone. Flak. The Germans gave us the name for an aircraft defense gun, meaning a gun that shoots down aircraft. The NVA had radar-aimed antiaircraft guns with fuses preset for altitude. They didn't have to hit you with the shell. They had to stay alive and put the shells up. They'd explode. You'd drive into the explosion. Little red-hot screamers of casing spun into you. We're talking thin-skinned aircraft here, very vulnerable—hydraulics, electric lines, oil feeds, fuel feeds.

You lose your fluids, you go down. Of course, you can sustain a body hit and lose your own fluids, i.e., acids, brain sauce, bile, phlegm, blood, the sticky juices that you need to keep inside, and down you go. Lose a pod of rockets as they blow your ass out of the air. Lose a life. Two lives. No chutes, somebody says on Guard, and some people in your flight don't eat meat that night because it looks pretty much, some of them figure, like you, just as you hit.

Schelle's Face

WHAT I wonder is if she says what she says with me. She was always pretty wild in the sack back when we did that. We don't do that anymore, together. She'd whip her head back and forth, say crazy words out loud. But she was always modest beforehand. What did I know? We got married when we were kids, just about. What did I know what women wore to bed? I always expected shiny things, satiny things, and garter belts and underwear with lace and holes all over. Schelle always wore pajamas. She still does, with me, in our house. But what does she wear with the others? I keep seeing them.

But I also can't see them. I know she's in bed with a man I probably know, though there are no guarantees. I might not know him, after all. But she's in bed with him. Last night or tonight, or last week, tomorrow: Schelle is in bed with someone I am not. What I wonder is: does she put on a transparent red body stocking? A shortie nightgown and no underpants? Does she walk around the motel room hotel room storeroom at the hospital empty operating theater room in his house check one fill in others naked or in sexy clothes or in pajamas that she wears at home or with nothing on under a raincoat unbuttoned? Does she jump on him? Do they kiss romantically and tilt onto the bed and make slow love with courtesy and gravity and real affection? *Love?*

Maybe it's a vengeance fuck.

If she's gaining vengeance on me, who's *he* scoring on?

Maybe she doesn't think of me, I think.

But I see her. I look at the curve of her ass into her thigh where I always used to put my hand in bed. I see her mouth on his neck because she wants to love his flesh and drink his life. I see her mouth all over him. I hear her breathing. I see her tongue. It's like a movie closeup. I see her, I see the parts of her. I never see, no matter what I see them do, I never see Schelle's face.

The Ping-Pong Net of the Sheriff

THE sheriff's department has a large jail in Randall, which is fifteen miles southwest of Poole. Randall is the county seat, with courthouse, county office buildings, city cops, and of course the sheriff, who polices the county. Remanded prisoners, violent cases, nutcakes, and overnight arrests end up here unless the state cops take them. This was where I went for my *pro bono* murderess, who was of course innocent because she was my client. Advocacy, we call it. You do your best for your client, I do my best for mine, we dogfight in court, and whoever wins is right. Not just the winner: *right* in the eyes of the law. Don't tell *me* about might not making right. Because if I lose, I'm wrong. Try a murder, lose the case, go down on appeal, and she's in Bedford for twenty-five years. Doing the tango with ladies she might not elect for the dance, given a choice. It is about being given a choice.

We had a new sheriff, and his men had new uniforms. Cheap

uniforms. Polyester and horsehair, they looked like. And they were tight. So these big high school jocks and state police flunkouts and former city cops upcountry for the clean air and cheap land, and of course the good guys, as well as full-time bullies and all around beasts, all of them walk stiff-legged, pulling at their pants when they ride up, sticking fingers in the collars of their shirts. And everybody's looking attentive. With a new boss, you look attentive. For the guards, who were not Rhodes scholars, this meant looking somewhat like a man with dysentery. The jail was new. It looked like a cheap motel with two stories. It smelled exactly like the old jail. You'd have thought they'd transferred, molecule by molecule, the old prison's cleaning fluid, hot TV, stale bathroom, and unwashed body perfumes.

A desk man checked me in. We talked about the Jets. He said, "They win, I'm a rich man."

"They only lose," I said.

"That's why I keep not retiring. Go on in," he said.

"Bet the Jets over the Giants this weekend?"

"Yeah, and next week it's Mexico over the States."

"I'll take some of that action."

"Right, counselor. You go ahead in."

I got patted down by an Affirmative Action guard in the anteroom. She was about my suit size, but six inches shorter. She used to work as a waitress at a bar on the plastic-concession-store strip going north outside of Randall. She'd worked her way through some farmers, and through community college. She was her own new and improved model. She looked inside my briefcase, and she checked my glasses case.

"You want to look in my shoes, in case I'm smuggling in illicit socks?"

She said, "What?"

"That's all right," I said, "you keep up the good work."

I went up a flight to what they liked to call the women's wing.

They had two cells down a short corridor from the Office for County Disaster Planning. It was almost never used. In our county we did our disasters *ad hoc.* The office was in the jail, I'd been told, because there were shotguns and shells and .22s. In case of disaster, unlock cabinet, remove weapon, load, and run amok.

The monster guard brought my client in and sat us down at what looked like a dwarf Ping-Pong table, complete with two vises and the net that ran between them. It was half as long as a real Ping-Pong table might be. "Hands on the table," the guard said, "or on your lap. No touching. No transferring any object or substance across the partition."

"Okay, ma'am, if I sometimes put my finger in my ear—just the pinky, please, and kind of *scratch* now and then?"

She looked the way she used to look in the bar, I thought. She'd looked just about this perplexed and mean when she'd take your order. She said, "Fuck you."

I told my client, "The recent collapse of artificial barriers to jobs has given the work force a new confidence, as you can see."

She sat down, and then the guard left her and stood not quite close enough for us to hear her stuffy sinuses.

I said to the guard, "We've gotten off to a bad start, and this will exacerbate the problems in our relationship. Your hearing this conference would constitute an infringement of my client's interests. Furthermore, state law requires that you stand, and I quote, 'No fewer than one dozen yards'—that's thirty-six feet, ma'am? down there at the end of the hall?—'from lawyer-client conferences.' " I'd made it up. "I vow to you that we won't pass contraband across the sheriff's Ping-Pong net." I said to my client, "Do *you* so swear?"

The guard said, "Fuck you." But she moved three or four spaces back.

I looked at my client. She was small, short, and slender, very pale. Her hair was the color of what you'd get if you mixed the tones of a just-washed carrot with the dark gray of one of those wet river stones from the bottom. It was very glossy, very red-orange, her eyelashes were pale, her brows a little darker. Her face was square, verging on thin, and her long, narrow nose made it look thinner. Her eyes were very large, either brown or some kind of green-with-brown, I couldn't tell. She had stubby fingers on small hands. She kept her hands, as instructed, on the table. She had them clasped and on the edge. In her short-sleeved, collarless aquamarine polyester prison-issue house-coat, she looked bony and ill. It wasn't her best color.

"Estrella," I said. "Or is it Ms. Estrella? They weren't clear on the phone. Marcus Brennan. I am appointed by the court to represent you and to advise you. There isn't a fee, the public defender's office is picking up the tab. Well, there isn't a tab. We take turns. I'm volunteering. What I'm trying to say, don't worry about money, all right? Except: do you *have* any money?"

She smiled. It was pretty washed out. She was exhausted, and she probably hadn't slept. The smile went away. She said, "I have very little money. I'll give you what I have."

"No," I said. "I was wondering about bail. I don't know what the circumstances are yet—the charges? So I don't know if we're talking suspicion, presence at the scene, et cetera. Suspicion, and with a good record, maybe we can make bail. But you need the whole sum, or you have to give the bondsman a percentage—"

One of her little hands was in the air. I waited. She said, "I was on the scene. I called 911, the sheriff sent a car, the Randall police sent a car, the state police rolled in a little while after they did. Everybody took turns trying to arrest me first. I told them—"

I slammed the table. She jumped. The guard made adenoid

noises. "Sorry," I said. "I'm not angry at you. I was assured that your rights had been protected."

"I don't have any rights," she said. "I don't need them."

"That makes it easier," I said. "They'd prefer you not to have rights."

The guard muttered and I said to her, "Your career is on the edge, lady. Say one word, now or later, make one move on or near my client at any time, and I will see that you become the substitute German shepherd for the arson squad. You will spend your middle years on your hands and knees with your tail in the air, sniffing for flammables at building fire sites. Understand?"

I turned back to my client. She was beaming. Color came into her face, even her lips, which had been quite pale. Her eyes looked lively for an instant.

She said, "What?"

"You looked very pretty. That's what."

I watched the color drain. "Great," she said.

"Yes. Okay. I'll find out what the arresting officers said, and the scene-of-crime people. That'll mostly be state, with some stuff, maybe photography, done here. I'll make sure—they did Mirandize you, didn't they?"

"The reading-you-your-rights thing?"

I nodded.

"After a while. In the car, going back, I think."

"I'm going to leave you a pad and a pen. I want you to write down the sequence of things that happened when the police came. Everything that happened, words you remember, things they said, things you said, from the time you called the Guard frequency."

"The what?"

"Sorry. The 911."

"All right."

"I want to take a long statement from you. But just for me. I'll write it all down on another one of these yellow legal pads, okay? Just for you and me to use, nobody else."

"All right."

"But what I want you to tell me now is, did you do whatever they're going to tell me you did?"

"Yes."

"Did you want to do it?"

"Yes."

"Did you *plan* to do it?"

"I thought about it. You know, I thought once—more than once: I said to myself, I might end up killing the guy."

"Did you plan it out?"

"Are you kidding?"

"That's right. I don't know the particulars, do I? Ms. Estrella—"

"It's Estella."

"Sorry."

"Estella is my, it's my first name. My last name is Pritchett. Estella Pritchett."

I wrote it down on my legal pad.

"Who'd they say you killed?"

"A man. A person I'd been seeing."

"A lover?"

She nodded. Her face was dark again.

"Your lover's name?"

"Lawrence Ziegler."

"Larry Ziegler? You were dating Larry?"

"I was sleeping with Larry once a week. I work, I used to work, I guess, with the Department of Social Services. I live outside of Dolgeville, in the hills. I swung through here every week, seeing certain clients. I used to meet him at that horrible motel they never paint?"

"Yeah, yeah, the—the Rocky Run, the Stone's Throw. Right? Stone's Throw. God. It's a dreadful place. You used to meet him there. And?"

"We made love."

"Regularly."

"Yes."

"Now, Larry Ziegler. We're talking about the man who owns—owned—the radio station in Randall?"

"It's a terrible station, isn't it?"

"Light and Easy Bad Rock 'n' Roll of the Last Hundred Years or something. I can't listen to it. I get headaches from the DJs. They can't talk English. They don't know how to *read* it."

"Larry trained them personally."

"So how come you ended up, you know—"

"There's a question. I met him at a Rotary luncheon. I went with a marshal to serve a subpoena on the father of one of my clients. He was, he—how do I say fucking his daughter?"

"That's a reasonable facsimile right there."

"He was the usual barbarian. We served him. Larry got in his way when he went after me. After he knocked the marshal down."

"He was a big man."

"Yes, he was."

"Strong."

"Yes. What's wrong?"

"Nothing. Nothing."

"You were thinking of me and Larry. He's so, he was so tall and broad. You're not that much smaller than he is, are you?"

"But we're not in bed."

"No, we're not. We're in jail."

"Tell me."

"Excuse me?"

"Tell me what happened. We'll go over all of this, everything, later. Again. Many times. But now, tell me what you did. What he did, what you did, you know."

"You look at me—you think I'm some stupid rich man's piece of ass, the way you look at me."

"Estella. Ms. Pritchett. You're nobody's except the county's right now. You're not even your own self's self. The only judgment passed will be by the jury."

"There's a *trial*?" she said.

"My aching ass," the guard said.

I turned and I pointed at her. She backed up a step. I turned to Estella. She was smiling that same smile. It went away, the color went away, and she said, "I was feeling sorry for myself. I apologize. And I can't blame you for your opinions. Didn't I just work very hard to earn them?"

"Forget my opinions. Tell me what you did."

"And you'll try and tell a jury I *didn't*? We'll actually have a trial—"

"Go to trial, it's called."

"And you'll say to them I didn't do it?"

"Maybe," I said. "When we figure out what truth we're telling, then we'll work on how to tell somebody that particular truth."

Long Distance Lines

I WAS Schelle's reconciliation project. This isn't fair to her. But I was. By "fair," I mean just. Even accurate. She must have had so much in mind about us once, and maybe now, even. But I was the way she healed the United States of America. She joined the Vietnam wound with a pressure bandage made of her and me, then Mickey. The pilot and the peacenik. I thought we were like two gigantic drawings you see if you're up in the air over those places in Europe or Central America. The woman figure has these giant dugs and big pelvis, and she's all about all woman things. The man has a huge cock and balls, he's all maleness. You put them together and the earth is healed, nature's healed, the ground is fertile, the crops start to grow. I felt like I was up in the air looking down at us. Two big figures made out of the stuff the ground was made of. White figures on the brown-green ground. All tits and balls, everyone better, America shipshape because Miss Rochelle Courbet announces her marriage to airplane driver Brennan, ex of the Marine wing at Da Nang. I thought she thought that. I think. I see her mouth on the corner of another man's mouth, just the edge of where his lips meet, the side of his face. Can't see his face, can't see all of hers. Mouths only. Feeding on each other. Rochelle Brennan née Courbet, stepping out on her old man. Frankly, he doesn't deserve better. But it's hard, isn't it?

Isn't it.

Still, she works on her monument to him. To the dead. To the broken-up, allegedly healed, and somehow healthy United States of America. Last week a baby with a 104-degree fever is turned away from a hospital in the Bronx. The baby has AIDS, the doctor says 104 isn't that surprising, come back tomorrow. Guess where the baby gets to tomorrow? Tomorrow medicine. The new, improved medicine. Avoid all passive and inflexible methods, said Sun Tzu's student, Mao. This is Goblin, being flexible, regretting the war and what they call its "toll." This is a toll call.

"Mickey," I said. "Mickey, it's Dad."

"Oh. Daddy. Hi. Is Mom all right?"

"Mom's all right. Jack's all right. And I'm all right. Are you all right?"

"Great. Great."

"Great," I said. She and I were awful at this.

"So—what's up, Daddy?"

"I was working here in the office, and I thought I'd give you a call is all. I missed you."

"It's late, Daddy."

"Too late to call?"

"Too late to work."

"Oh, you know me. I get kind of involved in the stuff."

"And Mommy's there all alone—"

"No," I said, "she's out."

"Out?"

"I think maybe she learned it from me. You know, a bad habit, sort of. She works pretty late a lot."

"Oh."

"So tell me, Mick. What are you doing? Still flashing your feet?"

"Still. And still taking lessons. And still not getting callbacks. And still serving canapés to creeps. The same."

"And you like it."

"Love it."

"Great. Mickey."

"Yes, Daddy?"

"Would you ever come home anymore?"

"Daddy."

"Am I nagging?"

"I was home over Thanksgiving. I was home a dozen times during the summer."

"Yes. I meant to live."

"Oh. Oh, I don't want to live in Poole. I can't live in Poole. Nobody lives in Poole."

"All your high school classmates? Jack and Mom and me? The other couple of thousand taxpayers in the village of the damned."

"You know what I mean. I keep—I *choke* there. This isn't supposed to insult anybody, Daddy. I can't *breathe* at home."

"We do know how to create an atmosphere," I said. "You keep hearing, when you start raising kids they keep telling you, 'Never take it personally.' They mean when kids tell you to kiss off, when they get snappish and annoyed. You know what I mean. Never take it personally. I never could not. I never could *not* do that."

"You got insulted when I left?"

"No. Not—"

"Hurt. Your feelings were hurt?"

"Yes," I said. "I have to admit that. You cross-examining me, Mickey Brennan?"

She did me the favor of laughing like a kid who was talking to her father on the phone.

"Yeah," I said, "so everything's fine up here. And you're doing okay."

"Super, Daddy."

"Superdaddy rogers that. You need money?"

"Only in large quantities," she said.

"I sent you a little check today."

"Thanks, Daddy. I can manage, but thank you for it. I can also spend it pretty well."

"It's for something you don't need. You know? I am *not* telling you what to do with it. But I was thinking, when I was writing it, you ought to buy something you don't a hundred percent need."

"Fun," she said. "You're saying, 'Have fun.' "

"I am."

"I am, too, Daddy. Don't worry."

"Never," I said.

"Thank you for calling."

"I should get off now?"

"*No.* I meant *thank you.*"

"Thank *you*, Mickey."

"I'll talk to you, Daddy."

"You were the national reconciliation, Mick."

"Excuse me?"

"Other stuff, too. But."

"Daddy?"

Don't buy sneakers with it.

"Buy yourself something nice, all right, Mick?"

You break your foot in sneakers, the bone doesn't heal right because you didn't get enough support.

"Bye, Mickey."

"Bye, Daddy. You're okay, right?"

"Okay."

Differential

ON THE other hand, the people in the neighborhood say he's a hero. The hospital staff says the kid always had some kind of fever—"Sometimes the reasons were mysterious," a nurse said. Fever of 104, it spiked the next day to 105, kids get those. All right. Kid's born with a damaged brain, he's got AIDS, the mother's bound to be concerned. Tell her to give the antibiotics time to work and this Hispanic Bronx lady gets worried over a fever that lasts a while. It all depends on how you look at it.

Like the fellow not that far away, upstate a little and west a few, they take him in for killing eleven, twelve, thirteen hookers or drifters, some count like that. One little boy, the rest girls. Some of them small, some big, all of them not too old and not too happy, considerably dead now. "Cops Baffled," the headline reports. Roger that. "It's very difficult to get inside the head of a person like this," a police chief tells us. He liked to kill them and drop them in the river and sit above them on the bridge and eat. He was a big eater. Went into food service work after he was paroled for killing an eight-year-old girl a while back. New, improved food service.

So his mother tells Associated Press that he was "all right, just a normal boy. Then he went to Vietnam," she said. "He got sick because of the fighting they made him do," she said. He got sick, he got to be a guy in his forties, he got to killing these kids by strangling them, and then he got arrested. He did a plea on second-degree, not like my Estella Pritchett. On the other hand, she only buys it for one count if I lose; the upstate hero copped to eight.

It all depends on how you see it. It all depends on what you say. Schelle used to tell me, "I'm growing an old lady's throat."

I used to tell her, "Nah."

So what I wonder, now. When she's wherever with whoever it is, when they're there. Does she face him when she takes her clothes off. Does he unbutton her. Does he tear her stuff down her body. Or does she turn away and hide her tummy and hips and make a joke. Does she hide in the darkness and strip to be hot on the cold sheets. Does she ask him, "Do you think my stomach's—" No. She couldn't. "Do you think a woman's throat—" Negative. She'd be unfunny. She'd be breathing hard, not hiding it. She'd let him have her breasts and groin and stomach and to hell with everything. She would give them. She gives them. She does. She did. Then he went to Vietnam.

Fastball

THE AIRCRAFT just bucked. Billy's shouting about missiles on the screen. Nice spotting: all I had to do was look down the side through my canopy and watch the next two floating up. I tried to kick in the afterburner but it didn't respond. The 20 mm began to fire off. Or the rounds exploded. I wasn't shooting it. We bucked again, but this time it was a missile in the wing armament configuration shooting off on its own. I tried to turn left and get us out over the water. I figured we could take our chances with the sharks. What I didn't want was some pissed-off farmer doing a number on my nuts with a pitchfork while I'm tied up in some tree by my chute lines. Assuming the chute would open. Assume it, I said. Assume. The aircraft was very slow to turn. When I did kick it around, I did a dive. Negative. Started to. Flaps stuck. I didn't need to read the instruments, but I did. "Hydraulics are gone," I said to Billy. "Get ready, but don't trigger it yet, roger?"

He was crying. We could have used a guitar back there. The kid could really holler.

My flight leader is calling, "Goblin. You have flames a hundred feet off your ass end plus up forward."

"Repeat forward? Goblin."

"Baseball confirming forward. You just let a missile go."

"Goblin felt it. Shit. The weapons are firing off."

"Hit it, Goblin. Baseball going to Guard. Reporting your exit. Have a safe trip. I will follow you down."

"Watch the SAM fuckers down there, Baseball. Who did flak suppression for us? Goblin."

"One nearsighted pilot, Goblin. Baseball switching to Guard."

"Baseball, Goblin heading out and hoping. Billy," I said.

"Billy. I have negative control. We are riding pig iron. Time to fly without aircraft."

He made half a syllable's sound. I don't know what he was trying to say. The aircraft jumped sideways, but he must have triggered before he got hit. I heard his canopy blow. I heard the seat blow up the rails and over. The aircraft jumped again. I had no electronics. I yanked on the low grip and tried to sit back before the seventeen g's went up my spine. *Three,* I counted. I was thinking, You can hurt yourself this way. *Two. One.*

Very painful ejection. Bad slam on *One,* up and down my back. My legs went numb. I saw the seat fall away from me. I couldn't feel anything on the backs of my legs. I tried to look down and downwind for Billy. Found him. He was leaning down and over in the shrouds of the chute. No motion. Welcome to the Big Solitary, I thought. I tell them I thought that anyway. Welcome to the Big Lonesome. I went for the radio in the forward right pocket of my vest. I didn't want to be alone there. With Billy, I was alone. That was one dead kid, riding like meat on a pendulum. I couldn't make my neck work well enough to look up for Baseball. I figured he'd be there. I wanted to call him and say, "Baseball, this is Goblin. I am in the chute. My RIO looks dead. I am not, repeat not, clear of Slope Country." Instead, I fumbled with the radio. I dropped it. Goblin going in, I said to myself. Goblin reports that he is in the soup.

They look pretty, coming up. If you follow them all the way, you see the propellant flaming, you see the smoke of the exhaust. The thing is, they don't just rise to you, though they do that. They make these little shifts in flight. They rotate because of the vanes. When they're coming at you and you know it, you can see the spin. Like a batter watching the fastball come at his head. You pick up the spin. But what they do then is, they expand. They open up visually. They're all of a sudden *there.* You've been watching the fastball, staring into the cobra's face. Then: *there.*

Then Billy's dead. Then you're talking into your head. Going down too fast. Hitting too hard. Feet collapsing up through the tarsals the shins the kneecaps up the patella femur pelvis into the bowels driving them through the lung heart up into your head where everything's stuck.

You Are Here

ESTELLA PRITCHETT wrote it as a letter. I sat in the office and read the letter from a formal friend: Dear Mr. Brennan. Well, we'll get past that. We'll be informal friends. It happens, my interrogator told me, that even enemies learn each other's hearts. How, he asked, can such knowledge become less than certain friendship?

Name and rank. You forgot your serial number this time, he told me. Can it be that you secretly desire friendship already?

Just mercy. Name and rank, *number.*

When you fell from your murder plane, also there fell maps, documents, great secrets. We know everything.

You know how to read a map, you can find yourself right here? *You Are Here.* That's the secret you got.

Dear Mr. Brennan. Yes, okay, foolish love affair, loneliness, embarrassment, sure, et cetera. Major lies, I figured. Because she wasn't denying the big one. She wrote that she did it. She didn't say how. She didn't say why. Well, she lied about why. Possessive, cruelty, sadistic torments, uh-huh. She was half a step ahead of me, but not by as big a step as she thought. She was doing wife abuse without the wife. He was kicking her around, which maybe Larry Ziegler would have done, you can't ever tell. So she was defending herself. Self-defense or justifiable homicide, extenuations, maybe a woman judge, she thought, maybe a sympathetic jury. Dear Ms. Pritchett: lie to me and your ass is bare in the wind.

It certainly wasn't the first time a client tried to get away with name and rank and serial number. It wasn't the first time a client lied to me before a trial. It wasn't my first murder trial. She was, however, my first redheaded female client to lie to me in a murder proceeding. Dear Mr. Brennan. Lies in ink on yellow paper.

Monument

THIS WAS in the summertime, nearly three years ago, when I chucked the office, chucked the calls and callbacks, chucked the appointments and Ruthie and the typists, and came home at two or three. I did *not* hope to find Schelle in our bed with some squat, hairy man from the hospital. Though most of the doctors talked as if anything that forked at approximately the loins was fair game for them. And *wanted* them. Maybe so. Maybe Schelle was having one. Maybe one was having her. How do you figure the difference? But that summer afternoon, not as hot as a city, but hot enough in a town upstate, I came home because I was tired of solving other people's problems.

Schelle's car was in the driveway, the windows were up, the front storm door open to let the wind blow in through the screen door, and there was music in the house, symphonic music. She listens to it in the office, too. I sometimes hear it when we talk on the phone. Sometimes it gets loud or dramatic at just the right time, and I tell her we sound like a soap opera.

This time it was nice, not too loud, it didn't get in the way. There was pleasant music in the house. Schelle wasn't in the kitchen, which surprised me. Half of our life seems to take place in the kitchen. I read that once, that 89 percent of adult life takes place in the kitchen, especially in happy marriages.

Well.

She was upstairs, she was alone, and still in her linen suit jacket and wrinkled skirt and stockings. Her shoes were off, her shirt undone a few buttons, and she'd pushed her sleeves back. The bedroom air conditioner was on, but the light in the room was yellow with sun and it filled the air to the corners of the walls. She looked sweaty and in the middle. She looked the way busy people do when you interrupt them: they don't mind *you*, but they'd rather be doing what's before them that isn't you.

I remember that I saw the book I'd been reading in bed. It was open, face-down, on the bedside table. I'd left my light on that morning, and it was still on. My pajamas peeked out from under my pillow. I thought that I ought to put them in the hamper.

It was one of my legal pads. Yellow and ruled with faint green lines, like this one. She was writing with a plastic pen in red ink. I could see from where I stood, even though she did try to move her forearm over the letters. I could read Quang Tri and Dong Hoi. I thought I could.

"I had an idea," she said. Her face was shiny with sweat.

"Me too. I thought, Let 'em all plead for themselves, and let Ruthie rough out the contracts, and let her write me down a stack of messages to call back."

"You're playing hooky?"

"I guess I am."

"Me too."

"Wanna go to bed with me?" I said. She blushed. She always did.

Her face was red, not only from the summer heat. She began to unbutton other buttons. I thought she might slip her legal pad into the drawer of her bedroom desk, but she dropped her shirt on top of it instead.

I said, "Schelle. Listen." We were both quite still.

We continued to be still.

Then she bent for her shirt. She turned her back to me and, holding both arms up behind her, slid it on.

I said, "Schelle." We were still again.

"It can't be easy for you, either," she said.

That was when she was beginning to work on the monument. That was three years ago. Now there are merely weeks left.

Her Attorney's Recognizance

BUT NOT unheard-of, I'd assured the judge. He was the one I'd hoped we'd draw. His full name was John Backus, but the court clerks and a number of attorneys called him Johann, as in Bach. We were in his elegant Greek Revival courtroom. And it was *his.* He was in the firm-to-fascist mood. Dust floated up in the light every time he wiggled in his high-backed swivel chair, showing me his annoyance. He was a difficult man, a strong judge, and he truly admired women.

"Only because her innocence is so obvious to me, sir."

"You've been practicing law too long to talk like that, Brennan. But if you *have* to do some kind of starry-eyed-kid-at-the-bar act, would you spare *me*? Motion to dismiss is denied, but you knew that. Change of venue is laughed out of court, and you knew *that.* Are you trying to insult me? Now, you get your bail approved reluctantly. Not because I don't buy it that she's a pillar of the community and a comfort to motel owners countywide."

I noted those comments, and he stopped.

"They're on the record, counselor. Everything's a matter of record. You try and appeal on the basis of casual remarks made in the absence of a jury, you hang your ass out to dry *and* you face disciplinary hearings in front of the county Bar. I'm not fooling with you, understand? I'm buying it she won't flee the jurisdiction, you'll hand in her passport. I'm sure you can offer comfort and proper guidance.

"But bail? Standing her bail? Jesus, Brennan. Mark. You, ah, you feel like you know what in hell you're *doing*?"

I didn't answer.

When Attila the Guard brought her out to me a day later, she had makeup on, and her hair was combed up and back. Her face had more depth, more planes. Her eyes looked larger. She was wearing wrinkled clothes, all black—black boots, black tights, a short black skirt, black wide belt, black ribbed sweater with little white buttons. Instead of a coat she wore a ski jacket, black with a red-patterned collar. Her boots were the cowboy kind, with high heels, shiny black reptile leather. She took long steps, and she looked at me once, on her way from the guard, then went ahead and past me. I followed.

When she turned right in the parking lot, I tugged her shoulder left and aimed her at my car. She sat inside, looking ahead. As soon as I got in, I smelled perfume and soap and shampoo. I thought I could also smell her skin.

"Do you believe me?"

"No," I said. "Maybe a little."

"Which part?"

"That you killed him."

"And the rest is—"

"I'm not telling you what it is or isn't. It was a terrific read. It helped me fall asleep one night, so I'm grateful." I was driving. She held the safety belt in her hand, but didn't snap it home.

After a while she let it go. "I can get a ticket if my passengers aren't belted in."

"I'm sure you can fix it," she said. "You don't believe any of the rest of it?"

"I believe you killed him. I know he was strangled, and you said you strangled him. That's what I believe. And maybe what you claimed as your 'extenuating circumstances.' God, I love it when civil servants fill out forms. Even if they're arrest forms. 'Circumstances.' I do believe there were circumstances. It's the extenuations I find it somewhat difficult to buy. He was abusing you. To put it mildly."

"Mildly," she said, looking with a little agitation when I turned.

"I don't know if Larry Ziegler would do that. Would have done that. He was not a nice man, though. I'll give you that."

"Thank you."

"So why were you screwing him?"

"Because he was not a nice man."

"Thank you," I said. "How much do you weigh?"

"Excuse me?"

"Answer, please."

"A hundred and six. Maybe less. The sheriff serves, exclusively, corned beef from a can, vegetables from another can, or canned sauerkraut. Maybe a hundred and three now."

"Let's pretend it was a hundred and six at the time of the murder. You did say you murdered him?"

"Killed him is what I said. Murder or not is up to you, I'd say."

"You aren't stupid. And you're right."

"Yes. To both."

"And you're wondering why I'm asking questions like the ones I asked you before."

"No. I assume it's what the jury will want to know."

"Good. Will I be able to give them answers?"

She might have shaken her head. I couldn't tell. She looked up and over then, and asked, "Why did you bail me out?"

"So I could get you to the Stone's Throw Motel."

"No. I mean why did you put up the money?"

"Because you're broke. You don't manage your life well. Any of it. Do you?"

She didn't answer. She stayed in the car while I went into the Stone's Throw office. I didn't need to rent the room. They'd have let us in, I'm sure. But I did put money down.

It was very dark inside, and it smelled of other people. The smell made me think of the insides of their bodies. I turned the light on and slammed the door behind us. She jumped when the lights hit. It was a motel room, a little small and a little cheap, but like most motel rooms in every respect. Too many mirrors, as usual.

"This is the same room?"

She said, "I guess. I think so. They're a little hard to tell apart, you know? But I think so."

"Then this is the bed."

"It follows. Yes."

"Where was he?"

"On this side. Near us. Then—"

"That's what I want, damn it. The *thens.*"

"Then he was in the middle."

"Right. Good. How? How did you get him there? You said he—you tied a rope around his throat and you killed him with it. How?"

She looked me in the eye. Her color didn't change. She tilted her head back and looked hard at me and talked. "I kneeled on his chest or, you know, the insides of his arms."

"His hands were up? Fighting you off?"

She shook her head.

"Where were his hands?"

"He cut me," she said. "He broke the skin. He bruised it and beat on it and then the skin broke. I was bleeding. Sometimes he choked me, with his hands. Once he put a pillow on top of my face and leaned on it. For a long time. A very long time. I thought I was dying that time. Look," she said.

She unzipped her ski jacket and dropped it off her shoulders. She undid the buttons at the top of her sweater and she pulled it over her head. Her brassiere was black, mostly lace, it looked like. Mostly holes in the lace. The black clasp was in the front, and she removed it. She held it in one hand and she looked at me. Her body looked at me. Her stomach was pale, her breasts were pale. The nipples were large and dark and very hard. There was little extra flesh at her stomach, where the wide shiny belt pushed in at her, or on her shoulders or where her breasts ran into the top of her ribcage. The gray-black-ocher mottling was at the tops of her breasts and along her upper arms. Still holding her brassiere, she turned, and I looked for the crossing pattern of cuts and scratch marks, as if cats had been at her. As if she'd been attacked. Her pale, muscled back was smooth, unblemished.

"Larry hurt me," she said.

"I see. Yes. Would you put your clothes on, please?"

She shrugged and her breasts moved. "Touch the cuts," she said. "They're barely healed. You ought to know that. They're what he did when I felt like I had to—defend myself."

"Extenuations," I said. I touched her back. The skin was very hot, and she flinched as though my hands were cold. I kept them on her back, both of them on her back. She moved against them, and they slid over her shoulders, they went around her arms, they were on her breasts, they were cupping her breasts. Her nipples were like pebbles, and she made a sound as if I'd hurt her. I stopped moving.

She said, "No. It's—"

I moved my hands again, and she turned, she pulled at my collar and pinched the flesh beneath it as she did.

She kissed me by biting at the corners of my mouth, by pulling on my lower lip with her teeth. It hurt. I bit back and we were on the bed. When I tried to undo her belt, she shook her head. She pulled the hem of her skirt up, and I yanked down at her tights and underwear as she raised her hips. I reached down, but she turned me. It was as neat a move as if she'd been wrestling for points under NCAA rules. She reversed me. Her hand was in my pants, and on me, and then she brought me to her, almost into her, and I felt her hand at her own body. And then she was over me, riding like a little jockey, her *knees on his chest or, you know, the insides of his arms?* This time her knees were lower. The smell was hot perfume and just-baked bread.

I took off. It was a vertical drive. I wanted to *leave.* I was yearning up. And she had lied like a pilot telling stories on the ground.

Lists

Liquid-cooled Westinghouse radar dish (813 mm)
CNI package
Radar altimeter
Autopilot
Air-date computer
AIM-7 Sparrow missiles
AIM-7 Sidewinder missiles
M-61 20 mm gun
Wing pylons (max. cap. 16,000 lbs.)
Maximum speed: 910 mph (only in prayers)
Initial climb: 28,000 feet per minute (ditto prayers)

Ferry range w/external fuel tanks: 2,300 miles (who cares?)
Response time to MiG-21 or SAM missile: not quite quick enough

Ground in Which the Army Survives Only If It Fights with the Courage of Desperation Is Called "Death"

SO SUN TZU instructs us on the Nine Varieties of Ground. I was in death. Roger. I had a nylon rope I could climb down if my hands worked. I knew I couldn't move my legs—hadn't since the seat blew out and my back went numb, the thighs without feeling, a tingling in the knees or shins, someplace down there. I hadn't moved my hands since I dropped the radio. I'd been told to pack a spare. I couldn't remember if I did it or just nodded when told. I came down into the trees and didn't raise my hands to protect my face. I was screaming out little fear things. My feet hit the big branches and drove everything, it felt like, up into my gut. Stuff whipped me in the face and head. I couldn't feel anything anyplace.

Then I could. I didn't want to, and I could. I could hear them too, they were close, less than half a mile, maybe, splashing, slashing brush, coming on. Die, Yankee dog. They told us farm people would be more apt to kill us right away than the units near the cities. Pistol in shoulder holster, I told myself. Pull the gun. Don't do a radio deal. Don't drop the weapon. I was swinging again. The shroud lines were stuck above me, and I was ten, twelve feet or more above the ground, and when I moved I began to swing.

Goblin swings, affirmative.

I had the gun, though. I was crying, stuff was running out of my nose and down my face. I hated it that they would shoot straight up into my balls. I tried to lean forward in the harness and aim below me. Take out a squad of pissed-off farmers and the odd militiaman plus sundry NVA regulars with a .38 revolver. Roger.

When I leaned, I was swung into the tree. But when I hit it, I could feel. The numbness was leaving. I wasn't paralyzed. Time to run, Goblin.

I stuffed the gun back up into the holster and made sure the strap was snugged. I told a foot to move, and it did. Everything hurt, all over at once now, all the bones were aching, the way bad muscles do. I had charley horse of the bone. But I was able to get the Kabar out of its boot sheath and start to saw. I had half the lines cut away when they went quiet. I figured they were close. I figured they were lying in the brush and watching me. I smelled them, I thought: a horse-and-barn kind of raw smell on the wind. It might have been me. I was running sweat. It might have been the bright green welcome-to-Mars vegetation. Bugs were up my nose and in my ears and eyes. I kept spitting them out. I should have waited, tied the line on to something, and come down carefully. But I sawed the last lines and threw the knife away as I fell. I didn't want to stab myself. Just then.

I hit wailing. That was another time it felt like everything was shattered. I thought of punky wood, all soft splinters. I rolled, though, kept on rolling, as if my clothes were on fire. Rolled into soft stuff, probably tiger shit, I figured. And an anthill, I swear it. They started biting my thighs. Eat on, I said like a U.S. Marine maître d', eat on. I could walk, so I ran.

You're supposed to turn your beacon on, hit the radio waves for a Guard chopper, look at your compass and map, collect yourself and your data, and make a dustoff RDV. Goblin reports a negative response. Goblin pulled his pistol out and ran like hell.

As close as I could figure, we'd been very near to where we should have been. Which means tight up on the Ho Chi Minh Trail in the northern panhandle, west of Vinh. Being in the zone meant being in the middle of beaucoup materiel haulers. People who didn't wish us well. Considering we'd just been laying the 500s into them. Hi, fellas. No hard feelings?

I did not run into trees. I did hit those hairy vines and bounce back and strike off 15 degrees in another direction. I did fall halfway into holes, probably monster snake holes, I figured. I made a lot of those *Eee* noises you make when you run around in somebody's terror dream. There were a lot of grassy hummock places that I tripped on. And there was always furry, thick, high brush I couldn't push through. I figure Goblin did a solid 180 degrees of panic starts and stops. Maybe covered a quarter of a mile, total, in any single direction. Bounced into bushes and stumbled over vines. Wore wide white flowers in his buttonholes and ears. Came screeching to a stop like Roadrunner at an ambush.

Negative ambush. It was only six very small people with dark faces and dirty, ragged uniforms. They were backed up by a farmer with some half a scythe tool and a kid with what looked like a trowel. One of the soldiers carried, I swear it, a World War II U.S. government-issue Thompson .45 submachine gun. They could have just as well carried heavy rubber bands and rocks. Plastic pea shooters would have done it. I stood there with my lungs creaking. Smelled the gluey, dull stink of men in the jungle, sweating. Looked up to see if I could see the sun. Saw more trees. Some kind of dark bird moving out of sight. Flying monkey, maybe. Missing link between a flying squirrel and a pilot in a tree. Grounded pilot, now. Goblin. Dropping his pistol in the dirt and looking for a friendly face. Hi, fellas. Goblin surrendering. Goblin gives up.

Ferry Run

JACK STAYED late to participate in what they called Mock Trial. His teacher had never studied law, didn't know any. He was an expert in public speaking and in being creative. That was the year in the rural school districts for being creative. So one kid was the attorney for the defense, another was the prosecution, other kids were plaintiff, defendant, witnesses, et cetera. Jack was a witness. I knew the wisdoms. I knew the conventional wisdoms. What you like, your kid hates. What you want, he rejects. Basic theories of conflict, parent-child antagonism. So how come Jack was playing these lawyer games? I left work early to get him at half past four, a favor to Schelle, who couldn't get away. Mock Trial was held at the old elementary school for reasons I didn't understand, and the walk would have been a good distance beyond the edge of town. Schelle didn't want him out there with the local druggies, dusk coming on, we trust you absolutely, we just wanted to give you a lift, and so on.

So there we are. Jack leans against the door. I slouch under the wheel. I get the radio loud because ferrying Jack involves total silence. Negative conversation. Enough long silence to crack a hostile witness. Hard duty, loving a kid, I thought. Especially when your talent is minimal in that direction. Hardest duty: being a kid and living with me.

Jack, babe: I apologize for everything. Everything.

"Who's Deborah Harry?" I ask him after the DJ says her name.

"Blondie. She used to be."

"Like in Dagwood?"

"Huh?"

"Who, Jack?"

"A singer."

"Ah."

We're in the middle of town. Kids are standing outside our strictly American pizza joint. The bad boys are cupping cigarettes or tugging feed caps over their dirty hair. The girls who like a little danger are crouched at the window of a cherry-colored Camaro. They're laughing with a guy in enormous reflecting sunglasses. He looks like a joke about the state police. Jack looks straight ahead.

It's tough just breathing, being him, I think. Being any kid. Being *my* kid, I figure: hazardous-duty pay would not be payback enough.

"You want me to drop you here, you walk back to the pizza place, come home in time for dinner? Jack?"

"I don't—"

"I could let you have a few bucks."

"No."

"Okay."

"No, thanks. Homework, I have a lot of stuff to do."

"Right. Okay."

"Thank you, though."

"Hey," I tell him, "no sweat."

I turn the radio off as we turn the corner toward home. I wait for us to say some more. But we've said what we could, it seems. I hit the radio half a block from home. Somebody's forcing "ecstasy" to rhyme with "fantasy."

Eee. Eee.

"Here we are," I say to anyone, hitting the brake.

Jack nods. Here we are.

Latin

"HOW DID YOU get him to lie still for you when you strangled him with rope? What kind of rope?"

"Venetian blind cord." She was dressed. She was sitting on the desk chair, which she'd pulled up beside the bed. I'd wakened to find her watching me. Smiling. Putting on lipstick without a mirror and watching me sleep. "You sure needed to—relax. At the very least."

"How did you turn me over like that?"

"Oh, I'm strong. I'm small, but I'm strong. You're full of questions."

"In court, you only ask a witness a question if you know the answer you'll get. That's the rule. But I'm asking questions I don't know fuck-all about. Questions, answers, anything. Jesus."

"When you're confused, which strikes me as quite often, you furrow your brow. It's funny. It's vulnerable. You look vulnerable. A little less like the big lawyer man. Nice. And the answer is a pillow or length of blanket over each wrist. A piece of sash cord over each pillow, looped under the iron pipe of the mattress frame." I reached down below the mattress to the springs and felt the cold pipe.

"But Larry was big," I said. "He was a big man."

"Don't you get it yet?"

"Obviously not."

"Don't get huffy. Don't get mad." She leaned back in her chair, so that she was very low in it, and put her legs on the bed. Of course I looked along her legs. She knew I would. "What you have to see is it was part of it."

"Part of it."

"The hitting."

"Shit. The tying up, too. The—you two were—you're—"

"Don't name me. Don't give me a name until you know me."

"I'm *afraid* to know you."

She grinned, half lying with her legs apart. It was a girlish grin, sweet and spontaneous. Her eyes warmed and then went chilly again. "You never do know," she said.

"You tied him up because he wanted you to. And the M.E. didn't find the marks because of the pillows?"

She nodded approvingly. The dull student was getting less stupid.

"But if the two of you *wanted* to, if it was a—deal? Can I call it a deal? An agreement?"

"Lawyers," she said. "You make sex sound like interstate commerce. Call it what you want. We both were involved in what we did for each other. It *was* pleasure, after all."

"The pain was?"

"Good lawyer. Because you know *that* answer, right?"

"But why kill him?"

"Let's just say he hurt me too much."

"Back to your so-called confession. But what kind of lawyer am I, then, letting you tell me how to plead you?"

"You're a lawyer who just—Look, I tied him up the way he wanted me to." She stood now. She pulled her skirt up her legs, very high, and she kneeled on the bed beside me. I could smell the sourness of the clothing she'd worn on the day she killed Larry Ziegler. She was leaning her groin on my arm, bouncing a little on the bed. "I tied him up. I crawled down along him." And of course I was lying down for her, the sheets off me now. She said, into my stomach and then below it, her breath warm on me, "I did not do *corpus delicti*, counselor. Or *habeas corpus*. This is a question I know the answer to." Her breath on me. The glance of a lip. "Do you know any other Latin phrases I could use? Because that's what I was doing"—she did it, then lifted up—"just before I, well, did the other thing I did." Her mouth again.

Also disinformation. Also the lie.

We stood at my car and talked across the low roof. She looked very small. I could have been talking to my daughter, who was taller, in fact. Darker, of course. Looked like me, poor kid. Daddy's girl, I thought. I smiled because I knew I wasn't looking over the bright metal hood at anybody's girl but her own. Mickey might be my daughter, I thought, but *she* wasn't Daddy's girl either.

"What?" Estella said. She tilted her head. Her voice was soft and hoarse. She sounded like a singer offstage, between sets. She was full of color, her lips looked heavier.

"I was thinking, you had your blood for the day."

"Did I bite you?"

I shook my head. She smiled as if I were afraid of something that she knew wasn't real.

"Well, I'll have to remember and do it some time," she said.

"And then we tie each other down with little silk ribbons? I wear your underwear over my face? Or one of those rubber masks, with a zipper on it?"

"Not until you want to," she said. "And aren't you well informed."

"Was Larry?"

"Do you know the answer to that one, counselor?"

"No."

"He perverted us." Her eyes were mean again, her lips pale. Her mouth sounded dry. "He was at fault." She disappeared to sit inside the car. It rocked when she slammed the door.

As if it were her car, and I an interloper, I opened my door, leaned in, but didn't sit. "What am I pleading you? How? Are we seeing each other anymore?"

"Come in. Mark, come in. Sit here."

I sat. I closed the door. I buckled in. I looked ahead at the stained dark wooden wall of the motel, its low, scraggly privet, more wood than bush.

Estella said, "Larry mentioned you."

"We weren't friends. I didn't like him."

"Too big and beefy and German and Jewish for you?"

"He was always talking about the Nam. He wasn't Jewish, he was a vet. He made it his religion. Most of the men I know who spent time there talked about other things. I prefer that."

"He talked about you. You're a hero. He said you came home a hero, and he just came home."

"Everybody just comes home or doesn't. Everybody who made it through came home the same."

"Innocent is the answer."

"The—"

"To how you're pleading me. You know that. Self-defense. And we're seeing each other, yes. *Ipso facto.* Haven't you been looking for me? And I do know the answer."

Dead Man's Shoes

NEW, IMPROVED DRINKING. The man down south, or southwest, it doesn't matter. Mother's partying with a few people, and this five-year-old son of hers wakes up and comes into the living room. There's everybody in a sweat and all boozed up, and some guy in manmade fibers says to the child, "You all want a drink? We gonna let you drink some. You might as well learn early on how men do it. This here's Dr. Jack's sourmash, son. You drink it like a man, hear? Drink it down."

Gives the kid a vase or something, ten goddamned ounces of

sourmash. Boy goes into a coma. Surprise! All he does, then, is die.

Here's the snapper on it. Medics said they'd maybe have been able to do something if Mom and Manly had got the kid in sooner. "Sooner" is the kicker in the little AP item. Because then you have to sit in your office at night and try to look at the legal pad and all you see is somebody's baby hot and sick and having convulsions and not breathing well and being purple-gray on account of they have to finish the party or sleep it off or do a three-way number or they're scared.

They made you sit alone with a little pile of rough paper, it had bumps of wood or grain in it. And an old-fashioned pen with a square bottle of ink. You had to dip the pen in the ink and give them something. They always wanted something. They made promises. Medicine when you were sick. Food. No more beatings when they were in a beating-you mode. No more tin-ear wailing music when you wanted to sleep. No more bright lights. No guys whispering to you about snakes and rats coming up the latrine into you. Whatever you needed, they promised you. They always knew what you needed. They asked the questions when they knew your answers in advance.

True. The thing about building the house. True story. Maybe half of the guys I ever talked to about it did that. Built a house piece by piece, foundation to roof, all in their head. Kept it there. I never did. I'm no good with my hands. Not even in my head. I did other stuff. You had to do *something*. I tried to remember books we read in college. Names of guys I knew at Quantico. Various emergencies on the simulated-cockpit instruments. Country airfields I'd landed on. Women I'd wanted. Long list. Women I'd got to. Short list. States I'd visited. Number of singers in the Mormon Tabernacle Choir—how many of their faces I could remember from 1960, when I saw them one time. Lists. Real bony things to hang your thinking on.

Sometimes they demanded lists. Flaws in capitalist society. Reasons for U.S. involvement in Vietnamese affairs. Weaponry carried by the Phantom. Perimeter guard rotation at Da Nang.

My guy was named Phan Tuy. His guy was named me. I thought of him, often, as Phantom. When he talked about my airplane, every time, I smiled. Once in a while, when I did that, he had me beaten. So that if my thoughts were errant, he said, I would get my just punishment.

Just punishment. A favorite description of his.

He was skinny, of course, and his back curved over not quite in a hump. He looked a little like many of the rural poor in New York State, curved by scoliosis. It looks like a humped set of the roundest shoulders in the world. He was about five foot one, and his hands and feet were large for his build. He never touched me with them, but I sometimes thought he might try to stomp me to death. He wore huge American-issue boots, the heavy leather jobs the grunts wore. Phantom in the shoes of the dead.

This was what Schelle would commemorate. The Phantom who broke up the Phantom-less pilot. The flier who came to earth and busted a foot bone and lived in a compound on the northern panhandle for a number of bad months. This was what she'd been doing. As well as, without doubt, conducting her affairs. Doing her job. Being a mother. Trying her hand at wife. Raising money to raise a monument designed to raise the dead.

Ink and paper. And Schelle, the friend of my boyhood, a lodestone for what tenderness I might have offered.

She ought to be warned.

Body Parts

WHEN MARCH is halfway over, we get phony spring up here. You actually see the sun sometimes, and it's golden on the walls, it makes furniture glow. Then the clouds seal us over again. But you get your hopes up. You shouldn't. And the damp gets worse than the cold. We've come through the 25-below-zero mornings when the cars sound like old men dying if you try to crank them up. But it's worse, somehow, with spring on the way but not here, but you're hoping. You shouldn't.

Phony spring morning, and I was here half the night. Barely put anything down on paper, and I tried sleeping on the leather sofa you have to have in the country so they believe you're practicing law. It felt like lying on someone else's skin, and no one I knew. I walked the town. A few lights on—insomniacs and sick people, drunks asleep in front of late movies with cigarettes singeing their fingers. They wake up to smell themselves burning.

It smells, Phan Tuy said, quite like pork.

So this father comes in, and Ruthie makes me see him. He's in there early. I hear him walking in the waiting room before Ruthie gets there. Then she arrives, they talk, and she brings him in. He's round-faced, with a shave so close it's next to bleeding. He smells like cheap after-shave. He smells like Jamesway's own brand, cloves and recycled engine oil. He blinks a lot. His suit's at least fifteen years old, enormous glen plaid pattern, and it's made completely of polyester with a touch of bell to the trouser legs. His tie is thick and wide, dark red against the harsh white shirt and brown-green plaid. His baby fell. This is another man whose baby fell. When I heard that, when I smelled his coffee-and-panic phlegmy breath and heard that his baby fell, when I saw his eyes banging against the corners of the sockets like small brown pinballs, I stopped listening.

When they look like that and their babies fall, the child's in custody of social workers—Estella, say. They arrive with court orders and deputy sheriffs or marshals, they take the child away. Because the baby has hemorrhaged or been concussed. Arrived at the doctor's office or the hospital ER with an arm that was snapped like a stick. With abrasions on the face or cigarette burns on the stomach or back. Bleeding from between the legs. They smell like pork when they get burned. And the parents come in and they tell some sleepless lawyer, his face all smudges and shadows, about accidents.

He finished. He'd said something near the end, maybe at the very end, about so help him God.

"I hope he does," I said, tilting the chair down and looking at his necktie's knot as if I looked at his naked, stricken face. "I sure hope somebody does, you son of a bitch. You're entitled to it under law. But not from me. You have to purchase my services, and there just isn't enough dough for you to do that. You know what I mean?"

I thought about my four straightened fingers going into the gut, how he stood and wobbled, his eyes huge, his mouth open for a breath he couldn't take. In one of those Scandinavian countries, you talk mean to a kid, it's child abuse. *I* knew what I meant.

Like pork, and they suffocated first if they were lucky, Phan Tuy said. "If the jelly does not run properly, or only a drop attaches to the flesh, they merely burn," he said. "It is a mercy if they are engulfed. Then the air is burned away. They suffocate, but promptly, if you compare it to the pain of slowly burning. The infection afterwards, the consciousness of pain. Consciousness is finally the curse, you see. Hence our lights?"

It was a question. I'd learned to answer them. I nodded. I said, "Yes." The lights were on all the time in the tin shed they kept me in. No windows. Low roof. Bucket. The usual. My foot was broken, something in my foot was broken, it wasn't healing. The consciousness of pain. My knees ached all the time. Something had burst in the left pelvis. A chest muscle was torn, I figured. Nothing on the left side, nipple to breadbasket to balls to thigh bone connected to the patella connected to the ankle bone felt right or worked right. All of it hurt all the time. "All the time" meant more in Phantom's little establishment. Your eyes kept opening because of the light or the cold or the heat or you were outside a while and you used the trench and you thought of rats entering or exiting your body. Questions nonstop. Or answers.

Wobbling and sucking for breath. No breath coming. Animals using the body as a traffic interchange and the babies in Emergency with abrasions on their skin.

You keep thinking about wounds, the ligature around the throat, cutting through the flesh, the puckered edge, this is Goblin, Guard, Goblin reporting Mayday Mayday. You're late for school and your mother keeps calling your name. Not Goblin. No rank or serial number. She says, over and over, "Mark? Mark? Can you hear me? What hap—*Mark?*"

Coming up into it, through it, punching up above the cloud line.

"Schelle?"

"Mark, what happened?"

"Schelle?"

"You called me."

"We in the office, Schelle?"

"Stay flat, Mark. Yes. The office. Where else would you be?"

"I went to the office?"

"You stayed in the office. You called me at home."

"I thought I was sleeping late for school."

"You called me."

"What?"

"*What* what?"

"I said—"

"You told me you couldn't get a breath. You couldn't breathe. Your chest felt funny. Your fingers felt funny."

"No way."

"That Marcus Brennan, Esquire, could have a heart attack? According to which rules of evidence?"

"I'm healthy, Schelle. Sorry I called."

"Bastard."

"No. Sorry I scared you, I wanted to say. I'm fine. I must have panicked. I apologize."

"Do you think you can walk?"

"No hospital."

"Yes hospital."

"Schelle, it's *anxiety*. Tension—from, you know, the practice. It has to be. Lots of men my age do this."

"Also, they die. We're going to the hospital. Do we walk to the car, or do I call for an ambulance?"

"Schelle, I'm glad I called you."

"Yes. Do you know why?"

"I guess because you're who I call."

"I'm who you call. That's right."

"I'm sorry. I'm sorry."

I walked fine. She drove us there. The nurses in the ER said they ought to admit me and so did Schelle. They put me in an empty semi-private room. Schelle said she'd get me moved. Jokes about clout. It was Schelle's hospital, of course. The doctor came. Luwein. We didn't like each other. He asked the usual questions. I gave the answers. And she sat in a hard plastic chair while they took my blood pressure, did an EKG, threatened me with a stress test, listened to my heart and lungs, and took my pulse. Put me back to bed. I lay there, feeling cold in the open-backed gown. I kept my eyes closed. She knew I was hiding behind them. I heard her waiting. She knew I listened to her wait.

Schelle. The person I called. Wouldn't I come out of hiding for you if I could?

"So you will write your autobiography again," Phan Tuy said. "You speak of interest in Marxism in college. Clearly untrue. No boy interested in Marxism is admitted to the Marines. Or to the parent Navy. Am I correct?"

Respectful but a little arch: "Maybe I wasn't admitted."

"Marcus," he said. Fond reproach. He shook his head. The guard behind me stepped up as if to slap me on the ear again. I closed my eyes and tried to stay inside. He didn't hit me. When I opened my eyes, I would see a new thin sheaf of rough paper, another well of ink, another wooden pen holder and steel point. The ink would run on the page, the paper would soak it in, the letters would stray from their shapes. I would tell my round-shouldered Phantom the story of my life.

Rules of Evidence

WHAT'S ADMISSIBLE at trial and what isn't. You can't force a witness to divulge his history to his own discredit. Is he or is he not a witness to pertinent proceedings? Did he see them credibly? Can he report them credibly? If he's a rapist or a burner of old people asleep, the court is uninterested. The jury must be ignorant of who he was and what he did. It's who he *is* as eyes and a mouth. A man, say, is telling you about another man—what the accused, let's say, did, and to whom. Did he witness said events? Was he in a satisfactory physical position and condition to witness and remember? Is his eyesight good?

His memory? His ability to state his recollection? Admit the testimony.

You may *not* instruct the jury that this particular witness was cruelly made sad as a child. That his parents were eventually helpless alcoholics. That he cared for them during that period of his adolescence which ought to have been devoted to social growth and pleasures of an innocent sort. That his widowed mother, on being told by her son that he would leave her for the State University College in Binghamton, said this:

> Say it again [pauses indicate drawing on cigarettes, sipping iced vodka in gas-station premium glass bearing team logo and the name BUFFALO BILLS] . . . I want to hear about your plans. *My* plans . . . are to live in this outhouse made of Sheetrock and tin cans . . . and be cold all winter . . . hot all summer . . . and die of cancer. Which you *know* I've got.
>
> [Witness reverts to own voice] Ma, you cough because you smoke so much. You feel lousy all the time because you drink. On the job, off the job, you drink that cheap garbage—
>
> [In mother's voice] Get me some money and I'll drink whatsit. The Russian brand! Get me some *money*! I carry baked potatoes and horsemeat to . . . everybody's table in Austie's sixteen hours a day . . . so you can wear whippy shirts like that and fifty-dollar sneakers . . . you remember how your father died? He had no *shoes* on . . . You had shoes, he didn't. I rest my case . . . Except, I'm telling you—
>
> [Own voice] Ma. Ma? Please? I just want to—Ma, I need to get there. I *need* to.
>
> [Hers] Where? Name it, where I can't be, that we died making your carfare to!
>
> [His] Away.
>
> [Hers] Away . . . you cert, cert . . . You never sus*pected* . . . You carry a suitcase out that door . . . I'll shut you down forever. I mean it . . .

Like you got born without a mother . . . You'll do better than virgin birth! I'll say I never heard of you . . . Never know you again . . . If you ever come back once you're gone, and you come into this stinking room, I'll *be* dead, far as you're concerned . . . You hear me? And if I *am* dead and you ever come back, I'll make—you come near me, I'll make my body bleed.

Inadmissible.

Assuming any of it's true.

And yet it isn't as far to carry to the jury as the I-ate-too-much-junk-food defense. Or the I-overdosed-on-sweets-and-couldn't-help-myself gambit. They *worked.* A couple of homicides got manslaughter, time done pending trial, plus early parole. They're on the street. They're free.

The best defense is a good story.

Sortie

JACK, sitting in the salmon-colored chair in the new room Schelle arranged. I had privacy. Jack and I had privacy. He was pale and nervous, he looked sweaty. I was worried that he'd pass out. People get sick, visiting hospitals.

"I'm fine, Jack. You don't need to worry. Mom told you? Stress. Nervous tension. You know, all the usual modern stuff. You don't get sick, you get *worried.*"

He nodded in a peculiar way. But I knew him. When he opened his dry lips, when I heard his mouth clack before he spoke, I knew what he'd say. "I have it. I get that, sometimes. What you—"

"Your *chest* hurts? Your arm?"

He shook his head.

"I sometimes can't breathe right, it feels like. Before a test or something. You know?"

"You can't breathe?" The knife-strike blow, the four fingers stiff as wood, going in. His eyes enormous. Mouth pulling at what won't come in: breath. "Jack," I said. I whispered it. "Tension," I said.

"Yeah," he said. "That's what Mom said. She said I have to take a breath, just one or two good ones, let the air out easy, and tell myself something to make me relax."

"Good," I said. "Good." He looked at me: Schelle's face. My heavy chin and forehead, but otherwise Schelle's face—the graceful nose, large eyes with such milk-clean whites to them. The flexible lips, but not smiling. I waited. He waited too. We were watching each other. I said, finally, "So what is it?"

"Huh?"

"That you say, Jack. That makes you stop worrying so much about things. That helps you to breathe."

The small room, dirty as hospital rooms always are. Used tissues heaped in the pail beneath the sink. A dust curl near the sliding closet door. The empty eye of the television set on its wall rack. The closet half open, as I asked them to leave it. Nothing can jump out of a door at you in your sleep unless it's all the way closed. And the blinds drawn down. The high sweet smell of sickness and disinfectant. My tall, handsome son in his brown leather flier's jacket, sitting erect. My breathless son. The hand-strike going in.

"Oh," he said. A solemn smile. "I don't know. I didn't find it yet."

Dead Soldiers

JACK DROVE ME, and Schelle sat in the back. They walked on either side of me from the driveway into the house. I had a prescription from Dr. Luwein for something to make me relax. His words. Roger: relax. I was to take it easy. Simple to do. You just breathe out and don't breathe in. Goblin confirms. Jack sat in the kitchen and watched me sit in the kitchen until Schelle sent him out to his friends. First he had to stand over me, looking down. Red, confused, a baby in a big body, his heavy hand reaching lightly for the top of my head. It said all he could. He palmed my head like a basketball. He nodded and shrugged. "Take it easy, okay?" He said what he could. Schelle seized him to her. She hugged him hard. Her eyes were wet. Her mascara was coming down in streaks. The lines you get along the side of the craft after a midair refuel. Your ground man sometimes will rub at it with a rag if he's one of those finicky airplane fixers. Schelle watched him leave and went back to opening wine and cooking.

"I'm making roast beef. Mushrooms sautéed in oil with onions. It's probably bad for you. Us. But let's have a little cholesterol, all right? It wasn't your heart, after all."

It wasn't my heart, Schelle.

She put a half-full bottle of Italian wine on the table and two tumblers. "Want to make an exception to your rule?" She poured me a slug. Straw-colored, dark-tasting, raw. I poured more.

She was turned toward the sink. I watched her back move. You can see the muscles move if she's wearing a tight T-shirt or a bathing suit. Under a loose shirt such as she wore, you would know, anyway, that muscles were shifting. I wanted to see her naked. She stood still. Schelle knew. Then she went back to cooking.

I poured wine into her tumbler and slid it onto the chopping board beside the onions. Without looking at me, she reached for the glass and drank. As she replaced it, even though she looked away, at her work and not at me, I could see her eyes. The lines running down, black and wet. Wounds.

I said, "Schelle."

"I'm sorry."

"No. I wanted to say thank you. For taking me home. For staying here. I know you have work."

She said, barely, "That's all right."

"Because I'm fine. Thanks to you."

"You called me," she said.

"Yes."

I went back for the wine. Two more tumblerfuls for us, and the bottle was nearly empty. Schelle knew. She said, "There's another one in the fridge. I did some damage to it last night. You better be careful or I'll corrupt you."

I went for the bottle, emptied out the fresher one, uncorked the one from the refrigerator. We drank. She threw the knife into the sink. She dropped chopped onions into a black pan. She wiped at her eyes with the backs of her wrists.

"Strong damned onions," I said. I was standing next to her. The kitchen smelled of the cooking onions in oil, and of the powerful wine. I emptied the cold half bottle into our tumblers.

"There's more in the pantry closet," she said. "But I don't think you should."

"I'm supposed to relax. You heard my doctor."

"He did say that."

"He doesn't like me much, does he?"

"He's a friend, Mark."

"Oh. He likes *you.*" Not very tall, but a broad guy, big chest and shoulders, strong arms, big hands. His legs were short, his torso long. He had wispy hair in a choppy sort of crew cut. Thick glasses in black plastic frames. He always pushed them back on his nose. He smeared them. He looked at you through smeary lenses and he didn't like you much but he liked your wife. He told you to take it easy.

"We work together," Schelle said.

I was opening a bottle of wine. I knocked one of the empties over. Schelle turned. "Accident," I said. "Dead soldier."

"Soldier."

"We called the empties dead soldiers."

She nodded. "You always made jokes about getting killed."

"Except when it happened to us."

"Very funny," she said.

"Not when it happened."

"No."

"Schelle: your monument—"

She said, "Yours. Theirs. The people who went over to it."

"How do you know," I started.

"What?"

"Don't go through with it, Schelle. Don't let it happen."

"Mark."

"I know you worked your ass off on this. I know. It's a beautiful, wonderful thing to do."

She turned. She planted her legs. Under the dark long skirt and white apron, I could see the shape of her thighs. She smoothed the apron. She pushed her wrist at her eyes. I drank some wine. She reached for hers and drank some. "It's the least we can do."

"No," I said.

"The least I can think of," she said.

"Don't give it to me. It's good advice, Schelle."

"Thank you, counselor," she said.

"You shouldn't thank me. Really."

"You're right, I think," she said.

The Sons of the Pioneers

END OF APRIL, almost the end of winter while it's spring, and ladies in aprons tied over their dead husbands' cardigans stoop to crocuses in the mush of late snow. Estella's house: not a clue. No legless cats kept alive to call their pain. No dogs who cringe, no goldfish fed salt, no supermarket flowers beheaded. It's a small, locked-log, one-story house with high ceiling and big thermal-pane windows, a fireplace plugged with a woodstove unit, some soft old sofas and chairs, a lot of museum prints on the walls and some murky original oils, and nothing about torture, no analysis of suffering. Electric heat makes so little noise. Once in a while, the baseboard radiators crinkle and ping. The little kitchen's tucked away in the back, and from the bedroom you never hear the refrigerator cycle. When snow falls, you can hear its wetness on the windows. The wind nags at the chinking between the logs. You can hear yourself.

You can hear yourself wince.

You can hear her saying, "Want me to stop?"

Then you, saying, "No." Did you mean *Yes*? Does *No* mean *Yes* now?

Not as if she's a maniac. Who killed a man as big as you. With her hands. Not as if she's cruel. She's exploring you. She's loving you. Say *love.*

Yes.

Say *love.*

"Love." Hear yourself wincing it.

"Yes," Estella says.

Does *Yes* mean *No,* then?

The thump, across the house, of a bird flying into a window and staggering across the air to escape. Roger that. Turning right, I see it coming. The trick is to turn, now, *hard,* then dive, Billy hollering as usual in power dives, moaning and bubbling against the g's. G suit applies the pressure you need, keeps the blood from pooling, keeps some up in your head where you need to have it. See the instrument array. *See* it. Yes. I see the gauge display. Seeing nothing, seeing lights in a red filter, *Yes* for *No,* but you can't drop your aircraft, can you? So the flaps and the stick, Billy crying out—no, that's Goblin making the noise now, and up, coming up, turning, Billy at the radar. Roger, Billy. Goblin's in the saddle again.

Gene Autry? I'm back in the saddle again? Out where a friend is a friend. Damned straight, Goblin confirming: back in the saddle again. Along with the Sons of the Pioneers? Roger. Because this time *you* did the power roll and reverse, and Estella's back and arching under you. You're in the saddle.

Yes.

Meaning *No*?

The SAM goes past, Billy tracks it: wobbling, chasing the tail of its own exhaust, dropping to explode on the ground.

"We got the mothers shooting them*selves*!" Billy announces. Then he shrieks, "Launch! Launch! Oh, Jesus, there's two! *Three!*"

Goblin running away, folks. The ultimate maneuver: cut and run.

Estella: "Your legs are so strong. It isn't fair."

In the darkness, her eyes bright, her teeth, the silence and then wind, the coolness of her shoulders, heat of her neck and chest. "It isn't a match, is it? A contest?"

"Would you like it to be?"

"No."

"What would you like it to be, Mark?"

"Love," I said.

"You're such a romantic. You're such a boy. You blush like a boy, you try to please me like a boy. You lose your temper, like a boy, when I don't do what my lawyer knows to be best. And you keep wondering about me."

"Wondering?"

"About where I, you know, learned—what I learned."

"The art of love," I heard me say. Jesus, Brennan. *Jesus.*

"Oh, that's sweet," she said.

"I don't want you to tell me things," I said. "About your life. About, you know."

"You don't?"

"No."

"Really."

"No."

"Meaning that's right."

"Yes."

Estelle leaning back, away from me, and then she leaned in, her hair brushing my chest. Her teeth at my breast. On my nipple, and then hard.

"Ah. *Damn* it."

"You don't want me to do it?"

"No."

"By which you mean yes, I should stop? Or yes, you like a woman at your nipple like that with her teeth. Or, better still, best of all, you like me."

"Yes."

"Darling, what? Which?" Her teeth again.

"Goddammit, yes."

Dear Old Mom

THE METAL SHACK again, the heat beating in from its walls and up from the earth floor. The floor looked cool, moist. It should have felt that way, but it felt like a hot bath, just drawn. Steam. I thought I could see steam rising. Phantom in his crisp white shirt, his little rounded back, thin arms showing slack at the inside of the elbow where the sleeves were rolled. His face was young, the skin of his cheeks and throat was taut, but his arms showed his age. The muscle was slack, the forearm flesh vaguely rippled. He put the rough paper on the bureau with its missing drawers. He'd removed the drawer slides and backing to create a desk. I could see his feet on the stool on the other side. They were in the heavy boots. The guard behind me, who would start to cuff me at the ears soon, was wearing sneakers. Keds. Some American brand. Phan Tuy sighed and shook his head.

"There seems to be some truth in this story of your life."

I nodded.

"But lies as well."

I shook my head.

"You have just reiterated the truth and the lies. I wonder if you know which we must label which."

I waited. The sweat ran down and pooled at my belly. Soon, I wouldn't have any place for sweat to collect. Pretty soon I'd be starved and sick. When that happened, I remember I thought, Well, the sweat can run straight down to the floor. No point in using a middleman. But that would be when I had dengue fever. Now I was hungry and thirsty and scared, but I still looked American. I still carried more in muscle and tendon on my torso than half the guards wore on their entire frame all their lives.

"You refer to this happy northeastern childhood."

I nodded. Phan Tuy looked over his thick eyeglasses. I heard the guard's sneakers on the damp floor and I ducked forward. He slammed me twice, once on each ear. I said, "Ow." Then I said, "Yes, sir." The guard did my kidney, and I gagged.

"Thank you," Phan Tuy said. "Northeastern means, please?"

"North—yes." Big breath. "It means the northeastern quadrant of the nation. Of the United States. New York State. Beneath New England. Above the southern states like, uhm, Virginia? Florida? On the right-hand side of the map. On the Atlantic. Where it snows."

"You experienced snow."

"Yes, sir."

"Strangely, you do not refer to snow." Shuffling the pages. "No reference to snow."

"Snow is not unusual for me."

"Nor are you unusual for *me.* But I did request of you a full life's story."

"I apologize."

He looked up and adjusted his eyeglasses with his finger. I thought, You'll smear them. He smiled. "This is promising, Marcus. Shall I call you Mark? Yes. Mark."

I tried to smile back.

"Why do you call your childhood happy? What constitutes in the United States of America happy?"

Sometimes when he got drunk he didn't hit my mother. Sometimes he didn't hit me. He never burned me with cigarettes. Fathers do that. He never used a straight razor. He never sawed on my fingers with his teeth. Fathers do that. I was never ever raped by either parent. That can happen in the United States of America.

"It's hard to say, sir. It was typical. It was not unusual."

"What is usual, in that case? Mark?"

"My mother baking apple pies in the afternoon, sir. Smiling at me when I came home from school. I knew she'd start smiling when she heard my sneakers hit the front porch steps. I'm home, Mom. Milk, apple pie. She always wore a white apron over a housecoat. She always wore stockings and nice shoes. She always had her hair done up. She always smelled like baking and a little perfume. She always helped me with my homework. She always laughed about math. She always came to the PTA. She always came to see my class plays. She always came for parent-teacher conferences. She always came to school open house. She always took me to the movies on Saturday. She always let me go alone when I got older. She always made my favorite food on my birthday. She always gave me presents. She always baked cakes. She always let me have my friends come over. She always tucked me in. She always made me take a shower and she always tucked me in. She always let me listen to the radio at night. She always asked me about the baseball scores in the morning. She always listened when I told her about the games I heard from St. Louis and Detroit on the radio at night. She always made me a big lunch to take to school. She always helped me pick my clothes out in the morning. She always laughed. She always kissed me goodbye."

His hand in the air. Stop. Stop.

I heard myself panting. The sweat ran down. In the far corner, behind him, I thought I saw something move along the floor. I shifted my bare feet.

"Mark," he said.

"Yes, sir." Breathing hard.

He looked at a note he'd made. "Define, please, Pee Tee Aye."

The movement along the floor.

"Mark!"

Lee Beeton Palmer, tall in his Italian suit, dark gray, the

black and red tie, the white spread-collar shirt, loafers that looked as if they weighed half an ounce. "Hey, Lee," I said, wiping my forehead and noting how he noted that I did.

"You doing good, buddy?"

"Doing good by doing well," I answered. I often answered him that way. He always laughed the way he did: hard bark. He always rubbed a finger on his mustache, checking that it was there. It always was.

"Listen. A tip."

"We don't have a mutual matter, do we?"

"No," he said. "Not yet. That's why I wanted to wake you up here. I never saw an attorney sleep standing up in the lobby of the county office building."

"You want to sleep," I said, "you go to where the boredom is." The sharp bark again. "What's up? Which of your undercover narcs is breathing happy dust instead of air these days?"

He nodded. Nodded again. Then: "We have somebody in the high school. I don't want you to say anything to anyone. Maybe Rochelle, if you have to. Understand? Nobody. These are mostly working-class kids, some upper-middle types, doctors' kids, lawyers' kids. They probably aren't whackers. But whackers have to come from someplace, right? I want my guy out alive at the other end of this. He's got a kid, a wife, a dog—*two* dogs. A high school kid can kill a cop the same as anybody else."

"Lawyers' kids?"

"I'm coming to it."

I looked at his face. "You're there."

"I'm there," he said.

"Jack? My Jack?"

"Hey." He shrugged. "Anybody, these days. You know?"

"Lee. You're saying—your cop is saying—my Jack is doing cocaine? Grass? Black beauties? What, Lee?"

"He hears the name. He doesn't see the kid. Your boy. He doesn't see him use or hold. He hears the name. The boy's on the fringe of some ugly numbers there. We're busting into lockers tomorrow."

"Shit."

"What shit? You'll be doing major business by the afternoon. Not a word, Mark."

"No. Not to Jack."

"I didn't say not to Jack."

"Jesus, Lee. I appreciate this. I can warn him?"

He shook his head. His hand was in the air. Stop. Stop. "Don't make me an accomplice. I didn't say anything, and I sure as shit didn't hear anything. Your kid decides to go in extra early tomorrow, empty out his locker, flush it down, whatever he's flushing down, clean the cracks in his pockets out—you know. You know. He does that, I come in with the fucking U.S. Marines and blow the halls apart while the kids are in the Friday assembly, then I didn't know anything, I didn't hear anything, I sure as shit didn't see anything."

"God. Lee."

He looked unfunny for the first time. Not joking. Not experienced. He looked sad. No: moved. He said, "You know I lost a brother there. My baby brother. They mailed him home in one of those book bags, I figure, there was so little left. That's what his sergeant told me. They could have used a can from Prince Albert tobacco, there was so little left. You and my brother, you were there together. You didn't know each other. He was infantry, you remember. Just one more kid to send over so they can step on a Claymore—one of ours!—and get blown to shit. So they could lay enough of them down there, the reporters could walk on them and not get their jungle outfits splashed. You and him, that's enough for me. It's not for your boy. Tell him that. Tell him I'll probably end up busting him, he doesn't get smart. This is for you, Mark." He looked at me, and I thought he'd cry. Tough-mouth hatchet-face cop with tears in his big dark eyes.

I put my hand out to shake his. He grabbed it sideways, the way black guys used to do before they went to the Wharton School and bought your company and fired you because you weren't as smart as they were. I let him grip me that way and we shook hands like two men in country the night before Richard Nixon got nominated for President. Because the best defense is a good story.

"Mark," he said.

"Lee, I'm sorry."

"No," he said. "I am. Shit, we all are. You might want to send him around to me, or maybe I can come over some night, I can talk to him. You want me to do something like that?"

"Talk to him?"

"I can tell him to catch a little of his old man's action," Lee said. "He could do plenty goddamned worse."

"I'm sorry," I said.

Correction

IN FACT, you can't see them on the ground when you strafe. That would have been War Two, or Korea—slow-moving prop jobs, Corsairs, say, with the guns in the gull wings and a bomb or two slung underneath. You could come in and see them running. You could follow your tracers and watch them explode. *Pop pop.* But in the Phantom you were there and gone. Your RIO would look over his shoulder and see nothing and call out, "Maybe. I think maybe," but you didn't see it. It just *felt* like you did. I saw them in my sleep. I watched them explode.

I can see them.

Ruthie in clattering high heels, then running on her toes, we're that busy. In my office, I say, "When I hear your shoes bang in the hallway, before they hit the carpet, you know what I hear?"

She's catching her breath. "No, Mr. Brennan."

"Money. It sounds like money going into a piggy bank. You're the piggy-bank lady, Ruthie."

"Thanks, Mr. Brennan, I guess."

"I don't care about the money," I said. "We got enough, don't we?"

"I know that, Mr. Brennan." Studying me, because I sound a little nuts.

"I am," I say.

"Pardon me?"

"Just a little," I tell her.

"Pardon?"

"I keep hoping, yeah. What's up, Ruthie?"

"There are four people in the waiting room. They keep looking at your door. You know, waiting for someone to come out? One of them's awful restless. He's—swearing. The others, I—they do want so much to see you, Mr. Brennan."

"And I've been sitting in here doing nothing."

"No, sir. I assumed you were working."

"What's on my desk, Ruthie? Tell me what you see."

Her face reddening. Her hands pulling at each other. Glasses bouncing under her neck on their gold chain. "The same briefs I put there this morning."

"You know what I've been doing?"

"Not reading them?"

"*That's* why you're my executive secretary. Now I'm going to stop doing what I was doing."

"Thinking," she said.

"Got to do some of that every now and again."

"And I'll send the clients in," she said, happy with relief: I was about to let her go.

"One at a time would be best," I said.

Like a Man

ESTELLA was offering me a glass of wine in her dark kitchen. She's wearing my button-down blue oxford shirt half buttoned, but nothing else. Her house hot and silent, the moon spilling in across the long living room, the cork noisy in the house. "No," I said. "No, thank you."

"Whiskey? Tequila?"

"I don't drink," I said.

"Because you're driving. Me. You do that," she said, standing between my legs as I sat on the stool. She leaned her hair on my chest and rubbed her head against my belly and chest. "You do drive."

So of course my hand was at the short, clipped hair at the back of her neck. "Yes, ma'am," I said.

Standing again, looking in. "But you really don't drink?"

"No. Hardly ever."

"It doesn't have to do with drinking and driving, and you didn't think what I said was a clever joke."

I shook my head.

"You don't like it when people try to be clever."

"Least of all me," I said.

"Are you an alcoholic?"

Shook my head again. Like a man. The sourmash spilling down the child's throat, running out the edges of his mouth. The room falling on him, the taste of his own vomit and the sweet harshness that smelled like his momma's mouth when she kissed him on the lips. Everybody's lips wet with the hot sweetness. The laughter in the living room, and everybody lying on each other. Drink it like a man, son.

Estella: "Mark."

"Sorry."

"Tell me."

"I won't have any, thank you."

The long drive home in darkness, the headlamps pale from road muck in our false spring, the windows foggy with it. Squinting at the bright silver moonlight on trees and shabby farmhouses, on the moisture of the road, pockets of snow. Going home to Schelle and knowing in advance her curled shape, the tautness of her face even in sleep. How she will lie on my side of the bed, head on my pillow, as if she's waiting for me. All our lives together, she has waited, in fact. And on my side. The sound of her breath, the smell of her sleep. My lying against her, and her dreamy murmurs as if of love and as if it could protect us, Schelle.

Adjusting to Dead

WELL, of course the heat is going to get to a man. The sleeplessness will get to him. Though I didn't know after a while whether I'd slept or not. My eyes burned, they might have been open or closed, I didn't know. They burned, and the sun burned, though I didn't have to stay outside in it. I was in the tin shed for interrogation or the tin shed for not sleeping or the tin shed where you had to sit and lean over and that was all the room there was. After the diarrhea and the stomach cramps and the dengue fever you didn't have a great deal of belly to fold over so the sitting like that got easier. *Easier* is not the word. But you could bend that way. Things still pushed into the lungs and heart, they wouldn't work right. You could tell they wouldn't. The breathing was far more difficult and your heart would beat all through your body. You could feel it in your backbone and on the tops of the shoulders. They were getting to be mostly bone by then. And you smelled yourself only once in a while. It was like smelling a new place. Then you didn't and you worked exclusively on how to breathe. It didn't seem to work if you trusted your lungs to do it on their own. You had to concentrate. Shallow breaths worked best.

Then outside again, then into the interrogation room. Phantom with his dry skin, me running a lot less sweat than I would have thought. Dehydration was a factor. His curved back, the little wrinkled arm, small hand: a cup of metal, folding metal, something a grunt might carry, beaded from the cold of the water it held. "Please. Permit yourself to drink."

The look over my shoulder at the day's guard—too far across the room to swat either me or the water before I drank. Nodding my gratitude because I knew I couldn't talk, could only croak or cough. Nodding again. The smile on Phan Tuy's face that said how much I'd pleased him.

And *then* I remembered it, and why even though I liked him, because you had to like him, because he owned you—why I also shocked myself with my anger when he smiled. He probably wasn't going to kill me or hurt me too badly when he smiled, and I always wanted to weep or cry small words to him when he did, because I felt so *grateful*. But I also wanted to murder him. I knew that if I was close and if I had strength I would try to tear my way into his larynx. Because the smile, with its yellow, decaying teeth, its gaps, reminded me of the old man when he smiled. Daddy, don't *smile* like that.

"But we are not the creatures only of our parents, are we?"

Phan Tuy, gesturing from his stool at the paper with its fuzzy ink. My handwriting, sheet after sheet. "We are independent men. We make *choices.* The British say *take* choices. I have never understood that. Where would you take your choice, Mark?"

"Home."

Mistake, because he didn't smile the horrible smile, he nodded, and the guard was *there,* too fast for walking, but there and slapping the back and sides of my head. "You must never talk of home. You have no home. Home is closed to you forever. Picture your home, Marcus, burned to the ground. Pretend you are one of *us,* with nothing that has not burned twice. Where else would you take it?"

I don't know. Came out like "No." The nod, the guard's hard hand again. I thought I heard the high-pitched whistle of instrumentation malfunctioning. The on-board inertial guidance needed adjustment. I said, "Sorry. I'm not used to talking yet."

"Yes," he said. "Your period of meditation took its toll. Perhaps you should exercise. Would you enjoy some exercise, Mark?"

"Thank you." Bending my neck to stare at the ground. Whatever he asks, you do. Because this is one guy who isn't asking. Like a father, beaming over one of the early glassfuls while the ice still looks fresh and its sound is that *tock* going into the glass: "Who loves Daddy, huh? Who loves his Daddy?"

By then, you forget you drank the water. It's like you never heard of water. And you're going out into the sun and you're going to pile things, or dig things, or scrape furrows, or plant some kind of stemmy things in gassy, swampy, bowel-smelling ooze mud. And they're going to hit you while you do it. And your tongue's going to spread out again and fill up the whole of your mouth. While Phan Tuy smiles.

So you should really think of going home, one way or another. Dead might not be the awfullest idea you've had since you ejected. Dead could work. You could adjust to dead. One way or another, you think. Falling down and getting kicked because Phantom's gone and it's only you and the guard on your way to exercise fun-time leisure-hour outdoor entertainment for the smile pigs who carry the Garands and M-15s. Alive if you have to, dead if you can: go home.

Little POW joke, Goblin.

Roger the *little.* Goblin rogers *home.* Roger on the joke about adjusting to dead.

Discovery

THAT'S HOW you find out what documents your adversary will use, and what his witnesses know. Discovery is before the trial begins, and you're probing. Jack and me, unloading bales of peat moss for Schelle to use in the garden. The trunk of the car full of plastic containers and new tools. We get our gardens in late this far north. He was trying to carry too much because he wanted to demonstrate his strength, and because he wanted to highlight my feebleness. "You'll hurt your back," I said.

"No big deal," he said.

"Okay, fine. I appreciate the help. What's in your locker at school?"

I, too, was trying to lift too much at once.

Jack: "What's *that* supposed to mean?"

"If there's anything in there you don't want your principal or anybody else to find, you ought to go back to school and get rid of it."

"What're you saying—that I—"

"No. I'm not saying anything except exactly what you heard. And I'm not saying anything more."

"Well, that's a relief, anyway," he said.

"Do it, Jack. And nobody else better know what I just said. Forget ever not being grounded in darkness without even water or food. Understand? You say nothing. I'll drive you back there now. You want to go? There anything you want to get from your locker?"

"I forgot my social studies book," he said. Face flushed, eyes too wide. A baby in trouble. I saw the hand-strike, saw Jack trying to fold.

"I'll drive you back to get your book. You do what you have to do in there, you get your butt right out to the car. *Right* out."

He knew enough about reading my tones. "Okay."

"Okay," I said.

He mumbled a word that in English might have been "Thanks."

"Jack," I said, "for chrissakes, I *love* you."

He nodded.

I nodded back. We looked like those plastic storks they used to stick on the backseat shelves in sedans, nodding up and down into plastic glasses of make-believe water. I thought of Phan Tuy. Whenever he nodded they hit me. Jack turned away to the car.

Casus Belli

SCHELLE nearly never did this. Ruthie opened the door while I was in my swivel chair, back to the door, looking over across my spring binder, the stacks of documents and briefs, out through the window at this afternoon's real sunshine: buttery, thick, heavy enough to feel, if you walked outside, across your shoulders like something you hefted.

"Jesus, Ruthie," I said. "Come *on.*"

"I'm not interrupting you, Mr. Brennan—"

"Really? You're *pretending* to. It's a game. You make believe you walk into my office and I make believe I have to stop thinking about whatever it was I was thinking about."

"What I mean is, it's Mrs. Brennan."

"Here?"

"Yes, sir."

"She never comes here."

"No, sir."

"But here she is nevertheless, am I right?"

"Yes, sir. With a—somebody else, too."

"Mrs. Brennan and company?"

"Sort of, I suppose. Yes, sir."

"I'm going to turn my chair around, Ruthie, and stop thinking. All right? When you see me start to move around, you ask them to step right in."

I turned, Ruthie clattered, and then Schelle came in with her little surprise. He wasn't little, only thin, in wrinkled khakis and those big-soled shoes that weigh very little, a brown tweed sport coat, tattersall shirt, chocolate-brown necktie, heavy horn-rimmed glasses, and an expression of grave concern. He seemed worried about everything—disturbing me, shaking my hand as I stood to greet them, pronouncing his name after Schelle had said it—"Birnbaum, Sidney Birnbaum"—and then stepping back to let me talk to Schelle.

She said, "I'm sorry we surprised you, but Sidney could only fly in today, he called last night, and you and I never did get bases touched. So: surprise."

"Well, Sidney, 'surprise' is the word."

He shrugged. Through his thick glasses, he watched me with terrific intensity.

"What I wonder," I said, motioning him and Schelle toward

seats, "is what in hell *our* business is. You're on TV sometimes, right? The news shows? Have I forgotten an appointment, Schelle?"

"I was going to tell you."

"That would have been nice. I'd have enjoyed knowing it."

"My fault, Mr. Brennan," Birnbaum said. "Your wife, Mrs. Brennan—"

"A fine woman," I said. "Known her for years."

He didn't smile. He knew I meant no fun. "She's been in touch with me about the unveiling of the monument, the ceremony you're planning."

"*She's* planning," I said.

"Right. She's planning. The editors I work for are interested. A town reconciles itself to its past. The small-town slant, the regional slant. And the fact that you're a war hero and Mrs. Brennan, she said, was a protester against the war. The angles, if you'll pardon my coarsening things, are really nice." Now his lean, sad face brightened into a genuine smile. He was a man who loved his work. He was so terribly dangerous to me. "And the sentiments are real," he said. "No political bullshit, if you'll excuse the language. Real feelings. Good *stuff,*" he said.

I said, "Real feelings. Good angles for shooting."

"I don't mean to be offensive, Mr. Brennan. I know that this is mostly about Mrs. Brennan and you. At least to you. It's beautiful, it's a beautiful love story." Schelle was gnawing at her lip and looking out the window I'd abandoned for her. She squinted into the deep, thick light. "And that's what it *should* be. I'll write that into it. Hard. But the national angle, if you will: a specific moment in a specific time when a specific couple demonstrates the kind of feeling that happens all the time at the commemorative wall in Washington—I think sometimes it's too *big* at the national monument. Here we can see it small and plain."

"Small and plain's our middle name," I said. "But that was guano about your editors, wasn't it?"

He smiled again. He was a charming, smart man, this killer.

I said, "Guano's another name for bird shit."

"I'm writing the story," he said. "*People* expressed an interest."

"They don't use free-lancers, do they?"

"They'd use my stuff—"

"*Good* stuff," I reminded him.

"They'd use it as the basis for their piece. *Vanity Fair* says they'll look at it."

"If you make us look extremely foolish, unfaithful, rich, greedy, and fake."

"*Life.* Really. High degree of interest there. *Rolling Stone. Esquire,* very much. I'm in Syracuse on a piece for them, in fact. *Esquire.* The publisher who committed suicide after his lecture?"

"Good stuff there," I said.

"Mr. Brennan, I was in Vietnam. I didn't want to go. I spent half my life, it feels like, trying to stay out. They got me and I was chicken to go Canadian and I went. A full rotation, near the Song Diem Diem."

"You in on My Lai? That's the neighborhood."

"No. I was after. But we carried Zippos too."

"A very flammable place, Vietnam."

"Stuff burned."

"*Good* stuff," I said.

"I respect your experience and your bravery," he said. "I was scared all the time. I never had half the courage you showed in one day of captivity, one hour of escape. I swear I will honor what you went through and what Mrs. Brennan went through and what she's trying to do now." He stopped and very solemnly stared at me. He was almost as old as I was, but he looked ten years younger. His eyes got old, though, when he talked about his feelings. He hid them, and then they escaped, and then he looked his age.

Schelle said, "Mr. Birnbaum heard about us. Because of the ceremony. He approached me, Mark."

"Schelle," I said, "I'm not *re*proaching you. Or you, Mr. Birnbaum."

"Sidney," he said. "Please."

"*Casus belli* is a term they made us memorize in law school. You don't need much Latin once you get past"—I thought of Estella and her proud Latin phrasing—"uhm, *habeas corpus* and that kind of standard thing. I used to love *casus belli,* though. That which causes war. You understand: what precipitates a contest, a litigation, a clash of claims. Understand, Sidney?"

He looked at me with a humorous poise: he was used to people in his stories slapping him about the head and shoulders with talk. He was used to getting hit, then getting his story. He said, "It's a rugged-sounding phrase."

"Exactly," I said. "Rugged. Like yourself—a veteran who did his rotation and came back pretty whole, it looks like. And you can tell me you were scared, and maybe you were, but you don't look like a man who gets scared too terribly often."

He had long, dark lashes, and they actually seemed to flutter. He said, "I make a living doing free-lance journalism. I get by. Editors respect me sometimes. You have to be a little brash, I guess."

I said, "I guess. So what's your story, Sidney?" The best defense is a good story, Sidney.

"The story of my life, or what I'm going to write about you?"

"Neither. I meant what you're *really* intending to write about me."

"I won't know that until I'm done," he said.

"Jesus, Sidney, you're a goddamned *artist* is what you're telling me."

He laughed and showed his teeth. I'd given him real pleasure. "Will you let me interview you, Mr. Brennan?"

"When?"

"Whenever. Name the date."

"I'll call you."

"All right."

"Mark," Schelle said.

"No," Birnbaum said, "I'm sure that Mr. Brennan means it, and he'll give me a call."

"No doubt about it," I said.

"And meanwhile, I can start things at the Washington end."

I asked, "And what would that consist of?"

"Official documentation, maybe the debriefings they did when you got back? Where did you say you were?"

"They did a stool sample," I said. "Don't forget to get hold of that."

Schelle kept stroking her chin, like a boy with a brand-new beard. She looked sad and lonely, and I remembered how my greatest fear had been that I would die and leave her alone in the world, that she would be vulnerable without me. Well, I had not yet died, and here she was, lonely, vulnerable, not knowing where to look or who to ask. She looked like someone who needed to ask an important question, but didn't know how.

I said, "You want us to be in the papers, Schelle, honey?"

She said in a kind of whisper, "I think you should be."

"You deserve to be," Birnbaum said.

"Never mind," I answered him. "Schelle?"

In the same near-whisper she said, "I think you—yes," she said. "I do."

"Then fine," I told Birnbaum. "I happen to be neck-deep in a murder trial I'm preparing, and two lesser matters before the courts, and a *box*carful of documents for my clients. Would you leave me a card—well, I suppose Mrs. Brennan knows how to reach you, yes? Permit me the luxury of getting back in touch with you later on, Mr. Birnbaum."

"Sidney."

"Absolutely," I said.

"Mr. Brennan, I am on my way. I don't want to tie you up any longer. But where does that Latin come into play in all of this, if you don't mind?"

"It's the sort of now-it-all-begins thing I like to say to myself sometimes in the course of my practice."

"Now it all begins?"

Schelle said, "We'd better leave you to your work, Mark."

I said, "That's right, Sidney. Now."

"Really," he said. He didn't look confused.

Sticks and Stones

THEY SHOWED me the trick. Not that I could see it, of course, since I was folded forward, face as close to my thighs as I could get because the very low roof was hot, and the back of my neck burned in the darkness, burned without light, I told myself, when I let the pain of my gut and back push me upward. Cackling, are you? Talking to yourself, are you? *Yes.* I remember I coughed. I remember I couldn't say more. Lungs couldn't draw much. Thirst made the mouth not work. Maybe the voice was gone. If you don't talk except when people beat you, does your voice disappear? Didn't care anymore, because in the darkness and the heat, hotter than body heat, hotter than being sewed inside someone else's body while it cooked, over the roaring in the ears came their trick.

They used sticks, bricks, small stones, the butts of guns, the hafts of shovels and hoes—some or all, who knows? They beat on the tin roof of the room for solitude and consideration. "Room for Solitude and Consideration." It was a name. They had names for everything. Their eels were probably named. Their dicks and toes and guns and the teats of pregnant cows were probably named. The little hut they forced you into and folded you over and closed the tin roof with hasps on top of you had a name. They stood around and beat on it.

In the heat and darkness and the feeling of organs crushing one another like soft, pulpy fruit the blows to the tin went directly through the roof and into the head.

First they hit randomly. One started, more came in on the chorus, then they whaled away. Downed American running dog murderer of civilians and foe of the people's peaceful march to socialist independence crying up at them like a puppy to stars he couldn't see. Couldn't howl, though. A thick coughing noise if anyone heard it. I didn't. The throat tore. Mucous membrane, blood, pus, uvula, tonsil stumps, vocal cords, larynx, tongue. All of it coming up, sitting behind the teeth. Not enough liquid in the body to vomit. Jaw not working anymore, so the teeth stayed partly together, the tongue and lining of the throat and upper vertebrae couldn't come out. Sat behind deponent's teeth and took up room.

Stopped. And the sound came in to me, so I wasn't deaf yet. Sound of water in a kettle seething, almost at the boil. Not so. Sound of me. This was breathing. I am breathing, I thought. This is crippled breathing, but the body continues, I am not dead.

"I am not dead," I tried to say.

Local distaste for free speech. For coughing noises from the man in the box.

First stickman in the orchestra gave them the rhythm, and they all came in on beat number five. Goblin counting them, roger. Heavy slamming, everyone striking at the same time, on and on and on and on and on and on and on and on and on and on. Et cetera. Goblin sucking on his tongue and throat membranes and vocal cords. Determined to sing along. Pain of skull crushing, the temples shattering slowly, splintering, brain juice spraying out and up and onto the walls of the box. Sizzling in the heat. Frying. But Goblin singing back through it. Naughty child who's been locked in his room. Mommy pushing the cigarette into his palm to show him *You don't talk back.* Singing to his wounded palm the red sore rimmed with ashes. Singing for them to hear him. Or to comfort the cradled small hand. Goblin aloft on wings of song.

A while. Voice running out, and energy, the pain growing down and around like a new skin. The smell of frying meat on the walls. The huge noise collapsing him, except there was no place to go beneath the sound. The body unable to move any farther. The lungs like flat red bladders inside. The heart overwhelmed by the orchestration, beating only to the rhythm they struck. Goblin inside like a fetus. Waiting for permission to be born.

Then the roof lifting. Didn't know the sounds had stopped. They hadn't. I still heard them. Felt them, anyway, and flinched at the light, the sky, the ring of grinning men in black pajamas or dun-colored puttees, captured no doubt from the Imperial Japanese Army twenty-five years before. Lifted out. They wrinkled their noses. Apparently Goblin performed some intimate body functions.

Phan Tuy on his stool behind the bureau. "Mark, that must have been difficult."

Piece of cake. Tried to say it. Made the noise of someone gargling with talcum powder. Settled for what felt like a shrug.

"Others of you have complained of their time in the room."

Did manage to croak it: "Others."

"You are not alone here, Mark. Have I not informed you? How regretful."

That was a time I started to cry.

Mommy was sorry about the hurt on his hand. It was just that Mommy got so *angry* when he talked fresh like that. Surely he could see that Mommy loved him. She *hated* when he got hurt. Kissing the hand and if only Daddy could be *home* when he said. And *stay* home. Then all her boy had to do was not make these terrible things happen. Be polite and not say naughty things and be a *help.* We'll put some baking soda and water on it, no one would ever know he hurt his hand, poor thing. Poor boy. Lighting another cigarette.

That was a time I started to cry.

Where You Wanted to Be

THE PROBLEM, according to a doctor consulted by the prosecution, was that when the man "examined where he'd gotten to be in his life, versus, you know, where you wanted to be," he wasn't pleased. It ends up being a map problem. He started out for one place, he ended up somewhere else. Pilots do it all the time. You fly a T-38 out of a flattened anthill near Amarillo or Yuma, and you finish in upstate New York. It can happen. You can start out in upstate New York and land in upstate New York and still, once you figure things out, be downwind, upstream, and shy by half a million miles of where you wanted to be.

This is the new, improved navigation. This was the problem of the man who got caught after twenty years. He killed his wife and his mother and the three kids, he left word for his pastor, and he lit out for someplace else. He got there. There is always someplace else and you can often find it. He grew a mustache and married a woman who never suspected five dead people behind the mustache, and he got caught. Estella had no mustache to speak of, but the new, improved navigation seemed a way we could go. Your Honor, the defense moves for dismissal on the grounds that defendant was suffering a new, improved midlife crisis. Flying without instruments in heavy weather.

The fellow with the mustache bought himself a couple of guns once he saw his daughter was listening to heavy-metal rock music and was therefore under Satan's sway. She didn't enjoy church anymore, he felt. She dated bad boys. He test-fired both the .22 revolver and the 9 mm automatic. It was the son, he said in his letter to their minister, who gave him the toughest time. His young son. The kid, it seemed, put up a struggle. He killed the others with head shots from the rear. They didn't know. The littlest one saw it coming. He ran. He got caught. He fought his father. Daddy said it took him three shots to put the kid away. Killing the boy, he said, distressed him. Roger that. You're having a midlife crisis, the kid makes a scene, you end up distressed. This here's Dr. Death, son, you meet him like a man, hear?

Close enough. Dr. Luwein, the man who might love my wife, maybe was loving her in who knows which archly named motel or empty operating theater, watched me dress as though that were part of the examination: how the patient buttons his sharkskin vest and slides his suit coat on. Pushing his glasses back, blinking, moving his lips within his beard—it was like seeing some transparent microscopic feeding creature to note how his lips inside the layer of thick, dark facial fur would move on one another.

We sat, not talking. We considered each other a while. Finally Brennan, ever vigilant and witty: "Well?"

"Your shoes and socks, Marcus," he said.

Yes. Socks balled in wingtips, wingtips side by side, there they were. There I was, outside them, wearing my shirt and tie and vest and trousers and suit coat. "Right," I said, "right. I thought I'd—" Jesus, Brennan.

"Did you forget?"

Polite enough question, but not with that mouth saying it, the small eyes behind their lenses. Phan Tuy: Have you forgotten to tell me the truth, Marcus?

"What?" I said. Years of law school and a various practice had taught me the subtleties of rhetorical evasion. "Excuse me?"

"Your shoes."

"And socks," I said.

While I slid into the calf-length socks and then my shoes, crossing my legs to do the laces so I wouldn't have to bend beneath his eyes, I said, "Do all you guys get the same pictures of old-fashioned doctors and kids? Along with the off-yellow walls and the examination tables? There's one basic supplier, and you take what you get?"

In a sweaty small room, the treadmill roaring as it speeded up and, simultaneously, tilted farther uphill. On the computer screen, my heart was beating in valleys and peaks, the nurse was calling my blood pressure out to Luwein at the keyboard. Paper tumbled from the printer, the treadmill made me run, I heard myself heaving, blowing, felt the electrodes in their cups atop the patches of shaved chest and belly flesh as they wobbled, noted how my thighs began to cramp.

"How do you feel?" Luwein called.

Couldn't talk. Shook my head. They began to slow the treadmill, bring it level, take my blood pressure one more time, study me for dizziness or worse—the electric paddles in case of infarction lay to my left, on a small wooden bench.

And then, after he had gone away to read the printouts and returned, Luwein watching me sit barefoot, apparently dazed, while he pointed at graph curves. "You feeling all right, Marcus?"

"You're the doctor, Doctor."

"The cardiac stress test was fine. Recovery from maximum output was quick. Your heart's all right, I believe. Do you drink a lot?"

"I almost never drink at all. Just about never."

"Good. Sometimes the sauce can push your blood pressure up. It's only a touch above the last time. We'll watch it. And do you exercise?"

"At gunpoint."

"Walk."

"Walk?"

"Take walks. Work up a sweat. I can give you a regimen, if you like."

"The last thing I want from anyone is a regimen."

"Don't walk, then. Though you might consider doing what your doctor says."

"I'll take it under advisement. No insult intended. But I'm busier 'n hell right now."

"And at other times?"

"About the same."

"That's what I assumed. You know, chest pains, blackouts, fatigue, fearfulness—"

"Fearfulness? Who in fuck said 'fear'? Did I come in and talk about fear one night while I was sleepwalking?"

He smiled. Teeth and pink lips within the frame of red-brown hair with streaks of gray or white. "I'm not suggesting you're afraid. How about crankiness. Irritability."

"Goddamned right," I said.

"All right. I'm talking, anyway, about stress. Are you under pressure?"

"There are different kinds of pressure."

"Pressure makes coal out of earth. Pressure makes diamonds out of coal. It pumps blood through duodenal ulcers or blows it up through weakened artery walls into brains. Pressure's interesting. It makes a man get tired. It makes his chest sound like a kettledrum inside his own skull. It turns his arm and fingers numb. Men see spots. They hear Manhattan subway trains in Peoria soy fields. You get the idea?"

"You think I'm stressed."

"No, I *know* you're stressed. Who doesn't?"

"Schelle? Mrs. Brennan? You're talking about my wife?"

"Her, too. Can you change your schedule? Alter it in any way?"

"*That's* a question."

Prelim and Grand

I TRIED. The sheriff's deputies smirked, the state Bureau of Investigation detective stared at me, kept staring through the preliminary hearing. I said across the polished wood and gilt of the old county courtroom, "You have a problem?" Judge snarled, actually showed me his teeth. When John Backus showed his teeth, which embarrassed him because that's an intimacy, you backed away. I did.

But I tried. I challenged the D.A.'s assistant. She was a bitch on wheels, and a friend, an up-and-coming kid. I said, "Ms. Tillim, can we cut the crap and get to the horse?"

Backus interrupted by waving his hand at me. "What's that mean, counselor?"

"I don't know, sir."

"Good. I was afraid you knew something I didn't. Are you challenging Ms. Tillim's sufficiency of evidence? Let's see—I *might* be mistaken, but as I recall, well, as I *see.* Right here, am I wrong again? I see Polaroid pictures, very nicely focused, too, of Mr. Ziegler's corpse. Are there enough angles on that for you, counselor? Do you doubt it's a dead body?"

"No, sir."

"And I see a cassette of television tape on which we have all watched your client tell a number of people that she turned Mr. Ziegler from a chubby naked lovemaking partner into a chubby naked corpse."

"Larry would have hated to be called chubby, sir."

"Quite right. We owe him better. *Stocky*. Does that suit you?"

"Thank you, sir. About the confession?"

"You regard it as tainted."

"The tape does not show the defendant receiving her Miranda rights."

"A deputy will say that she did."

"Not established yet, sir."

"Agreed. No need to wave your arms like that, Ms. Tillim. *I'll* deal with matters of procedure in my court. I agree that an attorney for the defense could—would be bound by any code of ethics to—argue that the confession *might* be tainted. No attorney present, no Mirandization on the inculpating tape. Yes and yes and yes. However. The court *will* accept the sworn testimony of these officers, investigators, and even—you're thorough, Ms. Tillim—the log of the Randall Volunteer Fire Department, which sent its ambulance in response to the 911 call. There was a dead body, there was a woman who had been seen to enter the room with the deceased. *Ipso,* as they say, *facto,* Mr. Brennan. There's enough to bind over Mother Theresa, much less your client, for next month's grand jury."

Dee Tillim smiled, Backus gaveled, they held Estella for forty hours at Tillim's insistence while I posted bond, Backus on my tail for ethics, et cetera, and what it came to was the recently paid mortgage on the house. Backus set $50,000 as a favor to me. He could have gone a hundred, which is what Tillim and

Jake Brandywine, her boss, wanted. Tillim, tall, small nose, high cheekbones, expensive clothes, caught the judge's eye, I knew. He was very fond of women. Bright blue eyes, whitish eyebrows, a stern face: a German Catholic who went to church every day and whose saddest moment was Rome's decision that you no longer had to kiss the ring of your priest. He loved golf as much as God, his clerk once said. He'd been a splendid trial lawyer, a defending lawyer and not a D.A., unusual for a judge. He was fair a good deal of the time, and you couldn't ask for more.

So she was out. The grand jury was convened while I wrote and called psychiatrists to set up screening interviews. Jack smirking at Schelle's suggestion of a shrink and my jumping on her for it. Knowing that I knew what he meant. Roger. I didn't let her go to the grand jury, of course. Though Estella had a right to appear, I told her to waive it—better that than waiving immunity, appearing without your lawyer, answering all their questions. It's not like they have to work to *connect* you to the crime, I told her. We're defending with extenuations. When she asked which ones, I touched her or changed the subject. When she asked again, I said, "Duress."

"What kind of duress?"

We were in her bed, it was May now, and the usual early heat had set in. We'd have it for a week, then more rain, then a week or two of low temperatures, then late actual spring.

"What kind can you offer?"

She laughed low in her throat. Next to me, her short hair touching my shoulder but not on it, she said, "You know anything about me?"

"I'm willing to bet you were abused."

"Never."

"Never?"

"Never ever. Daddy used to tuck me in at night, kiss me good night, that kind of thing, but nothing else."

"They never put their cigarettes out in the palm of your hand?"

"No! Jesus, Marcus."

"They never came up behind you and smacked your head until you thought you were in church with the bells ringing?"

"No."

"Because you had to learn to listen?"

"Listen?"

"You had to learn to listen. Anybody ever kick your ankles while you were standing opposite them so you fell down on the side of your face?"

"I don't want any more of this. I get enough on the job, Marcus."

"That's why you have the job."

"To hear that horrible shit?"

"Because of your childhood. Where did Daddy tuck you, Estella? What'd he tuck? How far up?"

She rolled over at me, onto me, she was on top of me, and with one hand she pinched my nostrils shut while with the other she pinched my upper lip. She turned the flesh hard and tears came into my eyes. I swatted her ribs, the side of her head, but she rode me with her thighs and knees, digging in hard, not falling away, and she buried her head in my shoulder. I struck her hard, struck her again, but the pain was terrible from my nose to my throat. *"No more,"* she said.

I let my arms go limp to signify surrender.

"Not any more of that."

I touched her buttocks with my fingertips. She let go of my face. "I guess you found that line of questioning offensive," I said, letting the air out and out.

"I take care of little children and battered women and indigent old men nobody loves, and you don't pollute that with your smut."

"Smut. Saving your life is smut?"

"They won't electrocute me."

"Thank you. You like twenty-five years to life?"

She lay still, still on me.

"To *life*," I said. "They won't play around with this one, Estella. Dee Tillim's ambitious. She's not a great lawyer, but she's tough. She wants to be a D.A. one of these days. You'll be part of her record. Larry was a respected merchant, the bankers loved him, he *shoveled* the money to the Republican Party, and you generate sex like a goddamned female bear in heat."

"Thank you."

"Some men hate that. Men on juries, *women* on juries, prison guards—and wait'll you see what you draw for company at Bedford Hills. You think they'll smuggle in *The Atlantic* fucking *Monthly* for you, Estella? They will rape you with fists. It's ugly."

"So are you, Mark."

"Thank you. How much time do you think you can do?"

She leaned her forehead on my chest and shook her head. "Why are you so hard?" she asked. "You feel so hard. Your penis must love imprisonment."

"Why are you thinking about penises now, when I'm telling you, we have to formulate—"

"This."

She slid down, sat partway up, and inserted me. She was ready, and I was too. What I wasn't ready for was, while I closed my eyes and arched, bucking up and into her, the open hand she must have swung from shoulder height. I felt one hand seize my shoulder, felt the other move away. Then she struck, my head wobbled, my mouth must have opened because I heard myself gasp.

"Don't you try that, with my father and abuse and all of that, Mark."

"All right."

"I'll leave you."

"Now, you mean, or in general? I hope you don't mean *now.*"

"Your cock is a compass. Isn't it?"

Goblin.

"*Isn't* it!" Her hand, slamming in again.

I said, "Estella."

"Don't you tell me," she said, holding my arms above my head on the mattress. "Don't you tell *me.*"

I opened my eyes. In the gray cool light of her bedroom, the heat everywhere but there, my body feeling cool in spite of the sweat I knew was on my forehead and my ribs, she rode above me. Her lips were pale against her pale face. She had gritted her teeth. The warnings came from between them. She was weeping and pressing down with locked elbows her thin strong arms that held mine onto the bedclothes. She rode me. She drove me. She hated me. And when she came, she shuddered, and her lips made a frown of disgust. Then she opened her eyes. She saw me watching. Her mouth curved sweetly.

"Yum," she said, smiling above me.

Lists

WHAT WE CAPTURED, according to the President's count:

Approximately 23,000 individual weapons, enough to equip 74 NVA battalions.

Approximately 15 million rounds of ammunition.

Approximately 14 million pounds of rice—four months' worth of rations for all enemy combat battalions operating in South Vietnam.

143,000 rockets, mortars, and recoilless rifle rounds—fourteen months' worth of combat materiel.

Almost 200,000 antiaircraft rounds, 6,000 mines, 62,000 grenades, and 83,000 pounds of various explosives.

435 vehicles.

12,000 VC and NVA killed.

What we achieved:

Eliminated threats to our forces and the security of South Vietnam.

Inflicted heavy casualties and losses.

Dislocated supply lines.

Cut off resupply from the sea.

Kept the guerrillas and the Communist main force separate.

Bought time for the South Vietnamese to strengthen themselves against a cunning and desperate enemy. As Sun Tzu reminds us: Quantities derive from measurement, figures from quantities, comparisons from figures, and victory from comparisons.

The ink spreading in the wetness of the air, the watery heat. It leached from its letters on the coarse, soft paper. I wrote it for him.

Because I had sacrificed the lives of children and women and old men.

Because I had interfered for fascists.

Because it was not my war.

Because the fascists were Christians who drank blood in great churches in France.

Because I fought from above.

Because they fought from below.

Because in their tunnels the shock of my bombing caused the water to rise and the soil to drop into their mouths.

Because injustices were my motives and my principles.

Because I was a Marine and therefore a specialist in the slaughter of infants.

Because the lure of my war was the repression of youthful republics and socialist states.

Because I kneeled before money in marble banks with great corridors.

Because I had lied in my confessions of personal history.

Because I had lied to him.

Because I had lied.

Because I had lied.

Parental Council of War

THIS TIME I parked in the doctors' lot, not the patients', and I walked down the administrative corridor instead of toward Admissions or the labs. It stank the same—old age, fluids, fear, all overlaid by the acid perfume of disinfectants. Schelle's office was small but she'd made it pretty: flowers I knew she plundered country fields for, pictures of me and Mickey and Jack, a framed drawing Jack had made of a long-dead Irish setter, her nursing certification, a letter from a boy who died of leukemia thanking her for her care. Music played from a little transistor radio she'd propped on a tan filing cabinet, something heavy and German and full of bass growls. She was staring in the music, under the humming fluorescent light, at piles of papers on her desk.

When I knocked she said, "Mark!" Her eyes narrowed into worry at once.

I waved my hand, my elegant, capable counselor's hand. "Everything's fine," I said.

"You feel all right?"

"I'm here for you, not the doctors."

"The kids?"

"Fine, fine. Not a medical emergency, anyway. I need us to talk, Schelle. I was up half the night at the office."

"I know."

"I know you do. I'm sorry."

She shrugged, and it was the proper sign: we were past polite demurrals about late hours.

"Can you get out now?"

"Probably not," she said.

"We need a council of war."

"We should talk at night, Mark. And in the mornings."

"You're right. I apologize." I saw her shoulders start to lift. "I apologize for the *apology*. I have a sense, I have more than a sense, of what I've been like."

"And for how long you've been that way?" Her eyes were wide, and she wasn't afraid, she was unembarrassed. She knew, and I did too, that we were past mere damage to feelings.

Nodded. Yes. Then: "I heard a thing a couple of days ago. About our Jack."

"Oh, shit," she said. "I hate it when people tell us about our kids. It's never great news, is it?"

"Why should someone want to come and make us glad?"

"What, Mark?"

"Come out for a drive. I think you should."

Looking at me, examining me, she said, "I see that you do. I believe you. Let me talk to some people."

"I'll wait."

"Yes," she said, and then she smiled. "I'm usually the one who waits. For you."

"I'm sorry for that too."

"Thank you," she said gravely. When she stood, in her dark tan short-sleeved dress with the low waist and long hem, a choker of thick ivory around her neck, I raised my brows. She said, "Not bad, huh? This is the usual me."

Smiled what I hoped was the sexy, sex-drawn grin, then gestured at the doorway with my head.

"A minute," she said, reaching for the phone, draping the white cord across her chest like a Sam Browne belt, holding the pose for me. I offered the grin again, then turned to the door.

She drove the Volvo. I huddled against the door, resting. The minute she turned the ignition switch, I'd grown exhausted, the way you do in a crisis when someone competent takes over. I imagined that my clients felt this way. Wondered if Estella did. Doubted it.

"What?" Schelle said, heading out of town.

I shook my head.

"More secrets?"

"More?" I said.

"Yes."

"I was thinking how glad I was to get here and sit in the car and just drift out a while with you."

Goblin orbiting.

"You look like two hundred pounds of poop, Mark."

"Thank you. One-eighty-five, according to Luwein's scale."

"Is that good or bad?"

"Only less."

We left the two-lane macadam and headed south and west, on one-lane unpaved roads, raising dust, driving into the low sun at four o'clock on a bright and cold spring day. All sorts of pink and white little flowers were in the pastures, and thistle.

"The state flower," I said when we passed a purple patch.

"That's about all you can get now," she said. "It isn't a good time for wild flowers."

"Isn't a good time for all that much," I said.

She edged us off the road and down a dry meadow track into a very old, uncultivated apple orchard. "Did you ever come here?" she asked, turning off the ignition, rolling down her window, gesturing for me to do the same.

I cranked. Told her, "No. I don't even know where we are."

"Near Plymouth. Kids come here to park."

"So why would *I*? How come you know about it?"

"Grim source. We've had two rapes here. One alleged, one we proved."

"The Hergesheim boy?"

"He beat her up, too. He learned that from his father, I think."

"The father—"

"Beats the kid's mother regularly. Didn't you ever see a little fat, round lady in the stores or on the street, always has a discolored eye or a butterfly bandage?"

"Jesus, Schelle."

"That was her boy. He was following in the old man's noble footsteps. God. He beat her, then he raped her, then he slugged her again to make sure she didn't talk. Your client helped her."

"Client?"

"Miss Pritchett? The murderer?"

"Murderess, they're calling her at the corner cigar store. Who is only the defendant until the trial is over. How did you know about her?"

"You told me. You said some things. Though even if you hadn't, I can't imagine word not getting around a major metropolis like ours."

"No. No. I wasn't trying to hide it from you."

"I couldn't imagine why."

"Of course not."

Schelle swatted and said, "It's the damned blackflies. They come earlier and earlier every year." She rolled her window up, and I did the same. "I'd rather sweat," she said, "than get eaten."

"Yeah, well, we're going to trial in maybe three weeks and I haven't got proverbial dick."

"Did she do it?"

"She was there, Larry Ziegler was there, he's dead. Murder in the first degree is out."

"Why? Didn't she murder him?"

"Apparently she *was* the instrumentality of his death. Murder in the first in New York is called intentional death and they'll give you life. Since a policeman wasn't cut to ribbons with an Uzi after six months of plotting on Ms. Pritchett's part, I think the D.A.'s little hit woman will go for murder in the second."

"What do you get for that?"

"Either the all-expenses-paid vacation to Barbados for eleven fun-filled days and nights or something between twenty-five and life."

"God. What's going to happen?"

"I have to find some shrinks. You know any?"

"Yes. So do you."

"I don't mean mine. I'm done with those guys. I'm—you know that, Schelle. I'm done."

"Okay, Mark."

"Well, don't—"

"No," she said. "Mark. Please."

I took a breath. I watched it mist my window, and I realized that I was sweating. "Yes," I said. "All right. No, I need some professional-witness kinds of shrink, you know what I mean?"

"You're pleading insanity?"

"I don't know. Something closer to that than sanity, that's for shooting sure."

"I'll look around."

"Discreetly. I'm sorry: I know you'll be discreet."

We panted a little in the glass box the car had become, and finally she said, "So, tell me. About the kids."

"Could you start the motor and turn the air conditioner on,

Schelle? I mean, we drive out to the countryside here so we can sit inside the equivalent of a little tin *shack.* Jesus."

She looked at me the way she does when I exhibit what Schelle calls an inappropriate response. Fucking A. Goblin under fucking *glass* confirms that.

I said, "A little claustrophobia."

"I'm sorry," she says, and she means it. The response is deemed appropriate. Schelle remembers the war, the entire goddamned boogie begins, and we dance in our heads while remaining in place in the gently shivering car.

"Schelle, Lee Beeton Palmer works for the sheriff. Do you know him?"

She shook her head. Her lips were pressed together. She was scared.

"Apparently they got one of their young-looking people into the high school after hours, hanging out in the parking lot, the pizza joint, you know. They do that sort of thing every now and again. Lee runs the operations."

"He's a vice cop?"

"He's an expert on drugs, I guess you'd call him a vice cop. It isn't quite that glamorous, but yes. That's good enough. He really knows about drugs, too. FBI training, state training, and he likes it because he hates drugs. He's simply one of those people who lines up on the right side."

"Oh, don't tell me our baby is—"

"No. He didn't say that. All he said was kids who dropped names dropped Jack's. Tangentially. Not as if he's dealing or buying in quantities, nothing like that."

"But he's involved?"

"Possibly. Well: probably, on the edges. This happened the other day." Told her about Jack, the locker, the warnings, the boy's frightened face.

"Oh, God. Will they be after him now?"

"I think he's all right, but I wanted you to know. And I wanted the satisfaction of your knowing I wasn't nuts when I worried about it. Whatever I am, whatever you think I am, I would enjoy your respect."

"You were good to Jack," she said. "You're a good father."

"I'm a horrible father. In a long line of horrible fathers. But I wanted you to know."

Schelle looked at me and her mouth grew soft—not weak, not worried even, but pliant. I realized how long I'd seen her face composed to rigidity by daily, maybe hourly, acts of will.

"You poor kid," I said.

She said, "We have to talk to Jack."

"We will."

"Together," she said.

Nodded. We were still wearing the seat belts and she looked at me the way a woman looks at you when she starts to unfasten her clothes. She pressed the release on her belt and pushed it from her. It clanged on the metal of the door as it slid into the housing. I pressed mine. Goblin ejecting. She moved along the seat to me. I grabbed first. Clumsy man, swatting her more than seizing her, but Schelle didn't care. And I was doing what I should have done. Pulling her. Kissing her soft mouth and feeling it open. This was Rochelle who had married me. Carried me. Kept hauling me through these bad times like a wounded man on her back. We were under fire and she carried me. Schelle was the veteran, I realized. The monument ought to be for her.

My face in her breasts, the smell of her perfume and soap and her skin, clothing hanging. Shreds, like shreds, the clothing burned and shot away and torn away, hanging on her. Victim. Survivor. Schelle.

"What?" she said.

Looked up.

"Mark, please: *what?*"

"There's nothing wrong." Whispered it. Thinking still of the hotel in Hawaii our first night together when I'd made it back.

And finally I just sat up. Schelle pulling her clothes to herself, embarrassed and sad. My wife was so sad. Reached again, as gently as I could, but she shook her head. She smiled the sad, terrible smile.

"Schelle. Dear Schelle." Like starting a letter from a long way away.

"Why did we come here?" she asked.

"You drove us. But listen."

"Always listening, Mark. I'm always listening."

"Yes. I didn't mean a smart-ass answer. And I know you are." Big hands moving all over the place, trying to tell her something true. "I know you are."

She nodded. "Good," she said. "Okay." Tears on her face as she looked out the driver's-side window and buttoned her blouse.

"You're beautiful," I said. Something true. The tears came faster. "We're still you and me," I said. "Jack's parents." Something true.

"Mommy and Daddy," Schelle said.

"That's right. Yes. I screw it up, but I believe that. I believe in that. Mickey and Jack. We're Mommy and Daddy. That's a good thing, Schelle. That's something true."

Her head turning fast on those words. Studying me. "There's that."

"There's that," I said.

Later I wondered how she'd known, so accurately, the route to the lovers' lane.

Callback

MICKEY SAID, "Daddy! How come you're *home*?"

"You mean, how come *I'm* home. Mom's working late and I'm not. I bottomed out at the office and I came home for aid and comfort and your brother's out watching a school play about, I don't remember—yes, I do: the Little Orphan Annie thing? Cute little songs about Hooverville and street people? You know. And Mom's working late."

"Yes. You okay, Daddy?"

"Don't I sound okay? How're you?"

"Yes. Well, you sound a little, I don't know, sad."

"Never."

"Okay. Listen—you're sure you're all right, so I can tell you my news?"

"I'm all right and tell me your news."

"Callback," she said.

"When?"

"No! Daddy! You go and you read for a part and you're humiliated, the usual, and you go home and there's nothing on the machine. You know? That's pretty much it, right? Except, I read for the part, I go to work, I come home and park my legs at the door and stump around moaning, and guess what?"

"Tell me, sweetie. Tell me good news."

"The light's blinking on the machine."

"A kind of Morse code thing?"

"Daddy! Listen."

"Roger."

Long silence.

I say, "Go ahead, kid. Please. Tell me."

Slower at first, but then excited again: "There's a message on the machine. I play it back. It's from the director's assistant, this ice bitch with her nipples showing through her shirt. Except this time she's nice to me. First name, not Miz Brennan. Lots of *please* and *could* and *would.* And they would like me to come down and read the part again, but longer. And the *playwright's* coming, too!"

"So you got a part, right?"

"No."

"What'd you get, baby?"

"A callback, Daddy."

"Which could get you the part."

"It could get me the part. But I don't care! I never *got* a callback before! It's starting! I do care. I do. I want to get it. But a callback's a start. I know it."

"Don't quit work, sweetie."

"Thank you for the vote of confidence."

"No. Now, you know what I mean. Your lawyer's advice."

"You're right. I won't. It wouldn't pay enough to let me quit anyway. I'll work around the show if I score. Daddy, I could *score.*"

"What's the play about, sweetie?"

"Oh. It's this guy with AIDS, and his lover—you know, his friend. And the friend's sister comes to town, and they're—it's in New York. It's set in New York. The sister's name is Miriam, and she comes to stay with the friend, her brother, who she doesn't know is gay, and he begs his lover not to tell her, which is completely retrograde. It's wrong. Nobody would do that, except the sister still lives in this small town that the brother hasn't been back to in years? And he's afraid to tell their parents. And so he doesn't tell the girl and the lover agrees not to tell the girl, that he's just tested HIV-positive. You know, he's not like dying yet. And what happens?"

"Sounds great. Complicated. All that secrecy, people not telling things to each other."

"Yeah. You hate that, right?"

"What, Mickey?"

"What happens, Daddy? What do you think?"

"In the play?"

"In the play!"

"She guesses?"

"She falls in love with her brother's *lover*!"

"You do?"

"Me. If I get the part. I have to read this scene where I tell my brother I'm in love with his lover. Except I don't know he's his lover."

"Do you find out?"

"It's the saddest part. I'm glad they don't want me to do that tomorrow."

"I want you to be happy tomorrow, sweetie."

"Oh, I will be, Daddy."

"I want you to be happy every day. And this is wonderful."

"Daddy, I almost am."

"What, baby?"

"Happy every day."

"You really are?"

"Daddy, I really am. I must be a jerk, huh?"

"You must be living in the right place. Not in town, right?"

"New York's where I should be. Not away from you, Daddy. Mr. Take Everything Personally."

"But that's why you went there."

"One reason. It's part of growing up, you know. To do things like that. To say them."

"Now you're a grown-up, so you know that."

Mickey's voice changed, got huskier, more certain. She was somebody else. Somebody else said, " 'I know one thing, Andy. You're what I know. That's a thing to take home from New York. That's a souvenir and a half, isn't it.' That's Miriam. Meet Miriam."

"Jesus, Mick."
"See?"
"You're *good.*"
"I love you, Daddy."
"You do?"
"Stupid."
"Mickey, I've got this case. It's gonna kill me."
"Not you."
"It's gonna kill me, Mickey."
"I'm running, Daddy. I have to go run, and yes I'll be careful. Three of us jog together now, and one of us always carries Mace. And nothing's gonna kill you. I'll call about the callback when they tell me, and I love you and Mommy and Jack, you'll tell them?"
"Tell them?"
"The callback? Mickey to Daddy, Mickey to Daddy, do you read me?"
Confirming that.
"Daddy?"
"Mickey."
Out.

Defense

I WAS LYING on the office sofa, my head on the soft Mexican pillow Schelle had brought for me. It went with the Mexican pots and the donkey blanket that hung on the wall. She said at the time that I needed more color in the room, that lawyers were dull and their offices dull, their cases too, she'd said, referring to her nursing stories about painful deaths and the sadness of beholding the deaths' beholders. I was lying there, and Estella was walking around the office. She had a terrible energy that night. It was near the end of May, the office windows were open to high breezes and a cool, clear night. The cream-colored drapes blew in. Papers under weights—rocks Schelle and I had collected, old inkwells, two rectangular glass lozenges that held colored pictures (Niagara Falls in one, a cameo of Jefferson in the other)—were rustling. It sounded like autumn. I thought of dried leaves. It sounded as though Estella were walking around through piles of them, kicking them as angry kids might do. She paced.

That night she wore a dark skirt that came almost to the floor, some kind of open-toed, low-heeled shoes, a short-sleeved cotton sweater that picked up the mossy tones of her skirt, and a very wide leather belt with a big round buckle. The skirt had pockets, and her hands were in them.

I said, "It's standard. You filled out the form when you were arraigned. You told them you couldn't afford an attorney, then you told them you made a sizable salary. Anyway, you must have been known to some of the court officers, to the sheriff's people. You're a social caseworker, for chrissakes, Estella. They're going to know who you *are.*"

"No," she said, rounding my desk again. "It's not that I don't qualify. I didn't think I did. I don't have any money in the bank, I owe on my car, my stove, my dishwasher. You know. But no, fine—I don't qualify, then I don't qualify. It's that they told *you,* and *you* went ahead, but no one told *me.*"

Her angular face was blotchy, her hair looked ruffled by the winds that rattled the papers on my table, that blew around the black spring binder. When she took her hands out of her pockets, it was to clasp them in front of her. She moved her wedge of knuckles before her as she spoke. "Isn't it *my* life? *My* defense? My bloody *choice?*"

"Yes. But, well maybe I was wrong. I did assume you'd want me to continue as your attorney."

"Oh, don't sound stiff and righteous and hurt, will you?"

I said, "I wanted to continue the way we were going."

"All right," she said. She sounded tired. "All right."

"But did you?"

"Yes."

"For sure? I can get you someone else. They won't waive the fee, but I can help you out."

"I said all *right*, Mark. Thank you. All right. Yes. Thank you and thank you."

I closed my eyes. I'd been telling her about psychiatric testimony, confusions that juries were prone to when the defense and the prosecution had conflicting experts in matters like these. I'd been leading up to the shape of my so-called defense, and I was fairly certain that her anger was directed at that, at what she saw me formulating, and not at my having volunteered to defend her without a fee once the public defender and the D.A.'s office had found her capable of paying for defense.

"So how do you feel, Miss Estella? You happy with things tonight?"

"Asshole," she said.

"You're mad at what I'm leading to."

"That I'm crazy? Crazy's a little hard to live with. Can you plead me eccentric?"

"Not guilty on grounds of eccentricity. Why not? They do it with Hershey Kisses overdosing, with too many egg rolls, I can do it because you're not a usual woman."

"And I'm not."

"I know."

"Are you enslaved to me?"

I grinned. But when I looked up, she was watching my face and waiting for my answer.

"Jesus, Estella. Is that what you want?"

"Whenever you're ready," she said.

"I want you to tell me about your childhood."

She resumed her steady march around the room. When she passed the switch, she hit it and my desk lamp and reading lamps went off. I heard her beside me. I smelled her rich perfume, a harsh, oiled richness, and I heard her clothing as she slid inside it and kneeled beside my shoulders and head. Now my own hands were clasped, atop my stomach, to keep me from reaching for her at once. "It was nice," she whispered.

"No."

She whispered, "How do you *know* that?"

"You know it, too," I said. "Was it beatings? Burnings? Did they make you drink liquor as a joke at their parties? Did they kick you? Did your father—you know, did he rape you?"

She leaned down, and her face was over mine. She was talking with her lips nearly at my mouth, over my mouth, we were breathing each other's air. "It's never just rape," she whispered. "He loves you. He needs you. He wants to show you his love, and you have to prove yours to him. He whimpers. It's never a rape. How did you know? I mean, do you. How *do* you? Maybe it's something else. Maybe it's nothing."

"Maybe," I whispered back up. I could smell her lipstick. In the light of the office it had looked nearly black, it was such a deep purple-red. It smelled a little like crayons. I could smell that, and her breath, her dinner wine, the energy that beat inside her. It was like being next to a coal furnace, except her skin, I'd bet, would be cool. "But it's something, isn't it? It isn't nothing. It never is. Never. That's why you're in the business you're in. Because it's always never nothing."

She kissed me. Light, slight pressure, then away, then down again. I felt her hand come up my thigh.

"You can fuck my brains out, Estella. I'm pleading your childhood. I'm talking about your history. I'm maybe going to call up other people who've suffered that kind of abuse. I don't know, maybe cops, even war veterans. People who can tell them what happens when you've been mistreated, what happens years later. I need shrinks, I need better shrinks. I'm going to get them."

Her hand moved up.

She kissed me harder, and I waited, and then I felt her teeth on my lip, gently, then tighter, tougher, and then the pain.

I made some kind of sound, I know. She paused. "I'll stop," she said. "You want to talk. We need to do this. And I'm hurting you, I'm afraid."

"How afraid?"

"Oh," she said, "I'm terrified. Don't let me hurt you."

"No."

"No, you won't? No, you want to talk? No, you don't want to talk? No, I'm not hurting you?" Her hand wasn't caressing now, it was squeezing, and I winced, and her mouth came down again, her teeth. She said, between them, "Which?"

I said, "No."

She very slowly backed away, then slowly reached for my belt and eased it open, opened my trousers, pulled at the waist until I raised myself, like a baby being bedded. She slid my clothes down. In the darkness, my eyes were closed. I felt her stand, and then she moved so that she was lying on me, leg for leg, in her clothes. She moved to kneel on the sofa between my legs, which I moved to make room. I felt her skirt rustle, and then she moved up. It was clear that she'd come to the office with no underwear on.

"You're hard to get," she said.

In the darkness, I nodded my head.

"But I have you."

Nodded again.

"Don't I?"

I raised myself in her.

"Don't I, though," she said.

Then she slid herself down on me, and forward a little, and her small hand was on my face, at my lips, the fingers in my mouth, and then away. I felt her pull the Mexican pillow, and I moved as if in obedience to lay myself down without it. That, I realized, as we moved together and moved together and moved, was what she set on top of my face, and leaned her own face and fingers against. That was what she pressed down, cutting off my mouth and my nose.

I surprised myself by not fighting her. No: I noticed that I didn't fight, that was all. We moved on one another and moved on one another, and she pressed at the pillow, and all I did was hold my breath. "Incest," I heard her say. "Abuse." I tried to take a breath but I couldn't, and that was when it really began. We kept moving on each other. She said, "No. Whatever it was. Could be. Was, maybe. That's not the reason, necessarily." I heard my sinuses roar, it was something like a seashell at shore when you listen to it and hear the emptiness, call it the sea. I bucked up, and she rode me. I felt her lean against the pillow. I strained into her. "That's so fucking mechanical, Mark. It says they made me. Nobody made me. *I* made me. *I* made the choice." She said something else, but I couldn't hear the words. It was like being under the sea, under the emptiness, inside the roar. I heard the voice but not the words. All the feeling in my body went to my groin. It was such powerful pleasure, it almost hurt me. I wanted to scream for the pleasure of it, but there wasn't any air, and I rose to search for it, rose and rose and rose within her until I heard myself shouting. It was Estella shouting, though, and she pulled the pillow away and threw her face against mine, kissing me with small open kisses all over my face. Rewards, they felt like. Or gratitude. As if I had done something wonderful. As if we'd achieved something on the lawyer's leather sofa against which my naked ass made sticking sounds each time I heard it move in response to her continuing movement. The sensation, diminished now because I had all but exploded, still went on a little, and we moved. She continued to praise me with kisses. One day, I knew, she would murder me.

Hydraulics

PHAN TUY in the small sticky hut, behind his makeshift desk. His eyes were so dark and so small, his limbs so unmuscular, that his boots in their hugeness made his body seem even less important in that room. But it was his room, all right. Goblin, crawling with insects, too tired to blink them or brush them away. Three guards, little men beside Goblin, but larger than Phantom. None of them in glasses, and Goblin with his perfect vision. Fliers have perfect vision. And Phan Tuy reading the new revision of the latest revision of the ongoing and never correct life story.

"You did not tell me that you failed in college."

Swaying, unfortunately, because the room from minute to minute shifted. Goblin, expert navigator, forced to shift in response. "No." A whisper, because in the corrections hut there was no room to bend to drink even if they'd provided water. They had not. The throat stopped up. Tissue puffy from the beatings, and of course the thirst. "I failed a *course.*"

The delicate, intelligent, precise voice, as careful as the rolling to the elbow of his frayed white shirt. The small, unmuscled arms that he held cocked, as if he sat at attention. "You were inadequate? That is to say, you could not function at the proper and expected level?"

"Didn't do my homework."

"Homework," he said. He smiled briefly. His teeth seemed small, even in his small mouth. There was silver showing: Russian dentistry. "This is self-supervised learning you are required to perform at your home?"

"More or less." Coughing a little.

"You are uncomfortable, Mark?"

"Top of the line," I said. "Fighting fit." A mistake. "No resistance intended," I said. "An expression."

"Expression is much."

"I was careless."

"And in college?"

"There too."

"Mark, when did you become *careful*?"

"When I flew airplanes."

"And yet, in spite of your care you are standing on the ground. You no longer fly, hurling explosives down."

Goblin shaking his head, the throat gone soundless.

"So you remained in your college?"

"The state was generous."

"The state educated you?"

"For very little cost."

His nostrils widened, then drew in. The little eyes traveled the page, then returned to me. He shook his head once, angrily, and the guards moved in place. "More prevarications."

Goblin, shaking his own head.

"America is not a socialist state. America is a capitalist state. Schools are for the wealthy."

"Not all."

"For the privileged."

Just the head swiveling, throat sealed again, and just as well, because whatever signal he gave, the guard received it, and I heard him step forward to clout me. Caught me as my head moved, but the bone still received the hard knuckles and tensed fingers. Had to move forward a couple of paces to catch my balance.

"So these are lies. You have no discipline *yet*, Mark."

"In the state of New York, there are colleges." Coughing, and the words coming husky and ragged. "Poor people. Smart people. There are places for the less capable. Money not primary."

"You claim this enlightenment is a national policy?"

"State of New York. Like a province."

"I am aware of the state of New York. I have been to Paris and Manchester. I have studied the English and American industrial revolutions. Engels was in Manchester. Never, I think, in New York. And the province educated you. According to this document."

Nodding.

"Perhaps."

Nodding again.

"Is your voice impaired, Mark? The thirst?" He spoke to them in their language. One of them came close behind me and I flinched. Phan Tuy smiled a cheap hood's grin, a bully's delight, and it was a signal for them to laugh at me. An arm in a gray-green shirtsleeve extended a small tin cup. Warm water.

"Thank you." Always thank your host for courtesies: a mother's instruction.

"You are welcome. A joke: you are not." Phan Tuy, still pleasing the crowd, must have translated his pun. They laughed again. "You are not," he said, not smiling this time. "But here you are, and we must contend with you. This history is untrustworthy. You must write it again. Tell me, again, the story of your life. Be accurate about your early days. The child is father to the man. Wordsworth."

Goblin hanging his head, seeing the ink again, running on the soft yellow paper. The words again. Story of his life.

"We have an excellent program," Phan Tuy said. "An opportunity for you and your countrymen and other foreign people who are criminals. According to this document, you conducted an entertainment on a radio set for your college. This is true? This is customary? This is done? You have done this? You are speaking the truth? You are an experienced man in the operation of your college's radio set in New York State? Bing*hampton*? You have told me the truth?"

"I ran a little show. Played music. Talked."

"We have also ran a little show, Mark. Agents of our enemies, now in captivity, are permitted to earn our approval. There are *ways.* A capitalist radio program! You may earn medicines and rice. You are not wounded severely. You are strong. You are somewhat healed. You need no medicines. You may have rice. You may have tea. You will state on the radio program the follies of your officers and your President and the crimes you have committed in their name."

"Yes," I said.

"You agree to this activity?"

"Yes."

"You do not shout your name, rank, and the number you wore on your neck? You do not refuse?"

"No."

"Untrustworthy, Mark. You were willing to shatter the bodies of our children when that was your obligation to your officers. Now you lapse from your obligations. You did the one and now you do the other. This is illogical. It is suspect." He talked to them. I ducked my head, but nobody hit me.

"I'll do it," I said.

"Heroes do not volunteer to be treacherous."

"Not a hero." Goblin affirms. "Not."

"Liar," Phan Tuy said.

"Yes."

"You admit this?"

"Yes."

"Where have you lied?"

"Everywhere."

"When?"

"All the time."

He stared at me. His little feet in the heavy boots were swinging against the stool. The sound hurt me. He told them something. One of them hit me too hard on the spine and I went down. Knew enough to curl up, hands around the head, knees up to protect the stomach and balls. Didn't matter this time. They weren't kicking this time.

After a while, I raised my head a little, looked. Sneakers from America on their feet: old models and a few recent ones. Probably out of some African aid shipment. Maybe Armenian relief. Little feet in little sneakers. They spread apart, everybody was tensing for something, and I ducked down again. Goblin going to ground.

It was warm. It smelled a little like root vegetables. The three of them, standing closer now, pissing on me and laughing. They must have drunk a lot of tea to prepare for this session: Goblin's analysis. Phan Tuy was talking to me. Teaching me the lesson about this shame. I couldn't hear what he said. It was like rain on the roof, too loud. Then they stopped. Ran out of it. And I smelled myself stinking, a thirsty wet man.

"The *truth*," he was saying.

Afraid if I talked, their urine would run down into my mouth. I knew I would have to kill myself or one of them or all of them. It seemed correct that someone die.

Prima Facie

LADIES and gentlemen, this here's my kid. This is Mister Mark, my official kid. Everybody! Mark! Take a fuckin bow, boy. Bow boy. Bow-wow *boy*! Your old lady send you after me? Sendin a little boy like you, little high school boy like you, into a tavern like this? She drinks inna room. You know what I mean? She's a fuckin alcoholic. Talk about a bow-*wow*! Mark! You wanna sip? Kid! You wanna sip a something? You wanna sandwich, kid? Mark? You wanna Coke? Coke-Cola, something like that? Mark! You fuckin look at *me* when I talk! *Mark!* Atta boy. Atta boy. You wanna—you want anything? You tell me Yes sir, No sir, like a man. Like a man. You look at me, you tell Yes, you tell me No, you call me sir. Man looks at a man. Why you here? You here for something bad? Anything bad happen a anybody we know?

Good. Good. No, *sir.* At's good. So—

Well, *no,* a matter a fact, fuckin *no.* I am not ready to come home. To *what*? You ever think a that, kid? What I come home to?

No, *sir,* you say to me. Man to man. *Ev*erybody. Hey.

Nobody listens a nobody anymore. Listen: I gotta whisper it. They're a bunch a goddamn *drunks.* But I figure, you—gimme the matches over there, kid. Yeah. Mm. Now, *what* was it? You smoke? You wanna smoke? You don't smoke. No, *sir.* Good boy. Good man.

So tell me. Mm. School and shit. You okay? You doin okay? You doin what you should when a teachers say and shit?

Yes, sir. Good. Good. So, mm, how come you're *here*?

No, why'd I wanna go home?

Why'd I be finished tonight?

Why'd it be enough?

Why'd I be tired? I work all day, I get tired, I come in here, I *relax.* I don't get tired in here. All I gotta do in here, mm, I sit and I light these little fuckers up and I put em out and I take a little sip. You watchin me? Mm. Like that. I pull it in, I blow it out, I take a taste, I'm watchin Angelo there servin Fritos a people and some Schenley's, some whatsit, Black Velvet, you see em? No. This don't make me tired.

You want one? No.

Your fuckin *mother* makes me tired, is what.

Your mother'd make the Rip Van Winkle *Bridge* tired.

Where's at bridge at, you know?

You study geography in school, or what?

They don't teach you shit, do they, kid? Hey! Angie. Ange! Where's at Rip Van Winkle Bridge at?

No, I thought you'd know on account it's one of those Dutch, Kraut, whatever deals.

I'm a funny fuckin man, kid, uh? Yeah? Yes, sir? That's right. That's right. What's at on your arm? Over here. Gimme your arm. Gimme the *arm.* What's at?

What kinda bruise? Who did it to you?

Who twisted your arm?

I don't wanna hear it, you don't remember. I'm looking at your arm, I'm seein somebody hurt you, I wanna know *who.*

So re*mem*ber.

Now.

Nothing now, Ange. I'm talkin a the kid here, I want he has to remember who hurt him.

Kid.

Kid.

I don't wanna—

Kid.

No.

No way.

You don't talk like that up *my* nose. You don't—

I'm tellin you, Angie, nothing. And thank you. This is me and my kid.

Angie, I'm *look*in at the arm. Somebody twisted it on em, and I'm askin the kid, Who did it?

I know he said me. You listenin in, or what? I know he said, None a your business, Angie, *me.* Which is bullshit. Fuckin *bull*-shit. I am not twistin his arm. He *said* I twisted his arm, which is the bullshit part. All right. All *right*! You see it? You seen I let go? Which is none a your business, Ange, I'm tellin you *that* straight out.

Now, kid. Tell me. Tell the whole fuckin *bar.*

Kid.

Don't you turn your back, kid.

Don't you walk away.

Don't you—you stand, you talk like a man, kid. You look me inna fuckin *eye.*

Kid.

Kid—last warning. I'm warning you. Yeah.

Yeah.

Right back here. Right in fuckin front of me, uh-huh.

Uh-*huh.*

The Long Arm Up

ONLY A FOOL would let his client appear before a grand jury on a murder charge. Twenty-three citizens, some sleeping and others doing who knows what with pills, needles, some working as hard as honor-society students. And the district attorney presenting all the session's crimes, including that of Ms. Estella Pritchett, suspended caseworker, mistress to the chubby, rich, and perverted—*former* mistress: game suspended on the field of play on account of dying—and the grand jury, many-headed puppet for the D.A.'s office, handing up with the long, dutiful arm of citizenship any indictment that's asked of it. The county judge, Johann Sebastian Bach, plays it on his organ and I'm notified—oh, surprise!—we're going to trial.

It took me a week's fighting, and with Estella that meant actual fights, to convince her that she shouldn't appear before the jury. You're allowed to. It's your right. All you have to do is go into the jury room without your lawyer, waive immunity rights, and answer any questions they ask you without the protection of the rules of evidence. I screamed her into submission.

No, I didn't. Estella let me win.

I was the one submitting.

The jury handed up Estella's indictment. Goblin on the air again, talking to psychiatrists all over the state, and those in several other states, and she sat in chaste and muted clothes and answered their questions, filled out their questionnaires. She wore no makeup when she interviewed the shrinks with me. She was on the calendar of the court, she was almost in the citizens' hands, and she sometimes nearly did as I told her.

So we are deep in the preparation, we are so far under the surface of normal civilian life, it's like breathing water instead of air. In the daylight, there is Ruthie and her pattering shoes, the boots with manure in the waiting room, the telephone calls from realtors, the Rotary lunch, the bills to explain to clients, the bills at home from two motels I'd never heard of—you pay them, you do not ask Schelle why she'd use a credit card to cheat on you, and you watch her sad, dark eyes when you see them, which isn't often, and you think of her unhappy mouth opening on a man who isn't you. You think of Schelle becoming happy in the darkness of a rented room. And, in your own nighttime, there is the binder, the legal pad, the ink. And Estella, coming into the office at night dressed in a man's gray suit, or a suit for women cut like a man's, complete with vest and starched white shirt and patterned tie that picked up the suit's subtle flecks. Her makeup is artful: she looks like a man who gets a thrill from wearing women's cosmetics. Her lips are thick with red-pink lipstick that carries a hint of the suit's gray tones. Although it is a hot night, her necktie is drawn up high to the collar, and the collar is buttoned. She wears sunglasses in the late night.

She says, "I'm in disguise."

"I'm working on your case," I tell her.

"I'm the caseworker around here."

"Estella."

"Call me Steve," she says.

"Estella."

She walks around my desk and stands beside my chair. Steps back and turns it. Stops it by stepping between my legs and standing, legs together, close to the edge of my seat. "My name is Steve," she says. Her voice is hard, her throat sounds tight. She moves up closer between my legs, spreading them. Her hand, with nails colored to match her lipstick, goes to the zipper on her suit. She moves the zipper down a little, up again, then down partway. "Steve," she says.

"All right."

She moves the zipper down. "Say it."

I say, "Steve."

She says, her voice tighter, crueler, lower now, "I wish I had a cock in here. I'd pull this zipper down and take out my cock and make you suck it."

"Jesus," I said.

"Would you suck it?"

"Jesus. Estella."

"Steve." Her hand left the zipper and she grabbed my ear and pulled, hard, down behind the lobe, and I went with the pressure until my face was against the hard cloth and the spiky track of the zipper. I felt her heat with my face. The hand moved, though the pain remained in the back of my ear and on the side of my face. The hand moved, went behind my head, and pulled my face in, gently now, against her pelvis, which was moving.

"Steve," I said.

"Would you?" Her hand was against my forehead and nose, then moving the zipper down, spreading the flies of the pants.

"Yes," I said.

"You would."

"Yes."

"Yes," she said. She stepped back, went to the wall switch, and turned off the office lights. I heard the cloth. When she came back, my eyes were accustomed enough to the dark, and I saw that she wore the shirt and tie and vest and shoes, high businessmen's socks, but nothing in between. That was always Estella. Nothing in between.

She walked between my legs and leaned against me. She said, in Estella's voice, "I wish *you* had. You know. Behind your zipper. Because if you did, I would unzip your zipper." She did. "And let it out up into the air. Oh, my. You *do*. Yes, and well, guess what."

I lay back and closed my eyes.

She squeezed it, and very hard. I sat up, eyes wide.

"Guess, I said."

"Ow. Estella."

"Guess."

"Jesus. Damn. *Suck* it! Ow!"

Her small, strong hand relented. She caressed me again. Her forearms leaned on my thighs. I felt her breath. "Yes," she said meekly. "All right."

And it was after such diligent discoveries, rehearsals of questioning, and preparation of expert witnesses that *State of New York v. Pritchett* came to county court as summer approached, and Schelle worked harder at the hospital at night, and I waited for Lee Beeton Palmer to call me with terrible news. He didn't. Sidney Birnbaum didn't call about his Vietnam story. Schelle sent and received letters about her monument. My monument. Goblin's monument. Estella hadn't put the pillow over my face again right away. But she mentioned it. And she'd do it again. I kept a careful eye on the watch, the calendar, any clock on any wall. When I'd been Phan Tuy's guest, it had been the same way—harder and harder to know which days had passed and which were coming. The court calendar helped, and the timetable to Schelle's unveiling by which I also counted time.

Chambers

SOME OF US called her Delicious, and some of us called her Dee. Her full name was Adina, she called herself Dina (with a long, hard *e* sound), and she was determined to be the first female district attorney in our upstate, Republican county, in which women were counted upon for their ovaries, vaginas, breasts, and sometimes arms and legs, but never for political office or abstract thought. So she'd said, again and again, at Party breakfasts and ABA conventions, over drinks after meetings and once, face to face with me, in the darkness outside her parents' big white Victorian house on the line between country and town, my car idling in her driveway, and the two of us holding one another's lapels on a very cold night. Our breath made a cloud around us. I'd kept thinking, You could hide inside it.

But Dee didn't hide. Her eyes were a little close together, but not crossed; her nose was small and slim until the bottom, where it pugged a little; her mouth was wide and thin, her chin was chunky, her throat slim but strong; her hair was dark brown; it hung to her ears where she'd paid someone clever to make it fold under and hang in place as if it weighed twenty pounds.

She'd told me, "You're an old guy, counselor, and I'm a young chick. We have zero future."

"I'm not old enough to be your father."

"Nor young enough to be my lover, I think."

"I was thinking of, you know, some friendly sporting, Dee. Not love."

"Well, fuck you, Mark. I was thinking of love, a little."

"Oh, you'll deny this, won't you."

"I never said it."

"I'd have said it," I told her, "only you said it first."

"You're a vicious, cunning man," she said. "You have a nice chest. I like a man with a chest on him."

"You're beginning to sound like one of the boys, Dee."

"I know," she said. "It's all they talk about: tits, money, and how their wives are tired of sex. Is your wife tired of sex?"

"Schelle? I wouldn't say so. No. Sometimes I think I've made her weary, but I'm not sure she's even tired of *me,* entirely."

"I'm twenty-eight years old, Mark. I'll be forty next week."

We were inside the cloud of our breath, and we were talking to each other's faces, whispering, shivering a little in the bitter windless night. Hers was the only house on the curve of the road, and there weren't any lights, just the moon and the headlights of my quaking car. It looked as though the frost had killed everything. Only stalks stood straight. We bent toward each other.

"You ought to get out, Dee. You should go to Albany, or New York."

"And be one of those bright women with a healthy stride going to work in a six-hundred-dollar man-tailored suit, running shoes and anklets, and a briefcase the size of the boss's? And live in a shoe box for a quarter of a million dollars? And meditate every night on either AIDS from casual sex or working late to show I'm part of the team?"

"Nothing's happening here, Dee. There's nobody here and nothing here, and you'll end up being, you know, like *them.*"

"God."

"Because you can't be the D.A. forever. You'll have to make some dough sometime. Shaking hands solemnly, with little bawdy asides, at community events. Going to Mass or a less exalted service on account of your clients expect it. And the basketball games when the high school team plays its long-awaited revenge match with whoever beat them six weeks ago. Dinner with the pols when they come down from Albany to see if we're still cannibals here, and just how much we'll do by way of kissing their asses for a bridge, or a solid-waste tip, or a waterworks. And never learning all that much law."

She hung her head. The top of it leaned against my overcoat. Her head swung slowly back and forth. "God," she said. "Don't come here and comfort me, all right? You'll end up staying here. I'll have to tell you how your belly's tighter than you think. You'll have to tell me the same, and that I'm splendid on the sheets. I'll get to count on it. On you."

"There are worse evenings," I told her.

"Most evenings probably are. But I think what I'll do, my gratitude for your big chest and your conversation notwithstanding, is go inside and drink a little anything and fall asleep on whatever's there when I fall. All right?" She squinted when she smiled. She'd done it since she gave up glasses and took to wearing contact lenses, and there was something endearingly middle-aged about the young face laboring to focus. She somehow looked as blurry as whatever she worked to see.

"All right," I said. I kissed the top of her head.

She sighed and smiled. She kissed me on the mouth. "And one of these days," she said, "I will do a case and a half. You know? Something they let me argue on account of something they can't control. There I am, then. And it'll be something, I don't know, *big*." She let go of my lapels to spread her arms and I was sad at the loosening. "Intentional death, child molestation, something vicious and snappy and pretty as hell in the papers. And whoever's D.A. will get old or sick or be hit by a comet, I'll run for D.A. on my strength as a protector of the community. I'll savage somebody's ass in the courtroom and swish my own into office a year later and take business trips to Miami, representing the county. And—"

I waited.

"And I'll be happy," she said.

I kissed her mouth then, and then her cheek, and I backed away and turned.

That was Dee: a second-rate litigator like me, except younger and, often, honest. Backus came in, motioning us to sit. Estella sat in a very old and sagging brown leather easy chair. She was dressed in dark brown—had she known?—and she looked slight within the darkness of the big chair's frame. I sat on a hard wooden chair beside her. Dee, near the side of Backus's desk instead of in front with us, sat on the edge of another big brown chair. She was wearing a navy blazer and a tan linen skirt, cordovan pumps that matched her gleaming cordovan brief bag. It had several brass or gold buckles on it, and it gleamed in the light that came through the three leaded windows behind the judge. He wore seersucker trousers and a rose-colored Lacoste shirt. His white curls, in a fringe above his ears, seemed to be in disarray. His broad face was sour, his blue eyes unhappy, his jowls pronounced.

"Thank you both, counselors. Ms. Pritchett. I appreciate

your coming down on a Saturday at such late notice. I'm grateful. My clerk worked hard to find you. Now."

He gestured at his chambers, longer than wide, carpeted not with something Persian, as was customary among judges I knew, but with a thin, long rug that in black and brown and white was made of Indian patterns, something southwestern, I thought. His shelves had jugs and pottery that seemed to echo the patterns, and there were photographs of a younger Backus with a sweet, homely woman his age possessed of a remarkably slim figure who looked like a dancer. Backus in uniform posed with her and Indians at what looked like pueblos.

He was chubby, but had long arms, big hands, long legs. Dee would like his chest, I thought. I could smell grass and sweat and maybe beer as he sat. It was one in the afternoon on a hot Saturday of the first week in June. My letter on the leather surface of his writing table caught the golden light he'd left to be inside with us.

"Ms. Pritchett," he said. "It is customary in court proceedings, especially during motions, for a stenographer to be present, even in chambers, when formal proceedings are conducted. From time to time I will signify, in the course of the trial, that conversations between your counsel and me, or Ms. Tillim and me and counsel for the defense, be left off the record. At that time, the court stenographer will stop using his machine and will wait. In this case, as you can see, the conversation is so *far* off the record, I have not required that the stenographer be present."

I touched Estella's arm. She nodded to him. "Yes," she said.

"No reply is necessary yet," Backus told me. I nodded.

"Ms. Pritchett. Most of Ms. Tillim's colleagues in the district attorney's office want to be judges. Surely her boss does. Surely he'll more than likely succeed. He is not here, by the way, because of his long-time familiarity with you through your work together in commendable prosecutions of child abusers and so forth. If I had been the family court judge, I would have recused myself from this case. We do not know one another, however, and Ms. Tillim and you are not friends or foes, hence her argument of the People's case.

"To continue. I was not a prosecutor, a district attorney or assistant. I was a defendant's lawyer. My practice was more sharply focused on criminal matters than Mr. Brennan's, but it was similar to his. I *defended* people." He folded his hands and shook his head. "That is why, for much of Friday, and Friday night, and a good deal of today's golf game, I thought with dismay of the communication I have here from your attorney. Are you aware of its contents?"

"About the jury?" Estella asked.

"What?" Dee barked.

"In time, Ms. Tillim."

"Yes, Judge."

"Thank you. So, Ms. Pritchett, you do understand what your attorney has requested."

"*I* asked for it," she said, as I had told her to.

"It was, surely, Mr. Brennan's idea."

"Oh, he might have mentioned it. He was tossing out all kinds of things one night, one afternoon. And he said it, I guess, with a dozen other things. I came back to it, though. He didn't like the idea."

"Didn't he," Backus said, looking from her to me, and directly through the lie.

"No," she said, chaste and frightened, a girl in a small woman's body, pinioned by the law. "No, sir. I thought—well, it's *embarrassing.* A jury would despise me for the terrible things I let Mr. Ziegler make me do."

Dee snorted. I raised my brows at the judge. He turned her silent with a look. "Sorry," she said.

"So I thought if I could just talk to *you.* You're a man. You have a family, a wife, daughters—"

"How did you know that I have daughters?" Backus asked.

"Courtroom chatter. I'm at the court—I was—a great deal. As you know. May I go on?"

He nodded. His face was red.

"And I thought if I, we, you know—if you heard my side of it, and I didn't have to tell it to a dozen strangers, then, well—" She looked at me. "Oh. Also, Mr. Ziegler's name was always on his radio. He was like that. Everyone *knows* him. How could they be fair? So, I thought, well, I guess I've said it all."

"Well," he said. "Except the entire *purpose* of this kind of trial is to *tell* twelve strangers your side of the story. It's essential, Ms. Pritchett. Your lawyer should have known that your questions about the jury's comprehension of the circumstances surrounding your case are insufficient reason to assume *entitlement* to waive a jury trial. And your lawyer should have told you that the reason for this trial is to see whether twelve strangers judge you innocent."

"He did."

"United States v. Houghton," I said, "1977, California."

"And that's it? He recited precedent and said we'll ask the waiver anyway?"

"I said I wanted to waive my rights to a trial by a jury of my peers, and he said Rule, uhm, Twenty-three of the Federal Rules? Is that right? He said I can't demand it, it's up to you, but I'm allowed to ask."

Backus shook his head again. He leaned back in his chair. "Your attorney makes a decent enough case in his motion—his alleged letter—for the complexity of testimony. When expert witnesses testify on psychological subtleties, details get lost. But they can be retrieved," he said. He leveled his chair and spread his arms across his desk to grasp the edges. He seemed to be pulling himself toward her and away at the same time. "They can read the testimony if they need to. We can explain it to them. Ms. Pritchett, I spent half of my life arguing to juries on behalf of people accused of felonies. Never, in my court, has a wrongful death case been argued only to me. I cannot permit you to sacrifice an opportunity to best represent yourself. I cannot permit your counsel, whose motives and behavior have been shaky from the start, to jeopardize you. I am risking overturn on appeal, as Ms. Tillim pointed out acutely enough early today, by conducting this crucial conversation off the record. Incidentally, Ms. Tillim's consent would be required."

"The California ruling," I showed off. "*People v. Terry*? Maybe an at least analogous fact pattern, Your Honor. Persuasive precedent, if not binding precedent?"

He ignored me. "But I must not risk your liberty. Brennan, goddammit, why are you doing this?"

I politely nodded to Estella. I said, "Judge. Dee. My client insists. She trusts your perspicacity and fairness. So do I."

Dee said—and what else could she say?—"Your Honor, I of course do likewise. And when the People win, I'd hate to risk an overturn on appeal because of failure to waive. I'm confident, Judge."

Backus looked at her. She smiled, squinting a little. She shrugged to signal her helplessness, and he gently dipped his head to tell her he understood.

Backus said, "Your attorney will write a letter for you. You will sign it. Your attorney will sign it. You will ask that your right to a jury trial be waived. You will state that your rights were thoroughly explained to you. The letter will be read in open court, and the district attorney's office will accede for the record. And I will then indicate my extreme reluctance to determine matters of fact and matters of law. You're either cunning, Mark, or a dog of a lawyer."

I didn't tell him which.

He said, "Formal motions, then opening arguments on—is it Wednesday?"

"Yes, Your Honor," I said.

"Discovery has been scrupulous, I take it. Ms. Tillim is always a careful prosecutor. Ms. Tillim, has Mr. Brennan been sly with you as well as with me?"

"I've got his number, Judge." Estella's head swiveled at that one, and both Backus and Dee caught the motion. Tillim, therefore, couldn't resist adding, "Mr. Brennan and I go back a long way, Judge."

"I'm going back to the golf course," he said. He turned his eyes on Estella, full bore: "Change your mind, Ms. Pritchett. Change your attorney's mind." Then he turned to me: "You better not be fucking up, Brennan. Pardon me, ladies. There is no other word for it."

Estella lighted her face up. She'd been pale, receding into the chair, into herself. Now the color came into her skin. Even her hair seemed to shine. Her oval face rode a little higher on her neck. She sat forward. In her whispery, dark voice she said, "Your Honor, I feel even more, now, after all these stern warnings—I mean, your *anger*'s almost religious—I am going to trust you."

Dee puffed her cheeks out silently and made her eyes wide with nausea. I saw the judge look down, and away, and then up. For an instant I thought he'd been on the verge of taking her hand. He shook his head.

Estella said, "Thank you."

He nodded unhappily.

Dee put her hand on her mouth.

Looking at me, but possibly addressing both lawyers—I saw Dee's hand retreat to her lap—he growled, "Watch it. This is my court. This is the law. It's *America*."

Fish

HEALTH WASN'T a factor, because it wouldn't improve. I'd get worse. Swelling under the armpits, stomach big with Christ knows what, but it wasn't gas from too many ribs with barbecue sauce. The knee and ankle were steadier but not sturdier. They'd possibly fold under stress. Bending over a tender gut in absolute humidity and 104 heat was stress enough. The music they beat on the box was stress enough. Tough and angry men who pissed on you and scuffed you with their sneakers was stress enough. The slaps on the back of the head were stress enough. Goblin reporting ditto on the writing over and over in the watery ink the simple enough history of his simple enough life: born poor, raised hard, flew wild, fell into their field like a stone. Not enough, Phantom said. Insufficient examination. Insufficient analysis. Insincere study of lapses and flaws.

Back in the little room by myself now. A cup of warm water. Half-raw rice in a wooden bowl. A tube of ointment, bent almost out of recognition, the tube metal, the label dark and light brown, the word *trenchfoot* visible. My reward for being the guards' latrine. I would have laughed. I thought of it. But I was thinking of murdering someone. Trenchfoot, so the joke would have gone, was the only disease I apparently did not have. Bad bones, bad gut, lice on every hair of my body, perpetual diarrhea, the hand shaking as it lay the watery words down for Phan Tuy.

Feign disorder and strike him. Sun Tzu, my only book, Professor Sadler of the University of Sydney my only translator unless you count Phantom. Miserable high hard old book, the brittle pages breaking at the edges and falling out. They slapped me behind the head for letting the pages break. Stopped reading it. Too dark to read most of the time anyway, or the eyes were going bad. It hurt when I peed, but I wetted down a few of the pages. Stayed on my feet.

Waiting.

You don't get to do a lot of that in an airplane on combat missions unless you're orbiting over the fleet or holding over a fire zone to see if they want you to take a battery out. Mostly it's happening so fast, the kid in back shouting, you shouting, people on the combat frequency shouting, aircraft appearing and disappearing. Kind of a magic show. Flattened against the seat, the g suit clamping down, the turn shoving you back into the headrest, and the little spots taking over your vision. Then everything sighs, the aircraft, the driver, the seat, the suit, and you're back in the saddle, blowing all your fuel margin on one evasion or attack.

Waiting, though.

Standing six or eight feet in front of the wooden door that swung in crookedly. So they would see no threat.

And strike him.

Slept standing up. An okay sleep, four minutes, five, as long as any I'd had there. Standing, and the door's movement woke me. Remembered everything. Feign disorder and strike.

Hand appearing, small hand, hard one, dark and muscled, grimy. The sons of bitches had the hardest lives. Then his eyes. Shoulder level, he was tall for one of them, the man I called Fish because of the hook-shaped scar near the edge of his mouth. When I saw his eyes, I was crying. Tears, Schelle. I made my mouth curve like a clown's. It felt like a clown's, painted with urine and earth, exaggerated, big and stupid, smiling through my tears. He looked at me the way you look at dogs that leap through the air to bite at their tails and snarl coming down.

Nodded. Goblin nodded agreement. Yes, I'm crazy.

Fish was one of the men who peed on me. Fish was one of the men who slapped and kicked whenever he could.

Yes, Fish. Nodding, tears running down.

Query: Where did Goblin get the fluid for the tears? For violating Sun Tzu?

Necessity, mother. He gabbled at me, I nodded again, pointed to my head and my balls, figured that would tell him something. What else could I be worried about, Fish?

The darkness of the hut broken into uneven chunks of light by what poured in behind him. The stink of my rotten body. Smell of Fish's unwashed skin. And real fish, also rotten, in the sauce they used. The smell of jungle and brush, wet soil, human ordure from their gardens. His eyes, banging up and down like a pinball game in process, striking off my tears, my eyes, my shaking knees, my hands hanging beside me and ending in fingers that trembled before him.

Fish's hand drawing back.

Right back here. Uh-*huh.*

In a little closer. Feign.

Strike him. The hand up at the waist now. Hand no longer limp or shaking. All the energy diverted now. No more tears. No more gut pain. Everything shunted through the right-hand collarbone (connected to the pen bone). Down the arm. Forearm hardening. Hand in the knife-strike. Four fingers rigid, and the thumb folding into the palm. Taut now. Everything taut.

Sliding into the solar plexus, Fish. You like that one? The hand in the knife-strike under the sternum. His plexus stunned, the paralysis radiating out. Mouth gaping, Fish. And your eyes so wide. And no breath, am I right? Lungs creaking away but nothing coming in. And you're down on your knees. This is Goblin, Fish. Hands on your nostrils. Surprise! Tearing up the nose until there's blood on my wrists. No sound out of Fish. The blood coming, and Goblin going next for an eye.

Disgusting man. Comes in here stinking of body odor, with

blood all over his mouth and barely a nose on him. Ends up looking out of one eye, lying on his side, breathing only out. The funny little noises: Ah. Ah. Ah.

Goddamned Lee-Enfield rifle, British gun from French soldiers, used against the Americans. Bolt-action .303 caliber, and no doubt the shells haven't been reloaded since the First World War. I'll take it, Fish. All my thanks.

See, the difference between this time, with eye mucus and nose mucus and blood on my fingers and hands, and any other time: I really don't care, Fish. Do not care.

So walk. The piece is so heavy when I do, I barely keep it up. Lay it across one shoulder like a boy pretending a soldier's march. The clearing is small enough to walk across in under a minute. Goblin counting: one Mississippi, two Mississippi, three Mississippi. The stinking garden where they plant in their shit. The trench latrine where they say they'll bury us. Three long huts at right angles to mine. The interrogation shed. Ah, Phantom. It should have been you I bled. It should have been you.

Goblin does not forget. Eighteen Mississippi. Looking for American fliers, other POWs. No time to search buildings. No joy in the prospect of calling out for Yanks. A guard in goddamned black pajamas and the usual sneakers, son of a bitch, walking around the corner of a hut. Hello, guard. Hi, American. Goblin gesturing: Here! Quick!

What does he do but walk over? No more feigning disorder, guys. No time for feigning. Goblin swinging the Enfield like a baseball bat and taking him down. A little boy. Not so little. Maybe thirteen. Thirteen? Goblin murdering a boy so young?

Reader, you bet your ass.

And into the brush, barefoot, running with other people's blood, maybe bits of bone and brain, on the Enfield's butt plate. Goblin isn't looking for souvenirs. He's striking south-southeast, or as close to it as the sun can show him. Goblin's a pilot. Goblin's on instruments now. Goblin's making for home.

Chicago and Paris

WE WENT to Paris, Schelle, remember? It was after the war, after we'd met and courted. I was chasing you, it was nothing but hot pursuit, and all the while you thought of yourself as being courted. In Chicago, we ended up in some joint under the Loop that smelled of beer and sour sausage and steaming newspapermen, something Goat, Nanny Goat, and you sat next to me at this long bar, and I said something like *I guess this is it* and you nodded: *Sure. Sure.* You nodded and I talked, then you talked and I nodded, and we acted like what we said made sense. Your dark hair, your blue eyes, the wonderful curve of your nose—all very soft, the blue not hard, the curve not cruel, the glossy blackness of your long hair drawing the sallow light of the tavern.

I guess this is it.

Sure. Sure.

And we went to Paris. Where else do hick children go when they marry, when they've a little in savings, and adequate prospects? Paris, via Air Ignorance. Stumbling, through luck and a benevolent travel agent, into the Hôtel Colbert, its dark brown marble and wood, the little lightless hallways, the small balcony over the narrow street that went two blocks to the Seine and, directly across, Notre-Dame.

We went downstairs to a little restaurant across the street, and in its jumble of small tables and mouthy Frenchmen, each of whom I thought was sneering, you said, "We're in the twelfth century. This building was put up in the *twelfth* century!"

What they said, you accepted. What I said, you accepted. Twelfth century? Fine: 1100s, and no further questions—why would someone lie to Rochelle? Vietnam combat? War in the air? Prisoner on the ground? No sweat. There you were: tall, dark and light at once, strong enough to fight a government and frail enough to succumb to me. You believed me, Schelle. You believe me now.

In the room four flights up the stairs, near the tiny desk where a girl from Vassar on her year abroad interpreted the maps for us, we ate stale brioches with bitter coffee and proclaimed them French and therefore good. We made love inexpertly and often, and once—do you remember this?—it was dusk, and we were learning to go out late to eat, like the rest of the tourists imitating the Europeans, we stayed in the room and we pulled each other into bed. You lay back naked, long on the heavy sheets that made deep shadows underneath you as they wrinkled. You stretched, then let your muscles go. Your hands were on the pillow behind you. Your legs were loose and a little apart. Your eyes were squinted. We were awfully new to one another.

Remember this? I stood at the foot of the bed and looked at you. You were the absolute emblem—Schelle, the very *flag*—of acceptance. You were open to me, at ease, unquestioning. Your body rippled when you moved, the muscles in your stomach and ribcage made you shimmer like a flag. It was the banner of defenselessness before the loved one. It was any goodness, every goodness, I'd despaired of. And instead of hurling myself upon you, or crawling up your legs, kissing them, both of which I'd thought to do, I stood at the foot of the bed. Remember?

You said, in the softest voice, "Is anything wrong? Did I—" And you moved to turn on your side or bring a leg up, as if to shield yourself. I'd studied you too hard.

I reached down and seized your ankles. We were like that in

the room as it grew dark. A couple of naked young adults, all but children, people of small experience. I saw us. I was *of* us, I was electric with feelings about you, yet I saw us as if I stood apart. We were so *tender.* I see us that way now, as if we were the children of Mark and Rochelle.

He pulls her left leg back to where it was on the sheets. She permits him. He bends to her feet. He kneels on the carpet at the foot of the bed, and he kisses the sole of each foot.

He said: "No. God. Schelle. What could be *wrong*?"

Remember this: he didn't, even then, want to lie, though he did.

The Temperature Drop

I MET Lee Beeton Palmer, as he'd instructed me to, in the parking lot between the sheriff's garage and the exercise yard for the county jail. Small jail, small yard, small garage—a couple of minivans painted red and white, two four-wheel-drive vehicles ditto, one of the county cruisers, the gas pump, the oily rags, the overhead well of engine oil, the jacks on wheels, extra tires, wall racks of ratchet tools. Thirty yards away, the yard, fenced in with Cyclone forty feet high and topped with concertina wire in looping rolls that gleamed tinnily under the spotlights mounted on the wall of the jail that was the fourth side of the skewed square formed by the fencing. For twenty feet up the Cyclone and painted barn red—we were in the country, remember—went the undressed one-by-ten lumber that kept the prisoners from visiting through the diamonds of fence link with girlfriends, local kids who sought their apprenticeship for jail, and messengers who bore drugs.

It was a warm night, and the moths and other bugs blundered at the spotlights. The single light on the garage above the doors was broken, or Lee had unscrewed the bulb. Thick-winged moths beat against it anyway. Talk about unrequited love, I thought.

I wanted to say that. So that Lee wouldn't talk about Jack, who stood beside him and who wore a blanket around his shoulders in spite of the heat.

Cops always put them on people who'd been in accidents or whom they'd been beating on, so all I said was "Shit."

Lee nodded. Jack looked at me. His eyes, in the shadows there, looked vast, I couldn't see the eyeballs, only the big holes. As if they'd torn his eyes out, and the sockets were gaping at me. Goblin on his way out of the compound, Fish. Remember? Like overcooked yolk, is what an eyeball feels like, but with a little more surface tension, a touch more juiciness, and then the blood, of course.

"What, Lee?"

Lee said to Jack, "Stand there."

Jack said, "Yes, sir." He looked at the ground—or his hollows and forehead pointed that way.

Lee took me gently by the elbow, the way you draw a woman through a dance floor crowd, if you go to dances, if you know how to dance. We went toward the open garage, and he drew me down. We sat on the front bumper of a van. He leaned his legs out, and so did I. He lit a cigarette and hissed the smoke tiredly.

"Are his eyes all right, Lee?"

"Sure, I guess. He didn't complain any."

"He's—"

"He's fine, Mark. Except for being scared shitless and thinking he's under arrest and his life is over. And he believes that you and Rochelle are going to use a fillet knife and take the skin off his nuts."

"And we are?"

"It might happen," Lee said.

"I think I'm going to tell you, at the end of your story, that I owe you a lot. Or everything."

"Well," he said, "not quite the mortgage, unless it's in the half-a-million range."

"Jesus, Lee, don't talk mortgage, all right?"

"Whatever you want, Mark. And you don't owe me shit and you know it. *You're* the one's owed."

"Please," I said. "Don't. No more."

"I'm the owee. Whatever that's called. Obligation's mine, Mark. Fuck. You'd do this for me. You *did* it for me. Your boy, anyhow, is standing in shit approximately up to his waist."

"It beats nose-high."

"Let's hope."

"Where?"

"You know the old recreation center that went bust, above the waterworks? Weddings, country fiddle bands, flat beer, and kielbasa?"

Nodded to him: yes, a couple of miles north of Randall and on the eastern ridge.

"We heard they were breaking in and throwing a let's-get-wrecked party for one of the girls who hangs around with the bad boys who don't work."

"Who're they?"

"Attrangiata, Leary, Wheatley, you know those families?"

"All big businesses in town. Lots of dough."

"The three kids I mentioned have been dried out twice, not once, twice. In the usual variety of overpriced detox Kids "R" Us hotels. Leary's done another stay for drugs. He's got the moral fiber of oatmeal. There weren't just three or six or ten of them. They had over a hundred kids there, Mark."

"Jesus. I never heard a word."

"These kids could have organized D day in total secrecy and won the fucking war if they'd wanted to. They're *smart.* Listen to this: they sold *tickets.* Ten bucks a throw. There was beer, there was blow, there was dope, there were little black pills and little reds, and there were at least five girls they were pulling a chain on."

"What, they were—"

"Gang-banging. Gang-raping, maybe. Who knows? The girls were out of their skulls. Would you call that rape, counselor?" He might have stood up and slugged me as he said it. His rage was so absolute: he knew what was right and what was wrong, and he hated what was wrong. I felt accused by his certainties.

"I'm so sorry, Lee."

"Huh? Shit. They all deserve each other, that's one way I comfort myself. The other is I puke a good deal. After one of these, I can't keep goddamned *water* down."

"You busted them?"

"Didn't you get the calls?"

"I was working. I was doing some tremendously involved research and I was at the other end of the office."

"The library part."

"That's right. I heard the phone ringing, but I kept telling myself—"

"What?"

"I should have answered, Lee. It could have been Mickey in New York."

"Or your wife. Or your kid. It's not my place, of course."

"But I should have."

"Yeah," he said, "I suppose."

"Jesus, Lee. And it must have been the parents of half of those kids."

"You could have bought an oceangoing boat with the

hourlies on those, counselor. It's a good thing we don't have an ocean for the next few hundred miles."

"Christ. I let a lot of people down."

"Important case, I guess."

"Yes."

"Yeah. So, anyway, I see Jack—"

"Was he—doing anything?"

"Jack's a baby, Mark. He was as far from the room with the girls as he could get. One of them, by the way, was the girl with the birthday. Her present's a half a pint of semen from the guys, in her mouth and her twat." He leaned over and blew out smoke. "I still want to puke. I've *got* a daughter."

"So do I," I said.

"Right," he said. "Right. And the boy."

"He wasn't in on the sex."

"Other end of the dance floor. Everything was dark except for a couple of lanterns and some candles. Kid was leaning against the wall. I think he was toking up some. We found a few stumpy little roaches near his feet. They could have been somebody else's. But he looked it. His eyes looked it. He had a can of beer in his hand. He was pretty much alone, Mark. You know? He has these friends, we see him with these friends, but the kid's alone, I'd say."

"Blood test?" I heard a voice, almost like mine, try to say.

"We had the right. But I hustled the kid away. I stuck him in the back of my car. He was so scared he was shivering, the poor little pussy. So: no *urine* test. It wouldn't be a blood test, Mark."

"I don't do all that much in my practice with drugs and tests, Lee. But I owe you everything. That's the point. I owe you everything."

"Not the point," Lee said, lighting another cigarette. I saw his mouth purse, then disappear as he closed his lighter. "Point is, the kid's drifting, Mark. I don't want to sound like I'm lecturing you. But this is serious business. You know that. He *could* have been screwing some fifteen-year-old. He could have been snorting coke off a fucking compact mirror with a razor blade in his hand the way they all learn how to do from watching goddamned television on the reruns after school. He's a loner, he's very mixed up, he needs some serious attention. He'll hang with the bad boys, he'll do something dumb so they'll let him stay around, and then he'll be in it. *In* it. And then I won't be able to do him any good. If he wasn't your kid, I might not have made the moves I had to make."

"I owe you everything," I said.

"I already talked about that. Did you hear what I said about the boy?"

"Yes. I promise."

"What?"

"I don't know."

He snorted his laughter out with smoke. He touched my shoulder. "You're a goddamned honest man. I'm always impressed with that. You talk straight."

"You do."

"What I think about, every time I think about my brother not coming home on his legs, breathing—I think of you. I think he came home in you. That's a heavy load to put on a man. But I think a lot of us feel that way about the guys made it back. You suffered what our people did, you brought them home with you."

"Lee," I said. "I wish he'd made it."

In the darkness he nodded. I could feel his shoulders move. He said, "You've been to the Wall. You know what they do. What we all do. We go to it, we find the name, and we put our hands or face on it. We feel them. We touch the proof of it. The—that they're always there. At least there." He stopped, and we waited. Then he said, "That's how we are with the guys who came home." He touched my shoulder again, just for an instant, barely.

We sat, and I realized, after a while, that we both were looking at Jack. He stood very still, his blanket around him, the survivor of a shipwreck, a car crash, the very bad collision between whoever he was or wanted to be and the world.

"You could have brought him to the office."

"I sent a cop there because you wouldn't answer the fucking phone."

"But you didn't send Jack."

"No. I wanted him here. If there hadn't been so many upstanding citizens at the desk watching their kids get booked, I'd have let him sit in line with the other shitheads. Anyway, a bunch of them ran into the woods. We didn't bother even looking for them. We were too busy putting the shitheads into the buses. *School* buses we had to use. Can you beat it? No. I wanted him right here. I wanted him to see what the compass led to. I didn't say a word to him, by the way."

"You didn't need to."

"No. Well, I hope so, anyway. You'll have to say a word."

"I will, Lee. I promise. I swear."

"Do you know what you'll say?"

"Are you kidding? No."

"God, I love you, Mark. You're the fucking most honest man I know. God bless you." He stood.

"No. *You,* Lee. Thank you." We shook hands. He took his long-billed cap off and ran his hand over his head, as if to wake it up. He smiled a sad smile, then walked across the darkness to Jack. He stood in front of him. I watched them. I listened, but nobody spoke. He was looking at Jack, and his big hand with its thick forefinger was in the air between them.

Finally, he said, very low, "You got to get to be a person, kid. Fuck all this child shit. You don't need it. Your old man doesn't need it. Your mother doesn't need it. You get to be a man-sized person." The finger stood there, and then he took his hand away and walked around behind the exercise yard toward the car I saw in the alley.

Jack didn't watch him walk away. He was looking across the darkness at me. I saw his hands on the edges of the blanket, holding them against his chest. I thought of being a man-sized person inside. I found my own arms crossed against my chest. Aren't we cold, Jack? On this gentle night?

For the People

DEE MADE her opening statement: what she claimed the people would prove. Since Backus was very much a man, she could talk about Estella as a sinner—back-road motel affair, perverse lovemaking, et cetera. On the other hand, we who had argued before him knew that Backus was an old-school gent who didn't like you to talk about women, even if you were one, in a demeaning manner. Furthermore, he loved the law: he wanted to hear about evidence and precedent, not about character, unless the defendant's character was a verifiable element in her motivation. And Dee knew, I figured, that every word she adduced to the record about Estella's psychology would give me grounds for summoning witnesses about how battered and torn she had been from the start. Dee knew I'd call them anyway. But she had to not legitimize what she'd term mumbo-jumbo by *introducing* the notion of a wobbly mind.

It was said that Backus took his tone from the courtroom itself. You climbed a softly spiraling staircase, wide and covered with the federal-green figured carpeting that also covered the courtroom floor. Old wood creaked underneath it all. The balusters of the curving rail were narrow hardwood. A bailiff sat on a high stool of oak, as you came to the top of the stairs and stood in the back of the room. Church benches, and corduroy cushions on the oak armchairs for the jury up front, to the left. The teacher's desk for the clerk, the littler of the court's microphones for Backus, and one for the witness, the oak tables with carved decorations on the drawers for prosecution and defense. And the wide, chest-high bench with its curved chunk of marble for Backus to strike with his gavel. The two-story ceiling of recessed layers, decorated plaster and pressed tin, long brass light fixtures, formerly gas lamps, their white bulbs milkily glowing at the room's austerity, not brightening it. The daylight outside pressed at the windows, the lights above us pressed at the gloom that floated like vapors that we breathed. Dark green walls above dark wood wainscoting, and the wooden outline of a Grecian temple on the wall behind the judge.

The building had been restored, of course, and at huge expense. Worth it, the community and the Bar had thought. We all felt a little proud about practicing in our ancient courthouse with its one courtroom and the wooden statue, in the lobby downstairs, of Justice—an anxious-looking giant woman who held the usual scale. It was all a little much for Estella. She sat down hard, and I had to pull her up when Backus walked in to be announced by the clerk. When he motioned us to sit, Estella breathed out hard as she did what he said. And then the calling of the case. And then Estella's waiver, Backus's grim displeasure, then Dee, for the People. Estella and I were opposed to the People, and we were truly not.

Dee was careful. She had dressed with delicacy—a dark gray, almost black, tailored suit with an oversized jacket, one of those floppy-collared shirts with a bow made of its own fabric at the neck, and shoes that nearly matched. She wore no rings or bracelets, only a man's watch on a black leather band. Her earrings were dots of onyx on silver squares that matched the metal of her watch.

May it please the court, et cetera. She formally introduced herself to Backus, who impatiently waved her to get on with it. Thank you, Judge, and so on.

Estella looked like Dee's bad sister—a long, loose-flowing skirt that was tight at the waist, a short open jacket, a white collarless shirt with embroidering at the neck, white stockings, black, low-heeled shoes. Somehow she looked like someone who had just slipped out of crotchless underwear and garter belt and black lace hose. Her small oval face and pointed chin were pale, unhealthy-looking: she might strike an onlooker as someone with bad habits or bad hygiene, though her teeth and breath, when she talked to me at the defense table, smelled fresh. Her long lashes hid her eyes a lot. She looked hard at Dee, as at an enemy, and I wanted to tell her to stop doodling on the yellow pad I'd given her. But her pencil was never still. She smelled of a dark perfume I remembered.

There were ten or so spectators behind us. I'd seen no one I knew well, nor, according to Estella, had she. Our witnesses would be downstairs in the lobby with the statue. I knew we wouldn't get to them soon. First, a woman I liked had to address a man I feared about a woman I slept with so violently that my body was scarred.

"Judge, the deceased—"

"You mean Larry Ziegler?"

"Lawrence Ziegler, yes sir."

"Lawrence. Certainly. Well, why don't you call him that?"

"I will, Judge. Lawrence Ziegler. He apparently had predispositions to violent sex."

"And you're going to prove that," Backus said.

Dee, letting a snap of impatience into her voice: "I am, Judge. As soon as I finish my statement."

Backus, with surprising mildness, said, "Then proceed."

"Thank you, Judge." Dee stood in front of her table, half sitting, but tall enough and erect enough to look respectful. She did that because her knees shook at the start of a trial, I knew. She read from her notes, then looked up as if she hadn't memorized them the night before. She'd settle down soon. She'd be dangerous, though she, as I, was not an excellent lawyer. "Mr. Ziegler, the People will show, liked what is called rough sex—a term we are prepared to define. He liked more than that, however: he liked his children and respected his wife, even though he was separated from her. He liked his business, a very successful radio station, and he liked his life. Ms. Pritchett deprived him of them all.

"For she too apparently participated in rough sex with some regularity. And yes, we will show that too." Under the table, Estella's hand gripped my knee. My leg was far too wide for her stubby fingers, and they pinched in tight. I patted her hand. I took her finger and slowly bent it back until I heard her wince. She moved her hand.

"We will demonstrate, Judge, that the accused was a regular abuser of alcohol and dignity."

"This is not a Sunday school," Backus said.

"The information is relevant," Dee said. He nodded. She went on. "And we will bring to bear testimony of law enforcement officers who were summoned to a motel to which, we will prove, the defendant regularly went to meet the deceased. Mr. Ziegler, that is. We will prove that Mr. Ziegler was found dead in the bed he had shared with the defendant. That the defendant was properly Mirandized, and that, afterward, she informed the officers that she had killed him. She *intended* to kill the decedent, Judge."

Backus said, "We consider intentional murder for people who shoot policemen begging for their lives. You're aiming at murder in the second."

"Judge, thank you. Murder Two. Yes, sir. We will prove it. The man is dead, she killed him, she said so, and she was of a disposition to do what she said."

Dee saw my face. I knew she was trying to remember her language precisely. I made the note, folded it over, and put it in my case file. She thanked the judge and wound it up and sat. Estella leaned in again, and I leaned toward her. She said, "She's right."

"What?" Whispering, while keeping an eye on the judge.

"About my disposition."

"Not a problem," I told her, telling the truth and lying at once.

Then, to Backus: "Thank you, Your Honor. If it please the court, defense will waive an opening argument at this time, and will reserve our right to make a statement at the end of the presentation of the case the People will try to make."

"*Will* make, counselor. I'm certain that Ms. Tillim will make *some* kind of case. Aren't you certain?"

"Your Honor."

I was certain. All she needed was a finger to point at the bailiff today or tomorrow. He would accordingly turn out the lights and switch on the county's VCR. We would see Estella tell them that Larry Ziegler died because of her. And he did. We would hear her voice shaking as she panted and said the fault was hers. And it was. All I had to do was protect her. Who, I wondered, had I recently protected? No one but me.

Horizon Line

I RAN ON FEAR at first, the adrenaline eating whatever nutriments were left in whatever flaccid fat cells the body had hidden near the bone. So the burst away from the interrogation camp was also the consumer of what I had left. Like afterburners: cut them in for combat, and you've a maneuver or two, and then you're out of fuel. As we used to say, you could save your life with a burst, and *then* go swimming in the South China Sea.

The bad knee wobbled, which meant ligaments, I later figured. Didn't figure anything at first. The ankle was bad, but it held. My *nuts* ached. They were swollen, didn't know with what, and the running was terrible. Kept wanting to vomit on the run, couldn't, so heaved and hacked while gasping, while half screaming, this little nightmare voice: Ah. Ah. Ah.

Ran headfirst into a tree. It was one of those very high ones that have vines on them and that never grow in the northern panhandle, they told us. I remember the guy, big rugged German guy with a ginger-colored beard and red hair. Drawled like a goddamned cowboy. Said he was from Virginia, but he sounded like a TV show about tough in the saddle. Showed us how to catch snakes and skin them. We met up in the mess once, and he found some kind of little potato bug in his food and stood up with a face filled with horror and disgust. "My *God*!" he said. "My *God*. This is insupportable." The Marines paid him to tell us how to survive in Vietnam. We did it region by region with him, and he showed us how to use the vines on these huge old trees that did not, however, grow in the panhandle northeast of Vientiane, one of which I hit face-first.

The concussion and the bouncing into the soft, dark floor of the forest settles your panic somewhat. You get to take a breath and consider because you are lying with your nose and lips mashed into the ferns and moss. No sound of pursuit yet. But why? Doesn't anyone care about a thirteen-year-old boy with his brains running down his neck and ear and that soft skin on his cheek? Isn't Fish beloved among his comrades? Good old Fish: he always kept an eye on you. Goblin giggling a little hysterically, wiping his fingers on the forest floor, unnecessarily. Fish still keeping his eye on me.

No more.

Goblin confirms.

Up again, nuts aching, stomach aching, head aching, the eyes not focusing well, but not much to see, really. The sparse forest. The trees that don't grow there. The watery wide sun. Stuff moving in the brush. It would have to take care of itself. I tried, once I was up, to lean my head back and take a fix on the sun. Made me wobble. Looked for moss that grew on maybe a northern side of the trees. Not there. All right. Pilots find their way. Goblin making a south-southeastern course. Goblin going *that* way, with no shoes, no shirt, the pants torn raggedy on the leg and falling down the hips some.

A tiptoe march, forcing the pace by falling forward but not falling down. Sagely working to avoid the trees. Scratching the belly a little on thorny bushes, but going through them anyway. Because Phan Tuy would send them for a long time. Eventually he would call them back. Goblin didn't matter much except in terms of pride: propaganda. Goblin didn't exist up here except as a function of Phan Tuy's words. Scary for you, Goblin: figment of Phantom's imagination, almost. Working around a blue-gray stony outcropping, an island in the forest, and thick roots at its base that look like snakes. Goblin walking over them. Snakes being the least of several problems right now.

And beyond the outcropping, the silent small woods going noisy with birds and insects behind him, like the wake, but in forest sounds, of a ship that pushes through a sea, the panhandle opening out and sloping west to east, if Goblin's navigation's right. Horizon. An honest-to-Christ horizon line. It could be in the White Mountains in New Hampshire, or the Catskills, or Mount Katahdin in Maine. A horizon line of blue stone and brown stone and hardpan earth, and beyond it watery blue low hills. There's wind here. Later the wind will be cold. Goblin shivering in the hollow of some hard-ass mound of stones. But not sweating, or worrying about the lack of fluids to sweat with. Goblin dragging his thickened tender scrotum and his busted legs.

Billy not alive in the shrouds, the chute swinging like a toy, a pendulum, his legs flopping when the wind gusts.

Phan Tuy requiring another history. Another life. "So this time tell the *truth.*" Which truth: Goblin. Which truth? Tell me, and I'll write it. Phantom's teeth, his little glasses, little hands, the big power in his brain: "What is correct, Mark. The correct truth."

And even Goblin, college-produced and Marine-induced, a flying officer, level and loyal. Goblin had to wonder after a while about why. Why fly in this place? Why bomb it? Phan Tuy knew. Made me write it again and again. Until I didn't know who Brennan was. Until I hoped I could write it one more time and this time find out.

Phan Tuy: he would have won.

Thinking of Fish, and the boy with blood and brains running down his broken head: maybe Phan Tuy did win.

The spreading ink. And Goblin walking, more or less, into a dusk coming down at him, and into the spreading cold, south by southeast, home.

Witnesses to the Fact

ESTELLA'S HOUSE was quiet. As usual, she'd turned out lights in most of the rooms. We sat in the living room, which was cooler than the rest of the house because it was shaded by a stand of old maples. I heard their branches scratch the roof as breezes built. Dark pictures in dark frames looked like blotches in the low light of two wrought-iron lamps in corners. She drew on the joint and it flared. She held her breath, pulled air on top of it, then sighed out when her lungs had scored. The ashy orange end looked bright in the darkness.

"I wish you'd have a little hit," she said.

"Never use stimulants. Really. You go ahead."

"Well, of course I'll go ahead. Isn't that presumptuous, giving permission like that? I don't need your permission. And what was that about the stimulants? Are we back to the missionary position, if you'll pardon my Episcopalian?"

"I'm sorry," I said. "I didn't mean to sound stuffy."

"You sure did sound stuffy."

"Yeah. I—isn't that right: I do get stuffy when people smoke dope and snort coke and all of that."

"You ever do a little coke, Mark?"

"No. I knew a man who used to smoke opium regularly."

"But you didn't."

"No."

"Coke's an ice-storm rush," she said. "Very powerful. You feel strong. You feel capable."

"But you *are*," I said.

"Is your necktie off?"

"Yes. Why?"

"I was hoping you'd start to relax."

"And you?"

"Oh," she said, "I will. I will. A little J for joint will do me. It's just somewhat dispiriting to see all those big men with bull necks march up there in their polyester uniforms and say they found you with your tits hanging out and a somewhat sloppy man in your bed who is dead and you killed him and you said so. Somewhat embarrassing."

"Embarrassing."

"I don't know the word. Naked. How's that for a word."

"Good word," I said. "Do you do a lot of drugs?"

"What's a lot? I never did any with you. Maybe you're a drug."

"Maybe you are."

She said, "I always thought you'd be too square for them."

"And I am."

"And you are. That's why I like you so much."

"That's why you love me," I said.

"Love you," she said.

"But all they were was witnesses to the fact," I said. "They weren't passing judgments. Even Dee wasn't."

"Dee."

"Ms. Tillim, the assistant D.A. Adina. She's a pretty good lawyer."

"Are you better?"

"Older. More experienced. Possibly more cunning. Not much better, though, I'm afraid."

"Will you keep me out of jail, do you think? Still think?"

"Yes."

"You're so confident about it."

"Oh, that's me, Estella. Confident."

"Tell me why you never drink or smoke dope."

I took my tie all the way off and unbuttoned my blue oxford cloth shirt another button. I stretched further, lying lower in the easy chair, my heels on a leather-topped ottoman. "Too many guys in the Nam used dope. Not many pilots. Most of them did booze. I don't know what to tell you. We didn't come up smoking tea, that's all."

"Smoking *tea.* That's right out of a Jack Kerouac novel!"

"I never read any. No, it was just a word I heard."

"That's what the jazz musicians used to call it," she said. "The black guys in Kansas City and Chicago. So the white guys called it that. Then everyone in Kerouac's novels and Ginsberg's dreams called it that. Then everyone who didn't read them. The word will always get out."

"I guess it will."

"You know, you sound a hundred years old, Mark."

"Square."

"Yeah. Except in bed. You're a little crazy there, you know that?"

In the darkness, I shrugged. She sighed around the smoke again. Then she said, "I really like that about you. You're a secret. You wear the official lawyer's suit, the tie, the wingtips, all of it. Briefcase, everything except a pinky ring, for God sakes. But you have all those muscles on you. And you know how to hold people very hard and a little *angry,* don't you? And you're always scared. Angry and scared. Aren't you?"

"I don't know," I said.

"Yes, you do. You know. And you are. And I think I understand you. I think you're a spy. Aren't we both? Isn't that what we are, Mark?"

Timetable

THE SCHEDULE tightening, the headaches worse. No more chest pains, though sometimes a kind of fluttery feel to breathing, and a little acid soreness down the center of the body, throat to sternum to gut. The plexus there, where the knife-strike went in and doubled Jack over, his eyes enormous, his mouth agape, poor Jack. Like a fish. I checked on the comfort of my witnesses at what used to be a Holiday Inn, but which was now locally owned, ineptly run, and a smashing success because the entrance to the rooms was in the back, in the parking lot, in fact, adjacent to the sheriff's lot, which was next to his garage and the prisoners' exercise yard. I'd made a joke to Estella about how, if she'd killed Larry Ziegler at the former Holiday Inn, she could have one-stopped it to her cell, then gone across the street to the courthouse for her trial. She'd bitten me, hard, on the back of my hand. I later told Schelle I'd caught it in a car door.

When you come down out of the courthouse, there's a two-story entryway in the center of the clean, square federal building. You walk down the steps, also of light tan stone, and you're parallel to the entrance to the sheriff's, and the jail, and you're looking over the village green. It's square, too, though crossed at an oblique angle by a stone path, which is crossed in turn, at odd angles, by other paths. The irregularity disturbed some civic mandarins, and they lobbied every year to tear up the green and turn it into a civil grid. In the skewed and odd-shaped patch of lawn a hundred feet to the right of the steps as you descended them, Schelle would have her ceremony. She would heal me, she thought, heal all of us, the local towns, the city, the county, the state, America, and some of the world.

The stone was already there. I saw it on the way to court. I'd seen it when I passed the courthouse on my way to the county office building where I'd register property deeds or run a title search on land a client had sold or bought. It was higher than a tall man. It was an icy blue-gray. Irregular in its mounding roundness, with pockets and glacial scars. It looked like a piece of the moon. A piece of Vietnam. She'd had the widest parts, along the top, about fifteen feet apart, slightly squared and beveled. The same had been done at the bottom. She'd had them do it on all sides. It was outer space, it was inner Southeast Asia, it was almost shaped, it was Schelle's design. On the high slanting side that faced the courthouse a man was going to carve certain words she had given him and would not tell me, or anyone else. The Veterans of Foreign Wars and the American Legion were in a steam of righteousness over her secrecy. She took their money and kept her silence. That's Schelle: gentle and pained, determined.

We were standing in front of the stone. It was Saturday, the court was of course recessed, and Schelle and I had put on T-shirts and jeans, had driven to the courthouse green to stand on the grass before the blue-gray stone and try to talk. Men and women walked their dogs and carried newspapers. Teenagers with boom boxes skateboarded the bumpy stone paths. Schelle poured coffee with lots of cream and sugar out of a Pizza Hut prize jug and we sipped from the kitchen mugs she'd brought along. The hot sunshine of the morning, hot sweet coffee, looming stone with its blank face: I wanted to award her something, offer a consolation to my wife. Her T-shirt was plain white, as were her jogging shoes. Her jeans were old and faded. She wore no jewelry but her wedding ring and a watch I'd bought in the duty-free shop at Orly years before. Her hair was swept from her forehead and gathered in back. She wore a little lipstick. Basic Schelle.

"You have to have music, Mark," she said. "This is America. Those are American veterans' organizations, congressmen, statehouse politicians. They don't perform an act involving two voluntary muscle movements without playing an anthem and saluting a flag. So it's either the Boy Scout band, which is two trumpets they'll never harness, plus a drum and a saxophone if the kid isn't at music camp this year. Or else we let the Tenth Division send some of their musicians down from Fort Drum."

"No Tenth Division," I said. "Those guys are real soldiers."

"So are you," she said. "So were you."

I shook my head. Didn't I, Schelle? Didn't I try to say it then? Again?

"No," she said, "Marines. I know. But you know what I mean."

"You're seeing someone, aren't you, Schelle." Flat statement, no accusation, but no phony lightness in the tone.

She hung her head. She let the remaining coffee run from her cup and onto the grass, and she watched it.

"Schelle, it's not a *charge.* I'm not doing it like a fight. I've had these, I don't know, visions of you. Dreams. I keep seeing you kissing a man. I can't see his face. I don't see any more of you. I don't hope to. I mean, it's not as if I'm trying to *pry.*"

She looked up at that, and her beaked nose and angry eyes went happy. I hadn't seen her very happy in a long time. The expression faded, but slowly, like the glare in your eye of a flashbulb. "You're always so formal. You're always so polite. Even when you're making me truly and certifiably insane. Your wife's sneaking around with someone, and you don't try to catch their bodies in the act, only her—what? Chaste kisses? Little pecks? Is that what you see?"

She reached with her empty hand for mine. We stood in front of the monument she'd planned. Her skin was cool and familiar. I knew all the lines on her palm. In her throat, at the neck of her T-shirt, the pale soft skin was jumping hard. An infallible lie detector, that pulse in the throat.

She said, "Never mind. Do you doubt at all that I love you?"

"No," I said. "Never."

"Do you agree you've been something like insane in your work schedule. Client conferences. Witness briefings. Trial rehearsals?"

"Yes. And before that."

"Yes," she said. "And we've seen doctors?"

"Because I've been difficult."

"At the very, very least. Yet we've stuck together."

I nodded. Yes.

"And," she said, and then her voice caught and her eyes filled. She stopped. She turned her face from me, but forced it back. Her eyes had spilled over, her cheeks were wet. I would have reached to wipe her cheeks, but the cup was in one hand and her hand held the other. She shook her head, as if to shake the tears away. "And we haven't had a marital life. A sexual life. Whew." The head shaking again, the sound of something trapped in her throat. "For a very long time." She stopped, bent to the canvas bag she'd brought our coffee in, and with a paper napkin she blew her nose. One hand was free now, but she was down and away, I couldn't reach her.

I shook out the coffee mug and dropped it into the bag. With both hands now I reached for her. She stood. In the green, in everybody's public day, we embraced. Her breath was hot on my neck, her lips wet. I said, "Your nose is cold. You're still healthy."

She snorted a kind of laugh and shook her head. She whispered, "Mark, it isn't—"

And then the word: *tolerable? terrible.* I couldn't decide which. I didn't want to ask. *Tolerable* meant so much. *Terrible* was a very small reprieve, but surely a lie. I didn't want to know. I said, "It isn't?"

Outside the courthouse and next to the stone, Schelle kept her face in my neck. Schelle shook her head. She breathed like a child with a cold.

Someone passing in a car thought us cute or annoying. They sounded their horn, and Schelle's grip shifted, though she didn't let go.

Testimony

DEE'S WITNESSES had simply spelled it out: the phone call, the motel, the deputies who'd caught the call, the state police log, the officer who'd assisted, the EMTs who'd found a dead man but had taken him anyway, pumping at him, jolting his heart, to the hospital ER where a physician fifteen minutes after they'd arrived pronounced him dead, and then the sheriff's deputy who'd asked her what had happened, and then Estella's words, in his notebook and on his videotape. He said to the court, "She said they were playing rough. She said, 'He hurt me. I hurt him. I think maybe I killed him.' "

Brennan for the defense, crossing the deputy: "Joe? You and I know each other."

"We do, Mark."

Dee, rising, though still small under the twenty-five feet from her shoes to the ceiling, "Judge, this isn't Smalltown, U.S.A. Do we have to listen to this kind of just-folks nonsense from counsel for the defense?"

I looked back at the spectators. Jack: third row back, among the day's larger crowd, his face white, his eyes big, playing hooky to see the old man work. To see something, anyway. It was the kind of room designed to make you feel alone under the heavens and under the law, but close to your fellow beings. You'd have to answer for your crimes. Jack felt near, looked far and unwell. To Backus: "I was trying to establish a rapport with the witness, Your Honor."

"Would you, Mr. Brennan, work on establishing a line of questioning? Rapport is the least of our problems here."

"Thank you, Your Honor. Joe. Mr. Furmin. What did the defendant say about her rights?"

" 'Are you kidding?' "

I looked at the witness, looked at the judge. He frowned at the deputy.

Joe said, "That's what she *said* to me. I told her her Miranda rights—"

"Told them or read them, Joe?"

"Read them."

"You said 'told.' "

"I meant 'read.' "

"You held the card in your hand and read it aloud?"

"Well. I held it, the way you do. You know. But I, all I needed to do was say the words. I knew them by heart."

"You think."

"Well," he said. He blushed like a schoolboy caught in class. "I guess you can always make a mistake."

"Did you? This time?"

"No. I don't believe I did."

"Believe. Can you make a stronger statement than that?"

Dee: "Is this badgering, Judge? Would you call it that?"

"You will please watch your tone, Ms. Tillim. I'm not on the stand. State your requests or complaints and I'll deal with them. And the answer is no: I overrule the objection. Proceed, Mr. Brennan."

"So you hope, believe, pray, whatever—"

"He's putting words in the witness's mouth, Judge."

"Sustained."

"You did say 'believe,' I believe, though of course I'm not one hundred percent certain, Joe. Did you say 'believe'?"

"Yeah," he said, disgusted with me. I used to make jokes with him at arraignments. We used to bet on whether he could stay on his diet, which he couldn't. And here I was, attacking his professional competence in public.

"So, then, Joe, you believe you read—sorry, you didn't read them, did you. You believe that you *stated*—"

Backus wriggled slowly in his chair and leaned forward, one hand up to stop me. "I will take it as very clear, Mr. Brennan, that the deputy might have gotten the Miranda warning to the defendant, about her rights, at the time of arrest, in a flawed or incomplete form. It is possible. I understand that."

"In which case, Your Honor, I respectfully move that this case be dismissed, since the defendant's arrest may well have been conducted in an unconstitutional manner such that she jeopardized her protection from self-incrimination."

"I'll take it under advisement and rule at a later date." His tone suggested that I not get my hopes up. "Proceed with this witness, if you've further questions."

"Joe, the defendant stated to you—"

"It's on the tape, Mark. You *saw* it."

"Thanks, Joe. She stated, and all of us saw and heard her do it, 'I think maybe I killed him.' She didn't say 'murder' or 'planned to kill him,' did she?"

"No."

Dee: "May I object once more, Judge, to the line of questioning? It's irrelevant. We did hear for ourselves what the defendant said."

"Overruled," Backus said. "Mr. Brennan, because he thinks I am slow to notice such matters, wants to be certain that I understand that premeditation, indeed anything but accident, *may not* be inferred from defendant's statement. Am I making progress, Mr. Brennan?" He stared at me with displeasure: *You made her waive the jury you pretend you're talking to,* his face said. "Do proceed, please. And do, please, rely on my wit a good deal more than you seem inclined to."

"Thank you, Your Honor. I wished only to be certain that it was crystal clear about the defendant's possibly flawed Mirandizing, as well as the relative innocence of her inculpating statement."

"Relative," Backus said, breaking it into three very separate syllables. He motioned me on.

I thanked Furmin, who looked at me with no affection, and I took my seat at the counsel table. Estella, dressed in white cotton that clung to her, mugged a "Not bad" as I sat. I motioned with my hand that she wasn't to respond facially. She nodded, closed her eyes like a chastened child, and looked forward.

Dee's witness, her fruitcake, against whom I'd set my fruitcakes later on: Dr. Marian Abbott of Albany, a professional expert witness whom I'd seen in two other cases and whose ads I'd noticed in the *New York Law Reporter.* She was competent and, since she lived and practiced a few hours away, she wouldn't cost the People too much in expenses. She took the stand in her powder-blue suit, a stocky woman in her sixties who was balding. She'd built a carapace of sprayed blue-gray atop her scalp, and I felt sorry for her. She had a mole near her lip, and she fingered it nervously during her testimony. Dee led her through her credentials. I interrupted to say that the defense would take her credentials as read.

Dee asked her about her review of the case, the number of hours she had spent on the review, her study of the tape, of pertinent arrest documents, medical reports, so on. Then she got to it: "What makes people hurt each other in bed, Doctor?"

A snicker went through the spectators, and Backus looked up as if someone had farted or belched, then he sighed into their embarrassment. He said, "Never. Never in my courtroom." I looked at Estella, but she was watching the judge.

The silence was a chastened one. The doctor happily spoke into it. "Psychosexual factors vary from individual to individual. In my practice, however, and in my years of studying these problems, I have seen that we deal essentially with feelings of powerlessness. A need for redress. The demand is that one be *acknowledged.*" She held her hand up, silver bracelets slid down her arm, and when she moved it down they jangled on the oak armrest of the chair. Though the witness stand was a foot and a half off the floor, she still looked as though she needed to sit on a telephone book to see us all clearly. She pointed in a practiced lecturer's admonition. "Sadomasochistic relationships concern the power of selfhood. The breaking through to the partner's autonomous being—or the insistence on being broken-through to. The self must be recognized, say these actions. The, we would call them perhaps, perversions. And therefore, I would suggest, it is about infancy—about loss and the requirement that, in terms of the acknowledgment, the loss be made good."

Backus was taking notes very quickly and copiously. He studied Dr. Abbott and tilted his glasses at the moment that she looked at Dee and tilted her own. It occurred to me that we all should be wearing Groucho Marx noses and eyeglass frames, and I buried my face in my hands an instant. When I looked up, Backus was watching me, and I smiled.

Dee said, "Thank you, Doctor. You used the term 'perversions' just now. In customary sexual practices, then, the making of what is called 'rough love,' the inflicting of pain on a sexual partner—that is not considered normal?"

The doctor shrugged. "What is normal is what most people do. Most people do not do this."

"Your Honor," I said, standing, "if it please the court. I don't know why we're discussing these practices when no evidence about them has been introduced. Where does the A.D.A.'s line lead? Where does it come from?"

Dee said, "Judge, it has been stated clearly in this courtroom during Deputy Furmin's testimony—has Mr. Brennan such a short memory? The man said—we could read it to you, Mr. Brennan. The man said she said—your client, the defendant said—they'd been playing rough with each other."

"Your Honor. 'Playing rough' is a term introduced as a conclusion by the witness Furmin. Defendant never said it."

"You did not object, Mr. Brennan. Am I correct?"

"You are correct, Your Honor, and I'm at fault. I didn't think the A.D.A. would build a house of cards on that single clause."

"Phrase," Dee said.

Backus gave us both his cautionary glare.

"But I must object now," I said. "Especially since 'playing rough' has been built up by the prosecution to mean something it doesn't *have* to mean. If I speak disrespectfully to Ms. Tillim, I can be accused of 'playing rough,' and no one would accuse us of—"

Backus's hand stopped me. He waved us forward to the bench and covered the microphone before him. He pointed at the stenographer, and she stopped taking down our words. I heard the spectators rustle, moving with curiosity or boredom. Backus whispered to us, "This is terrible law, Ms. Tillim. I'm sorry. It is quite terrible. And you're no exemplar, Mr. Brennan. Ms. Tillim, I wondered why you bothered to introduce state of mind at all, given testimony on how and in what circumstances defendant was found. But that's your choice. I'm right, you're wrong," he said as Dee opened her mouth to protest. "You're young," he said, "and you'll learn this stuff. That isn't patronizing. It happens to all of us, being young, starting out, so on. But there you are. You're in a hole. You dug it. Mr. Brennan, shaky as he is, is in a position to bury you in that hole. My suggestion: get out of it with as little mud on you and your case as you can. Thank the witness, and sign off. Mr. Brennan will be merciful—"

"No, sir," I said. "I have some obligations here."

"It's your right," he said.

"My responsibility, Your Honor."

"Is there music to go with this, Mr. Brennan?"

Backus shook his head instead of waiting for me to speak. He looked at Dee.

"I may want to have this witness reappear at a later date, Judge," she said.

"A permissible precaution. I'll so note. Let's move it."

We went back to our tables. Estella stared at me, and I thought, The testimony's turning her on. Which made my blood pressure move. I felt my body change, and I thought, This line of work used to feel a lot different. I wanted, again, to grin.

Dee had her own plans, Backus notwithstanding. She quickly said, "Does the making of love lead to rage?"

"In the abnormal ways we earlier discussed?"

"Objection!" I said.

Dr. Abbott wanted to get it in. She blurted, over Backus's voice, "The rage builds up. These people do violent things."

"No!" Backus said, as if admonishing a puppy on paper. "You will dictate your actions according to my rulings, Dr. Abbott. That's not to be done, what you just did and said. Strike it."

The stenographer wearily nodded.

Dee quickly said, "Thank you, Dr. Abbott. No further questions. Mr. Brennan?"

I took my time to stand, consult my pad, which was blank. "Dr. Abbott, good morning." She adjusted her cat's-eye glasses and said nothing. She waited, chin up. "I noticed that in the course of your testimony you used no, might I say, professional language. No polysyllabic jargon, for the most part. None of those complicated words we expect these days from expert witnesses."

"They aren't necessary. And I have trained myself to speak simply."

"For juries?"

"Objection."

"Mr. Brennan?"

"A few more, Your Honor, then I'll stop if you don't see the line as fruitful."

"Overruled."

"Dr. Abbott? You speak simply so that juries will understand you? Yes or no, please?"

"Yes." Reluctantly. She was smart enough to see it.

"You testify a good deal before juries."

"I do."

"You advertise in various journals of the legal profession, offering your services as an expert witness?"

Dee: "Judge, he stipulated the witness's competence."

"Your Honor, I am not impeaching the witness's paper credentials, which I did indeed accept. This is a hostile witness, I believe, and her *competence* may indeed, I would hope, be examined."

"Overruled, Ms. Tillim."

The court recorder, a 150-year-old chain-smoker who retreated into a Zen trance to get through litigations, reread the questions in her flat, insane voice. She looked like a long piece of frayed, graying lace attached to a steno machine.

"Yes," the doctor said. "I advertise."

"Is the bulk of your income earned, Doctor, by way of such testimony?"

"I have a private practice."

"No clinical practice? That is, you're not attached to a hospital or public health clinic?"

"No."

"Were you ever?"

"Yes."

"May we know why you aren't now?"

"I prefer to work independently."

"Flying or driving from court to court to testify on what's normal according to your lights and what isn't?"

"That puts it—"

"Please," I said respectfully, "you must say yes or no." Backus didn't pounce on my "according to your lights," and I was encouraged.

She sighed. "Yes."

"Are your patients—the people in your private practice—do they lead normal lives?"

"If you consult an analyst, you probably aren't normal." She smiled, as if she had scored. She fingered the mole, adjusted her glasses.

"Are you married, Dr. Abbott? Do you have a sexual partner?"

Backus knew what I was after, and he stopped me. "You might object at this point, Ms. Tillim."

"I felt certain that you'd take care of it, Judge," she said unctuously.

"Mr. Brennan," he said, "a doctor need not engage in sex, or discuss his, *her* sexual history, in order to testify effectively about sexual matters. Your point about Dr. Abbott's, ah, serviceability is one I have noted. Your more vulgar further explorations I want ceased herewith. Clear?"

"Clear, Your Honor. I hope, Dr. Abbott, that you don't think I meant to insult you. I was confused about how you knew so well what was normal."

"Mr. Brennan," Backus warned.

"I've only one further question, sir. Dr. Abbott? When did you interview my client? Or attempt to? The defendant? That woman, at the table where I sat while Ms. Tillim questioned you?"

"She would, obviously, not have been truthful."

"You knew this in advance?"

Backus's head swiveled to Dee. She looked down, at either her notes or her hands atop them. The witness looked at Dee. I stepped between them.

Backus studied the witness. She felt his stare. She said, to him, "I did not feel it necessary to take the earlier commuter flight. I had seen the pertinent data. I usually do not speak to them."

"You don't like to talk with the people about whom you testify, Doctor?"

"They would only lie," she said.

"You always know this? They always lie?"

Dr. Abbott shrugged. She looked bewildered, she looked sad.

Dee puffed her cheeks out and closed her eyes.

The witness said, "People who live like that, you see, live unaware. They would not know what is true. It would take us months of analysis to progress to the truth. Must I catch the measles to treat the measles?"

"You were afraid you would catch a psychological problem?"

Backus silenced me with his hand. "I don't want this to continue any further unless it is essential, Mr. Brennan. And there *is* no requirement or custom that she interview your client. I'll see citations, though. I really think I've heard enough. Haven't you?"

"Thank you, Your Honor," I said. "Perhaps the A.D.A. wishes a redirect at this time?"

"I'll offer the occasions for questioning the witnesses, Mr. Brennan. Don't sound smug."

"No, sir. If it please the court, I've no more questions at this time."

The doctor wasn't crying, but she soon would be. She was all right. For most circumstances, she'd be fine. And if Dee could pump some language from her, remind her that there wasn't a jury to be impressed, but a judge to be talked to directly, she might salvage some testimony. The damage I'd done, that to the doctor aside, was really to Dee. She was young enough to think I had achieved something. Backus wouldn't, for long.

There would be a wedge of doubt about competence, a sense of the shopworn, the questioning of her judgment. But he knew that Estella could well have told the deputy she killed Larry Ziegler, and he'd know that people who kill people in third-rate motels aren't nuns.

Jack's face: I'd impressed my kid with my pony tricks. I was a wild buckaroo on defense.

Backus said, "We're getting out of here. Adjourn for the day. Ms. Tillim?" I could have tried for equal treatment: ask if I should be in chambers too. But I knew what he wanted. Dee was about to receive some instruction in the law from a diehard defense lawyer. And I was going to have to introduce my son Jack to the woman I wrestled in bed.

But Jack had already pulled himself jerkily to his feet and was walking away: balls of his feet, the swagger of shoulders—a kid who didn't give a good goddamn. Sure, he didn't. I looked at Estella, who'd been standing beside me and watching us as the judge left the courtroom. "Is that your boy?" she whispered.

I nodded.

"That's sad," she said, looking away.

Going Home

IN MY OFFICE that night, and this time with no lights, not in the library and not in the outer offices or waiting room and not in my own room. In my office, and on the floor, on the old oriental rug, its horsehair padding underneath as punishing as it was cushioning, the stiff bristles stinging me through the frayed weaving of the rug as though we made love on nettles and thistles and hawthorn barbs. I was rehearsing her for her testimony. We were talking about Larry Ziegler, about their lovemaking, and I said, again, "Tell me about your father."

"Have more pizza," she said. "Have a sip of my beer."

"No. Thank you."

"Why don't you drink, Mark?"

"I sometimes do. I used to. I just don't."

"You never do with me."

"I don't hang around with you for drinking. Tell me about your father."

"Tell me about not drinking. Tell me about *your* father."

"You first."

"It's irrelevant."

I said, "You've been in courtrooms too much."

"Well," she said, "it's not by choice. Though we wouldn't have met otherwise. Would we?"

"Would you have wanted to meet me?"

"I'd seen you before. You once defended a guy I was trying to put away. The D.A., Brandywine, was trying. I was there. I gave testimony."

"And I saw you do it?"

"I used to look different," she said.

I closed my eyes. I remembered one of the goat fathers, one of the studs of your nightmares who prided himself on seducing his daughter. Who denied it on the stand and in depositions and when they arrested him. Who wept in public and smoothly told his daughter in bed how to slide down onto him, sweetheart, like *that*, yes, like that, darling, Daddy's darling. "Your hair was black," I said. "It was even shorter, butchy and black and sort of crew cut, wasn't it? And you weighed more?"

She smiled. She was sitting in my swivel chair. I was in the client's chair at the side of the desk. She wore baggy khaki shorts and a maroon T-shirt and sandals. She crossed her left leg onto her right, cocked at right angles. "No," she said, "but you have a good visual memory. My hair was colored. It was very short, you're right. But it was dyed. And I wasn't fat, I wore padding in those days."

"In your *brassiere*?"

She laughed a deep, pleased laugh. "Well, where else would you do it to get bigger, you know. You know?"

"But why?"

"Oh, there was a guy I was seeing. Trying to see. Making a pass at. I wanted to catch his eye. He seemed to go for chesty women. It was very stupid. I had a low level of self-esteem, as that bitch doctor would say. I felt like shit about myself. My father, to sort of almost answer your question, had just died."

"And that was your response?"

"That was one of them. And never mind the others. And never mind the guy."

I took a piece of pizza with sweet peppers and mushrooms and sausage. It tasted like the smell of a damp cellar. "What'd your father die of?"

"My *God*, Mark. It was a *sick*ness. Nobody killed him. I didn't kill him."

"You should have."

"How do you know?"

"Because I do. Because I know. That's that."

"I'm not talking about it. Not with you. Never in court. Maybe you could get it out of me, but never anyone else and never in court and never anywhere, fucking *never*!"

She was up, my chair was spinning, she was at me and on me, slapping open-handed, but not like some unmuscled creature who wasn't used to fights. She kept her arms locked, she swung with her back, her wrists were strong and her hands were hard. She meant to punish me, not only shut me up. Instead of seizing at her hands, I ducked under them and into her, took her with my shoulder and drove her, my hands going around her buttocks and thighs. She fell, started to, and she at once put her clawed hands into my neck and ears, so she was holding on, taking me with her as we went. Almost before we were on the floor, Estella taking my weight and wincing, nearly moaning with the impact, she was tearing at my collar, at my shirt, and I was pulling her shorts down.

We wrestled there, fought hard, and she ripped into my back while at the same time, she was jamming herself at me, moving hard from the waist down, but not in combat.

"Jesus," I said. "Are we—"

"Shut up," she said. "Shut up."

"Are we fucking or fighting?"

"Shut up."

Her fingers went down to my throat. I reared, partly because of what our bodies did, but also because of her fingers, working at my throat, gripping at my throat. As I raised myself I squinted at her face. It was furious. It was red, and angry, there were tears and mucus on it, and the most dreadfully sorry cast to her mouth.

But she was strong. Those stubby fingers were strong. And she knew the carotid artery as if it were a homeward route on a map. Hearing went first, I didn't hear us panting, or the slap of our sweaty, slick skin. Then my vision dimmed. It was a sudden going-gray of her face and the objects in my darkened office. It was a filter slid over everything, then I simply didn't see. I bucked into her and onto her and she rose at me, and she was in me or I was in her and the concentration of every sense was in my penis. I felt as if all of me were there. I didn't feel her letting go of my throat. I felt a coolness enter my head as I came and came into Estella, who had arched, bearing us both above the stinging floor.

When we fell, it was somehow sideways. Somehow we were lying sideways, still gripping each other, still locked in one another, breathing harshly into each other's face. She moved first, after some seconds, to burrow her nose into my throat. She licked daintily at the sweat there, licked like a mother animal or an infant seeking its need. And then, a few seconds later, she said, "There."

That was what the recon squad leader, a sergeant, said, to me or himself or his team. He said, "There." He was a tall, skinny black man who wore a dark brown cowboy hat with feathers stuck in the band. I saw something gleaming on the front, and when I was up on my feet, later, I saw that it was a crow's or raven's head.

But I was lying on my side, curled and clutching my sore nuts and scraped belly. And he was standing above me with his patrol. They were all black. They were all tough-looking. None of them loved me. None of them had decided that finding me was a triumph for the forces of life, a defeat for the enemy and for death itself. I wasn't the pleasure of the day.

The sergeant was closest to me. He set a pump gun against a pack beside me and he squatted. "There," he said. "You back home, paleface."

"How," I said.

"*That's* charming," he told them.

Someone muttered, "Charming," and they laughed again.

"Name yourself," he instructed.

Told them: base, mission, point of shootdown, manner of imprisonment, means of escape.

"That's cool," one of them said. I was sucking on a canteen, choking and gurgling.

The sergeant said, "Drink all you want. We got a spring back here. We're going in. We'll be all right."

I held the canteen away from my mouth, against my will. "What about me?"

"Yeah?"

"You'll take me."

"You ever shoot a nigger in Detroit?" A tall guy, his back to me.

"No."

"You ever rape a sister on Kosar Road in Corpus Christi?" Short kid.

"No."

"Then you ain't white, you in dis*guise*. Shit, no, we won't take you home."

Everybody slapping hands. Goblin leaning back on his elbows and sucking the canteen, dripping over his chin and chest.

The sergeant said, "You got your pale ass whipped, boy."

Nodded.

"How long?"

Shrugged.

"You say you killed one of the slant brothers with your hands?"

Nodded. Didn't matter. Tough-ass flying Marine.

"That's good shit, you can do that."

I panted over the canteen. "It was time to get back."

"I can get next to that, time to get back. All right."

"So I go in with you."

"Prove you're a white-ass American upper-class shithead so we know you ain't some Russian mole."

"His snout isn't long enough," the one from Corpus Christi said.

"Isn't brown enough," another one said. He was angry. He was short and chubby and his face behind silver-rimmed glasses was handsome, nearly sweet. He wore a red rag over his hair, an earring in his ear, and a gold bracelet. It was wrapped in electrician's tape, but I could see the metal between the edges of the tape. He was very angry at me. At all of me. Any of me.

"Prove who I am?"

"Nah," the sergeant said.

"Yeah," the sweet face said.

"Listen," I told them. "I'm a fucking officer. I'm a fucking Marine aviation officer. I'm a motherfucking *captain.* Get me pointed straight, give me a piece to carry if you got one, and cut the fucking *shit.*"

"White U.S.A. male, for sure," the sergeant said, cutting each *r* hard, a joke about honky speech.

"Don't bother to salute," I said. I plugged the canteen. Rolled slowly to my hands and knees and climbed up the sergeant's trouser legs. Goblin going airborne. He held still until I was up. Put a hand on my arm to steady me, then pulled a stained but obviously cleaned shirt from his pack. I put it on.

He said, "A man wore that. A friend of mine. That's his blood and body waters, made those tracks on it. I keep it for him. You know, for his memory. So I never think of being nice to anybody, you know? Just hump the load and walk the road. Understand?"

"Thank you," I said.

"Fuckin *chuck,*" the sweet face muttered.

I told him, "Don't *you* bother to salute either, okay?"

Sergeant handed me a World War I model .45, the kind that officers still carried in the Corps and the infantry. "I took this off a captain who got killed," he said. "You'll feel right at home. I doubt you'll need it, but you look like you could use some assurance. Instead of that antique you brought in."

His eyes weren't as deadened as he might want them to be. His head was clearly filled with too much swamp and night and killing, but he was a whole person inside, under it. He'd just shrunk a little to make room for everything. That's what you did. I nodded and his bright, hard eyes saw me seeing him. After a while, he nodded back. "Don't shoot yourself," he said.

"On purpose?"

"On purpose, by accident, or half of each—that's *your* call, Captain. Just don't do it now, out in the boonies here. You wait till we get home, all right?"

Goblin: "Roger that."

"Roger that," the sweet face said. "Roger my black, sore *ass.*"

The sergeant took his hat off, wiped his head with a khaki handkerchief, stuck it back inside his hat, and put it, raven's head and feathers and all, back on. "A little grace note," he said, his tough eyes liquid and alert. "A little fashion bracer for those muggy days in jungle clearings when you never know who you'll meet on Claymore Street. Ka-boom. Let's go."

The chubby, handsome one said, "Don't you say *Roger*, Captain Pork."

Goblin, armed, looking back into the man's round eyeglasses.

Goblin taking the safety off with his right thumb, cocking the piece left-handed with the slide.

Goblin turning sideways to the kid and raising the weapon.

"You see," the sergeant said, behind me, talking to the kid, "they get their heads fucked, too. Understand?"

The kid had the M-60 at waist level all the time. I'd have been Salisbury steak and never have capped. But it was the roaring in my head, and the terrible sound of my own panting, sore throat. It was the simplest reason, really—that all of a sudden I knew that there needn't ever be rules anymore. Heard everything, now: flies and quivery insects with their high drilling sounds, and parrots, some kind of pig not far away, rooting, snuffling, the click and ping of equipment they hadn't muffled well enough, the hard, echoless *tock* of a weapon being armed.

The bristles of the carpet, the warm wet flesh, her breath on me. And Estella said, "We're getting there, aren't we, Mark?"

The New, Improved Divorce

THE ONE ABOUT the husband and wife who applied to family court because the boy they'd adopted three years ago, when he was eight, hadn't taken. They weren't satisfied with the bonding. The father's word: "bonding." Like bourbon bottled in bond. Like savings bond. Like glue. Like ducks with ducks and dogs with dogs and children with parents: bond. They didn't like their progress as a family. They thought they'd try divorcing their child.

There's always the hope they invited the kid to court to hear his parents ask to send him back to the foster home. Mommy and Daddy *love* you.

Caveat emptor, as we tell our clients, our children, our wives.

The country club's narrow, screened-in porch, where golfers and shoppers eat second-rate food and listen to the purr of golf carts: here I am at lunch, sliding the bacon from a BLT, pushing its lettuce onto the plate, and eating two thin rings of mayonnaised tomato with my fingers, dripping seeds on the tablecloth. I drink quinine water with ice and lemon. My client, Christine Conroy, wearing her golf duds and smelling of grass, deodorant, and the sweated leather of her hitting gloves, is eating about two pounds of tortilla chips in a melted yellow cheese that hangs in the air from her fingers and lips as she crunches away. She is drinking beer from a glass filled with ice and lime slices. Her hair is short, mostly gray, and her eyes behind tinted glasses are mean. Christine, who owns two movie theaters and a number of Victorian homes converted to multi-dwelling apartment houses, weighs a bit more than I do, and is worth one and a half million dollars more than Schelle and I and our lustiest pecuniary dreams put together.

We're talking of Christine's portfolio. She's boasting that her accountant has deemed her portfolio *healthy.* "I think she's solid now," Christine tells me, referring, with a slowly running trail of molten Velveeta cheese, to her certificates of deposit, her municipal bonds, her more volatile defense-industry and electronics stocks, her riskier futures investments, and her sizable holdings of precious metals and gemstones. "I want some junk," she says, "but my money people say that junk bonds are dead."

"I could never get too excited about low-yielders," I answer. I'm thinking of the Reuters piece reprinted in the Binghamton papers a week ago. "And I think they've run their course."

"Exactly," she says. "Exactly."

We nod at our wisdom and sympathy, we address our lunch, and then Christine, referring to the district attorney, says, "I was talking to Jake Brandywine a couple of days ago. They had a little reception, just a swollen office party, really, for his niece. The one who had the abortion?"

"You mean the kid who needed an appendectomy in New Jersey."

"Exactly the one. She came home, she was visiting her aunt and uncle, and uncle tossed a little reception."

"Jake always had balls," I tell her. "His theory is, when you step in a cow pie you clean your shoe off and tell the world you've discovered the secret of making gardens grow tall."

Christine says, "He was worried about you. We were talking, you understand, about everything under the sun."

"Wide-ranging talks of mutual benefit."

She shrugged and raised her gray-white brows. Her big head waggled and she made a face. "It isn't *all* jokes, Mark."

"No, ma'am. Is this the true nature of our lunch today? I thought perhaps you needed some legal advice. Giving it is a practice of mine."

"I should be charging you by the hour for this one, Mark.

Jake tells me that, in his expert opinion, you are sailing close to the wind. He thinks you could face disciplinary action for your conduct during this trial. Before it, even, he said—not that I understood a good deal of what he was getting at." She drinks her limed, iced beer and gasps with pleasure at the end of her long swallow. She wipes her mouth with her hand, then says, "Do you think he's out of line?"

I shook my head.

"Because I think he's saying *you're* out of line."

"I probably am, Chris. It's pretty likely. At least *unorthodox* would be the postmortem on this one, I think."

"So he's warning you."

I say, "I believe, yes, that's why he sent you."

"Mark, nobody *sends* me."

"Chris: bullshit."

She laughs and so do I.

I say, "Jake could always take this case. He could plead it. He could always beat me to a pulp in court unless the deck was stacked. This one isn't. I'm surprised he hasn't done it."

"He pleaded too many cases for your client. He thinks she's wonderful. He's maybe got a little, you know, heat in the seat for your murderess."

"Alleged murderess. Old Jake, huh? What's Geraldine think of *that*?"

"Come on, Mark. She knows he doesn't get walked on a leash by his cock. Jake's been the D.A. this long because he knows where *everything* should go. He's into power, not sex."

I tell her, "Sometimes they're the same, maybe."

Christine looks at me and shakes her head. "You're too young for this," she says. "Or too stupid. I don't know which. And you *look* terrible, by the way. Your eyes are *awful.* You know what you need, Mark? You need a good goddamned *attorney.*" She laughs, and the cubes in her beer bang the glass.

"Tell me," she says, "did she do it? Jake's honey: did she really do it?"

I ask her, "Do what?"

Andy and Miriam

RUTHIE BROUGHT the message in, risking wrath and wreckage and Christ-all knows what she might have thought about me and Estella. I told her how pretty her print dress looked, and she said, "I've worn this every other week for the last two years, Mr. Brennan."

"And I've liked it every time."

I really thought she sniffed. As if she could smell us on the office air. And maybe she could. But she smiled. A major virtue in Ruthie, her incomprehensible loyalty aside, is her fear of me. "Mrs. Brennan called while you were in conference."

"Oh, yeah. Speaking of that. That—what's his name? The contractor I was just with."

"Lloyd Hermann?"

"Hermann. Terrific. That's exactly what I called him. You know, like it was his first name? Herman this, Herman that. What can you do for me, Ruthie? Help me out. No wonder he looked at me that way. Listen: telephone his office in a couple of minutes, tell him that I asked you to remind him to send me the contract in question. It'll at least suggest I remember who in hell he is."

"A stroke," Ruthie said, nodding, and blushing a little at the daring of the word.

"Exactly. I knew you'd handle it. Anyway, he wants us to bring suit for breach, and I think it's a pretty transparent matter. Not that we'll ever come to trial."

"Why, Mr. Brennan?"

"Oh," I said. "Well."

The silence became a pause.

I swear it: she cocked her head like a dog that hears a strange sound. Then she straightened. She said, "Mrs. Brennan telephoned, it was urgent. She said that: urgent. And could you meet her in the rehab room? Now?"

"Now," I said. "You think they want me for aerobics, Ruthie?"

But I went over. Schelle, I ran for you from the start. I still would, if I could. The seasonal heat had deepened beneath an inversion that hung above the center of the state. Humid air that on some early afternoons beneath a watery bright sun smelled stale, breathed and breathed again, made everyone sweat. We all looked wilted, I thought, as I went from the doctors' parking lot through the lobby and down one flight to Physical Rehab. It was underlighted and ugly, painted in glowing pastel yellow, with low ceilings of stained off-white. The smells were of boiled vegetables and artificial flavorings in gelatin, of sweat. It seemed I smelled somebody's odors all the time, these days.

In the small gymnasium, people with damaged bodies worked on the myths of recovery: that they would walk without the parallel bars, or limp without their sticks, or sit without being held. Across the room, near posters of Olympics featuring Rumanian pederasts' four-foot dreams, a wide woman in highway-safety crimson sweats was forcing a boy to bend a knee so scarred I could follow the wormy lines on his leg from where I stood. He moaned, but bent to her instructions. She cheered him on. In the opposite corner, Schelle and four women were working out aerobically to taped instruction on a VCR. A woman encased in tights so hard and gleaming that her muscled body looked synthetic was telling them how to jump impossibly for a very long time.

One woman stopped. She sat down and looked as though she might vomit. Schelle, more or less keeping up, told the others to continue. I saw her wave them on, though I didn't hear her words. When she came closer to me, wiping her face with a towel, I saw that she had already started to cry. She shook her head, instructing me not to ask and, masking herself with her towel, she led me out of the rehab room and down the low, ugly corridor to a room I'd never seen.

It was small, oddly shaped, the same yellow and off-white, and loaded with folding furniture. One metal table was open. A legal pad, some pens, and a pile of leaflets were on the table. The leaflets said, *Sensible Eating is Fun!*

"Sure it is," I said. It seemed important to say anything, to somehow keep at bay the news she was going to deliver.

"Sit down, Mark, will you?" She wiped her neck, her back and arms. In her tank top and leotards, she didn't look synthetic. She looked like a muscular woman with skin that was mottled from toweling, exertion, emotion maybe. She looked handsome, and I wanted to tell her so. I leaned into the smell of perspiration and her skin, the powder and soap I recognized from home. But Schelle leaned away.

I said, "What?"

"You talked to Mickey about her play, didn't you?"

Nodded. Tightened inside and nodded, waiting.

"About Miriam and Andy, the boy she falls in love with who's her brother's roommate?"

"The callback," I said.

"The roommate isn't her brother. We know that because he lives here. Jack."

"Jack?"

"Mark, it isn't a play."

"She didn't get the—"

She watched me sit, thick and uncomprehending. She

watched what must have been a yellow glare of understanding come into my eyes.

"It isn't a play, you said, Schelle?"

She shook her head.

"But there isn't a brother?"

"The brother-person's a boy she waits tables with. They're friends."

"Friends."

"Just that. Only that. Buddies. He took her home one time for coffee, talk, you know. And she met his roommate."

"That's the play?"

"Except it's real."

"As in: real life," I said. "When she was talking to me, she wasn't talking about a play." Schelle shook her head. "She was talking about a friend of a friend. And she fell in love with him. And he's gay."

"Yes. Homosexual, that's right. And he has, you know."

Her mouth looked so dry. And she could not make the word.

"The boy she loves," I said. "Like the play."

"There *isn't* any fucking play, Mark! Will you stop talking about the play? There is no play."

"She lied about everything?"

"Except the plot."

"Which is true: that she loves a homosexual man who, oh please, Jesus, who has AIDS. He has AIDS. She loves a man who has AIDS. AIDS. AIDS. He has AIDS."

I watched my hands because I couldn't watch her face. The right was twisting the four fingers of the left, over and around, pulling so hard the base of the left hand's index finger turned white each time the right hand passed over it.

Schelle said, weeping openly and hard, "The poor man. I feel so sorry for her. It's so tragic and terrible for her that she—God, Mark, she thinks she *loves* him. It's killing her." She giggled and shook her head, she slapped herself so hard the handprint stayed on her cheek. "It's killing *him.*"

"And did they—you know, did they make love?"

"No."

"How do you know?"

"She said so."

"Yeah. She said some said-so's to me too. Like it was a play, Daddy, and I got a callback, Daddy, and it's a play about this man, Daddy, and Daddy I get to play the girl, Daddy—" I saw her disgusted mouth and I stopped. I thought she was going to hit me this time. "Schelle," I said, trying to find a tone someone might think of as reasonable, "Schelle, she went to such lengths when she lied about it, maybe she also lied about making love. She could *die!*"

Schelle only nodded. Her exhausted eyes, her lifted brows, said, *Brilliant.*

"She pretended so hard," I said.

Brilliant again.

"To not tell the truth like that. To make such a *story.*"

"She made the appointment to get the test for HIV," Schelle said.

"I thought she told you they didn't make love."

Schelle looked away. She said, "She should still have the test."

"So they did make love."

"God, counselor," she said. She looked straight at me, and I remembered how hard she could glare with those frighteningly clear eyes. "You've got us," Schelle said. "First time around on cross, and you picked my bones. Yes. I thought maybe I could keep it from you, but you got me. Yes. Our baby might *well* have had sex with a man who will die, and maybe she will too."

"Someone with AIDS who makes love without telling the partner beforehand can be tried for attempted murder," I said. "There's precedent. The soldier who—"

Her face stopped me again. When she saw that it had, she said, very low, "We are not talking about the law. Or what you'd call recourse. We are talking about our little girl. Her heart is destroyed, and maybe her body is. Her life. We're talking about her life."

"And that she couldn't tell me the truth," I said.

"No," Schelle said. She stood so suddenly that the motion in the dirty yellow room filled with furniture looked like an exercise on videotape. "No. Not at all. That is what we are *not* talking about, Mark. All right?"

"Just tell me. We don't know for sure she has it. Tell me that."

"We do not know for sure."

"She might be all right."

"I'm going to New York."

"Good," I said. "That's right."

"You take care of Jack. Come home, the nights I'm away."

I looked at my hands. They stopped, as if I made them uneasy.

"Mark," she said.

"I will."

"Maybe," she said, "maybe we'll all be all right."

"We will," I said.

Memo

LATE AFTERNOON at the office, and Dee Tillim on the phone: "You son of a bitch. I thought we were friends. I thought we at least were colleagues."

"Hi, Dee."

"Don't be calm with me. Don't be calm and smug and make me sound like a goddamned *girl,* Mark. You didn't have to make my witness look and feel like shit."

"The judge saw the whole thing. He sees everything. He knows what I did and what I didn't do. It was slightly cheap, a little sly, and probably it didn't add up to terribly much. You know that."

"She looked unstable. She sounded unstable. He's not going to find her a rock of certainty on your client's willingness to murder."

"Willingness wasn't the issue, Dee."

"Don't *do* that, damn it. This is the phone, not court."

"Then stop shouting at me. If it's between you and my client, you know I'll make the choice that makes things tough for you."

"Don't I. But I am talking about professional ethics here."

"And I'm talking about sound legal representation."

"You talking with your pecker is the only sound *I'm* hearing," she said.

Words

MY ARRANGEMENT with Jack, since the night Lee Beeton Palmer rescued him, was that he stay home in the evenings for a while. He'd been willing. He'd been eager. Schelle didn't know about where Lee had found him, and now she was in New York, and it felt as though we would never catch up. There was too much action. Too much traffic, Goblin would say. So: Schelle had gone to the airport, the little one a dozen miles away, not the airport in Syracuse. She'd flown a five-hundred-dollar charter to La Guardia. Jack was home with me. Estella was home with herself.

Jack was cooking for me. Big, and growing bigger, pale and clumsy and scared of me, of Lee, of the law, of himself, of his friends, of losing them, and of coping with their presence. He was frying eggs in too much margarine he'd cooked too hot. They were splattering in the oil, gurgling, beginning to brown before burning. I didn't tell him. I sipped a diet soda and leaned my shins on the edge of the table and watched him. I kept saying to myself, This is my son. This is my former baby.

He slid the mess onto cold, overcooked toast and squirted ketchup on.

"Want a slice of onion, Dad?"

"Not with my eggs, thanks, Jack. This way's good."

"I'm not such a good cook," he said.

"You do that thing with vegetable soup from the can on top of hamburgers."

"You remember that?" He smiled as he covered his lower face with strips of toast and smears of ketchup.

"You made that for us after the game. The night we drove up to Syracuse and saw the Chiefs play Columbus. Terrific Triple-A baseball. Get em rising, and—"

"You catch em sliding back down," he finished for me. He nodded. He blushed. Watching him, I finally understood: he was happy. Jack, my son, was *glad.* "Maybe we should go again," he said.

"Damned right," I lied. I was as sorry about that one as any of them. Sorrier, I corrected myself.

He slurped some soda and covered a belch. He saw me gather myself. His soft brown eyes had grown so watchful. Though they weren't the color of yours, Schelle, they were shaped like yours, they were sad like yours.

I said, "You can get out of this."

He nodded.

"The trouble it feels like you're in."

"I'm in it, all right," he said, looking at his plate.

"Yes, you are. The only reason you're not arraigned is Mr. Palmer. Detective Palmer."

"Because of you, in Vietnam."

"Never mind. The thing is, there was booze, there were drugs, there were underage girls, for chrissakes, Jack, getting bagged. By a bunch of thugs. That's terrible, what they were doing. Little *girls.* Mickey was their age, and not so long ago." Miriam, visiting her make-believe brother in a make-believe play. Callback. "Anybody. Jesus, Jack, people shouldn't *do* those things. What I'm talking about: don't admire that shit. It's shit, Jack. It's evil, it isn't anywhere *close* to halfway decent. You don't want to know those guys, much less earn their approval."

"Who says I'm earning their approval? They're my friends."

"They're nobody's friends."

"They're mine."

"They don't care about you. If they did, they wouldn't get you sucking on dope—yeah, I know about it, what in hell do you think the world's like, Jack, that I wouldn't know about it."

"Does Mom?"

"That you smoke grass? Yeah." I nodded, and it was like a blow to the face, I saw. His expression nearly broke, and I thought he might cry. The knife-strike going in, the eyes widening, the gaping, soundless mouth.

"I'm sorry," I said, "that it's all so tough for you."

He shook his head, and we were nearly back to nothing but words—yes you are, no I'm not, they are, they're not, et cetera.

"Jack," I said, "if anything happens."

"Huh?"

"What?" I said.

"*What* happens? What? I don't—"

"No," I said, "listen. Have a little patience with yourself, is all. It'll be all right. Girls, school. Really. Have a little—just *wait.* If you can wait on it, you'll be a happy man. Sometimes sad kids are happy grown-ups. Can you—never mind. This isn't what I wanted to say."

"What'd you want to say?"

Because he needed something, didn't he? He was thinking maybe I'd slip him a clue, a key to something. He still thought maybe when the old man talked that something came out besides words. He was admitting that. Maybe. And maybe, too, there was no way to do this. Goblin switching to Guard: I have *nothing*.

Said, "I love you. I'm sorry."

"For what?"

"Jack."

"Dad. Thank you, all right?" Then he rose. He said, "She's guilty. Everybody knows she is. She's a whore. Your client's a *whore*." Pushing away from the table, leaving me with ketchup and the oily eggs, leaving the room. Everyone had someplace else to be.

The Braid

JUST OUTSIDE of South New Berlin, New York, near the quarry just off Old Route 8, which is a crescent off New Route 8: clapboard, little insulation, roof gone rotten, window frames moldy from the wet earth cellar, cornices crumbling, paint scoured off by upstate winters, wood turned silver-gray, which deponent remembers as the color of their lives.

It was not the color of his mother's hair, which even then was whitening. Her hair he thinks of as stone-colored, blue-gray going white, the blue of clay and certain rocks, the gray of old dogs' muzzles and the bass in ponds near home. It was his father who then drank the most, who was still sometimes kind, still sometimes sober. Now he remembers the house as smelling of moisture, of vinegar, the overheating woodstove in winters, the high, sharp smell of dirt in the cellar during humid summer days. Then, he thinks, he didn't smell it. Now he does.

He did smell his father, the yeasty, rich odors of beer and the cured meats his father would eat at the bar for his lunches and often dinners too, and the sweat of the day, and sometimes, when he raged, the stink, almost a bowel smell, that his father's body generated. It was oily, and it clung to you after your father had seized and twisted your arm, or thrown you out of the way, or gone directly after you, maybe with open hands, maybe with fists. That was in the days before his mother gave up or gave in and drank her way dead. That was when she got in between your father and you and got hit. That was when you escaped for a couple of hours at a time.

And at night, and once in the brown-yellow light of a kerosene lamp because they hadn't paid the electric bill, his mother would sit on the edge of the bed in his parents' room and braid her hair. She always wore white muslin to bed in the summer, white figured flannel in the autumn and winter. As deponent grew, as the parents worsened, the white fabrics became more stained, yellowed and faded and eventually torn. When deponent's father was away, as he so often was, deponent might do his homework at his mother's small birch table, rounded at the edges, the small square mirror attached to its back surrounded by a birch frame that held empty bulb sockets. Sometimes, if no one had been struck, and before she began to drink with deponent's father, the mother would sit on the edge of the maple-veneer double bed and hum to herself. Deponent did his homework and she hummed, songs he no longer remembers, but which she hummed or even sang, over and over, "Da *dee* da dum!" It was like sitting under a tree, he remembers thinking, or now thinks he thought, and hearing a bird sing the same glad song again and again.

And on a night when they had both been struck, but not too badly nor repeatedly, and when the light bill had gone too long unpaid, his mother sat in her bedroom and braided her hair, and sometimes sang and sometimes hummed, and deponent sat at her little makeup table in the soft yellow light by which it was difficult to see but good to feel, and he looked past his pen and the spreading figures on the harsh yellow paper supplied to him by school, and he watched his mother. Her eyes were closed. Her hands were behind her. In the dim light, on the cheap bed, with her cheek bruised and her rough hands dirty at the knuckles, she took her long, brushed-out hair in several strands and she wove them into a tight, dark, stony braid.

Deponent tried to follow which strand led to which. Her hair was quite long, and though for a time he could trace the path of a length, he soon enough lost track. He could see only the fingers working, and her hair in the yellow-brown shadows, her closed eyes, her swollen cheek, the shape of the whole as it built.

On that night, when he was nine, deponent thinks, she opened her eyes to see him regarding her intently. He remembers that her eyes widened, and filled with tears. He remembers worrying that he had offended or otherwise wounded her. He remembers his confused relief as she smiled a smile that altered her face and that deponent cannot remember having ever seen again.

Volunteers and Conscripts

THE SAME twenty or so people were in the courtroom on the other side of the bar. Spectators straggled in as Backus took his seat, then we took ours, and then I stood beside Estella, who that day, in a white rayon dress with a bold black flower print, in dark stockings and black shoes, with bold jewelry, looked too confident and self-involved for my comfort. She was small and she should have looked lost. She looked like a witch's familiar. She looked like the witch. I was grateful that we had no jury, but was worried about the judge.

"If it please the court," I told him. "The defense acknowledges that the People's case is cruel, but insists it isn't damning. Ms. Pritchett, a celebrated and widely respected social worker, carrying a heavy caseload of the needy and the victimized—and doing so, Your Honor, with distinction in this jurisdiction for nearly seven years—was compelled by forces traceable to childhood trauma of her own, when she could indeed have benefited from someone as wise and hardworking as she is now, to engage in an *affaire de coeur.*

"Her romantic partner, Mr. Ziegler, the decedent, was in the process of securing a divorce. There was no shame, then, in the liaison. Two consenting adults were comforting one another. Ms. Pritchett is not married, although she was, very briefly, at the age of seventeen.

"Mr. Ziegler was, and Ms. Pritchett is, open-minded in an open-minded time. It is common knowledge that what were once boundaries in erotic relationships no longer exist. Like the wall in Berlin, accustomed as we grew to it, those boundaries now have vanished. It is a new age, and tolerant citizens have grown to respect the private tastes and predilections of other citizens—although they may not wish to share them, or to know very much about them. Movie stars appear in what we once would have called a state of undress, but which is now acceptable public grooming. Words are used on television and in the press which once we banished from public utterance.

"Just so with the private expression of mutual need and affection between consenting adults.

"Sometimes accidents happen. Sometimes you pet a puppy too hard and he yelps. Sometimes you disturb an old dog as he eats and he snaps at you without thinking. Sometimes erotic partners may stimulate one another in ways outsiders consider rough.

"Indeed, the term 'playing rough' has already been—"

"Sir!" Dee, her face a shade of red that clashed with the red poplin blazer she wore with a navy skirt and a light blue blouse, had stood to object. Her expression was twisted, and under the dim globes on the high ceiling she looked like someone else. "Judge, I must with all respect insist. Mr. Brennan complained to me and to this court about that phrase, 'playing rough.' He called it a clause. He said that it wasn't admissible."

"Your Honor, we will stipulate about the complaint and that the clause is a phrase. The *phrase*, however, is on the record and has been throughout. It was introduced by the People. Your Honor admitted it. I assume you placed evidentiary value on it."

Backus was tired of us both. He didn't like me or my tactics. He knew I wasn't much of a lawyer. I made my money on farmers' disputes and land sales, the occasional suit for an obvious tort. I lived in the Register of Deeds and did real estate closings for a livelihood. He thought something more of Dee Tillim, because he liked women and because she was bright. And here she was, being goaded by me and letting me outslick her. This was country law, and Backus liked the suburbs. He adjusted the zipper on his robe, and I thought of Estella zipping the fly up and down on the trousers of her suit. I closed my eyes.

Backus said, "Mr. Brennan," and I opened them. "Thank you, but I will determine what I determined."

"Yes, sir. May I continue?"

"Ms. Tillim," he said, "you know that Mr. Brennan should be permitted to make his statement uninterrupted."

"But he's having it both ways, Judge."

"You're out of order, Ms. Tillim. Kindly remember that there is no jury present to impress. You must impress only me. I am not that impressible."

"No, Judge. Sorry," she said. She looked at me with disgust.

I smiled at her, said, "Thank you, Your Honor." I looked at my legal pad, the black figures rolling across it, and then I looked over my shoulder, because I felt something wrong. Birnbaum. In the corner of the angle of my vision I saw Birnbaum, back from Washington, back on my trail. Birnbaum knows, I thought. Birnbaum knew.

"Mr. Brennan."

"Sorry, sir. Yes. Yes." I looked at the page but saw only shapes. I widened my eyes, wiped at one as if there were a speck of dust in it, then squinted at my writing. "Now. We—yes: the term 'playing rough.' All right. In *County of New York v. Chambers*, what has been called the, ah, Preppy Case"—mustn't say murder—"the jury found that 'rough sex,' as it was called, was an extenuation in a very distressing and lamentable death.

"We will ask Your Honor to review the finding in that matter, and to examine the testimony we will adduce to this effect: that decedent did savagely beat the defendant, who was then forced to defend herself. That things, in other words, got out of hand.

"Furthermore, we will demonstrate to the court that the defendant's state of mind—an issue already referred to by the People in their use of the term 'predisposition'—was disturbed during this unfortunate set of events by what is called a 'flashback' to previous trauma. Specifically, defendant, as a child, endured severe beatings at the hands of her mother. Such a response is precisely within the parameters of reactions predicted in post-traumatic stress disorder. It is no different, Your Honor, from that endured by veterans of the Vietnam conflict and by veterans of the Korean and other wars." Backus had been a corporal in Italy and Yugoslavia at the end of World War II, and had been in the Judge Advocate General's Corps of the Army during the courts-martial for Korean prisoners of war who had been accused of turning coat. He had represented, to my knowledge, at least one accused GI.

"We will ask the court to understand, then, that the defendant, a good and socially useful citizen, had defended herself and had suffered a flashback to childhood victimizations—that the confluence of the two forces within her gave her no choice but to act in self-defense, and to do so with superhuman energy. The dreadful result was the death of Mr. Ziegler. Dreadful, sir, but understandable and, by a compassionate society, forgivable. Thank you."

I looked at Backus: zero response, a poker player's pan. Dee was puffing her cheeks out and shaking her head. I noticed the D.A. and his personal assistant just behind the bar near the People's table, and I hoped that he wouldn't decide to find an excuse to remove himself from recusal so he could plead the People's case. He was far too good a lawyer for what I was hoping to achieve. So was Backus far too smart a judge. But what, I wanted to say to someone, can I do? What else can I do?

Jack, among the spectators, pale and with his big eyes, was two rows behind and at the other side of the room from Birnbaum, who was looking down, no doubt writing notes. He looked up then, with his narrow handsome face, his round dark-rimmed glasses, dark hair, serious mouth. He smiled, but he gave me no pleasure. He nodded. I realized that I still stood at the defense table. "Sorry," I said, and I took my seat.

Backus lashed me into action, and I worked my first witness, Ms. Patt, a senior social worker with ebony skin and broad, graceful hands, who wearily testified that Estella was a good person in the office, that she carried a crushing caseload, that she worked hard for her clients, especially the children, that she should have been a mother in light of her dedication to kids. At that, Estella put both arms on the table, and her neck wobbled. I thought she was going to lay her head down. So Estella was a force on the side of the gods, a help to humankind, and a woman of kindness, not cruelty, we established. Perhaps.

Dee insisted on a cross, and I thought she might ask about Estella's social habits—did she pick up syphilitics in bars and jerk them off in public, so on. But all Dee wanted to establish was that the witness didn't know Estella socially, that they weren't intimate friends, that she didn't know what Estella did in her private hours.

What the hell: why not? "Your Honor?" Brennan for the defense, eager and innocent. "May I ask a question on redirect?"

Backus nodded, waved me on. I asked Ms. Patt, "Did you care what your junior colleague did in her very few hours off? They were few, I assume?"

"She works so hard. Well, we all do. She works on Saturdays, you know, and late into the evening. Sometimes you don't get them, the parents, unless you go around at night. I doubt she's got a lot of time, that's right."

"In those hours or minutes of what we could, I suppose, call leisure: did you, do you, think too much about her as a private person? Or did you see her as more of an arm of a public institution, someone trying exclusively to be of social usefulness?"

Dee: "Judge, if that isn't leading the witness—"

Backus: "It is. Isn't it, Mr. Brennan?"

"No further questions, Your Honor, and of course the previous question is withdrawn."

Thanked Ms. Patt, who smiled past me at Estella, nodded at Dee, who stared at me with something, I realized, approaching permanent distaste. Just wait, baby, I thought. Just wait for the *big* news.

I asked that my second witness be called, Dr. Guetterman.

When he was sworn and seated, when his aluminum crutches were leaning against the stand and he had folded his small legs and sat, smiling, a little man in a tan suit and maroon bow tie, a clean-shaven, pleasant, bald small man whose diminished body always increased my sense of his large and capable mind, I said, "Good morning, Dr. Guetterman. Would you mind, please, telling His Honor something about yourself?"

"I am Maurice Guetterman. I am director of outpatient counseling at the Mary Imogene Bassett Hospital in Cooperstown, New York. In addition, I conduct an extensive group therapy and individual therapy practice in my own clinic. I have published numerous articles on modes of therapy, several about childhood trauma, specifically the abuse of the young at the hands of parents, teachers, or relatives."

"Sir," the judge said, "there is that much of that sort of thing?"

"I'm afraid so. Yes. I think that early in his career, in the late nineteenth century, Freud saw this to be the case and then could not bear the information. He turned his back on it, and since then—no doubt his attachment to the charlatan Fliess had something to do with it, by the way—since then, everyone has more or less willingly turned his back to it."

"Thank you. That's shocking to think about."

"More shocking, sir, if I may, that we choose *not* to think about it."

"Quite correct," Backus said, "quite correct. Proceed, Mr. Brennan."

"Thank you, Your Honor. Thank you, Dr. Guetterman. In the course of your practice have you had occasion to examine adults who were abused as children?"

"Yes. Many."

"Did you find that in general the damage done in infancy or childhood had residual effects?"

"Not in general. Without exception. Each of those people was a damaged adult. Each was somehow dysfunctional. Each tended to repeat the actions of his parents."

"Was it only in the case of men?"

"Only in—oh! Indeed, not." He smiled each time he spoke. He enjoyed himself vastly, and he seemed to love his work, to be grateful for a chance to discuss it. I wanted to kiss his sweet round head. "I'm sorry," he said. "I use 'his' as a grammatical matter. Men *and* women were thus affected."

"Thank you, Doctor. How were they affected?"

"Children who were beaten might, and usually, alas, did, beat *their* children. Women seduced by their fathers or uncles became seducers, often of the very young. Sometimes they preferred homosexual liaisons, these women. Sometimes they were promiscuous. Often they loathed their sexual partners."

"Did any of the women ever simply live normal lives?"

"What is normal?" the doctor said. "So often, the term is moralistic, not scientific, you understand. Yet, by the way, I think we all have a sense of what normal *might* be."

"And, sir?"

"I tell my patients that if they can marry and be parents, if they can find satisfying work and keep their jobs, if their lives feel like something they might *volunteer* for, not be, well, *conscripts* in, then they are finding normality."

"And do some of these former victims, these women, find normal lives?"

"Yes."

"Many?"

"No. Not in my experience."

"Some, though?"

"I would say so."

"Ms. Pritchett?"

"I beg your pardon," he said.

"The defendant, sir. Did you have occasion to interview her?"

"I did."

"Where?"

"In your office and in my private clinic."

"For how many hours, sir?"

"A good number. I would say eight, perhaps ten."

"And you found, sir?"

"Your—the—she is a very intelligent, very determined, highly skilled social worker of the most useful sort."

"Useful in what way, Doctor?"

"She wants to rescue people. She knows, she has come with sadness to know, when they will resist rescue, or become unavailable to her efforts. She knows how to persist on their behalf. She works very hard for abused and neglected young people."

"Did you learn anything more, sir, besides her great benefit to the taxpayer and the community in general?"

"I learned that the young lady was treated, as a child, in a most cruel manner."

"By whom, sir?"

"So far as I could determine, by her mother."

"That treatment consisting of—"

He paused. He folded his little arms across his little chest and he looked down. Then he raised his head. The smile was gone. His brown eyes looked hurt. "She was struck, often and repeatedly. Sometimes with hands, sometimes with household objects—a clothing iron once, a broom handle, the cover to a pressure cooker, such things. She was denied her childhood."

I didn't look at Estella. I had told her to fold her hands and keep her mouth shut and look straight ahead. To get into a silent stillness and hide inside it until we were through.

"Denied her childhood," I said.

"Absolutely. She lived in prison, in a manner of speaking."

"You have testified, sir, that one does not escape these experiences."

"Correct."

"Did you find, therefore, that Ms. Pritchett is a psychopath, some terrible deviant who is a blight on society, as a result of her childhood?"

"As I have said, Mr. Brennan, quite the contrary. She is socially *useful.* She is driven to rescue herself, over and over, by rescuing the children she serves."

"Thank you, Doctor. And what the prosecution has called 'playing rough' in her, ah, her intimate life?" He looked bewildered an instant, and his small face actually turned to one side as if he sought to find who had said 'playing rough.' "Sorry," I said, "the term was introduced earlier in these events, before you were in the courtroom."

His face seemed to light with relief. He nodded. He asked, "The reference is to sexual domination, the use of controlled force, that sort of thing?"

"Yes."

"Yes," he said. "Such forms of sex play are thought by many to be attempts to recover lost power, lost authenticity. Feminist theory sees, in Hegel's terms, the need to be master or slave."

"You said 'sex play,' Doctor."

"Yes."

"It can be play."

"Of course."

"Can it get out of hand?"

"Oh, yes," he said. "Anything can. Women, making love to men in conventional ways, can suddenly feel threatened, even raped, if the intensity grows too great. Men can break down weeping while they are gently loved by a woman. There are large forces beyond the grasp of the conscious, Mr. Brennan.

Once tapped, and who knows what will effect that release, once set loose, they are remarkably powerful."

"And a woman such as you have described, in an intimate situation with someone fond of violent lovemaking—such a woman, whose childhood was as traumatic as my client's: could the partner become too rough or violent? And could the woman respond with a violent self-defense?"

"It is conceivable to me—let me say, first of all, yes. Yes to both parts of your question. Someone could be too cruel. People are often cruel, yes? Someone could respond to the cruelty with a feeling of emergency, of need to escape or to save herself. And, yes, she might relive her former tortured childhood moments."

"And otherwise, at other times, be a useful citizen in all ways?"

"Absolutely," he said.

"My client?"

"It is she of whom we are speaking. Of course."

"And all that could happen in response to lighthearted, more or less innocent sexual play."

"Without question."

"Dr. Guetterman, thank you very much. I've no further questions, Your Honor, at this time."

I had to sit, now, and keep my leg from lying against hers, and hope that Dee didn't think to ask about bondage and asphyxiation of the most innocent, playful kinds. It was time to pretend. As Birnbaum knew, it was always time to pretend.

The Part That Was True

So I WENT from outside Quang Tri down the coast to Chu Lai and out just ahead of the firefights to Saigon. They took statements twice. The session in Saigon lasted more than six hours, and they didn't start out friendly. Men in pressed uniforms who sat straight and took off their aviator sunglasses with reluctance were at best skeptical to begin with. The lieutenant who was my escort was unfriendly, too. I wondered what they suspected me of, and I asked them. We were at the square table in the air-conditioned room inside the embassy compound. When they moved me there, I figured I was being tape recorded for possible use by State or Defense. The embassy was a political site. They wanted me clean, I thought, so they could use me in the election. Apparently, there was fear that Humphrey or McCarthy could pull it off. That was what I thought they thought. Later on, an intelligence officer with a fused neck who looked like a huge albino ant thought I was safe to talk with, and he told me things. We were in the compound, drinking iced tea. He kept pouring brandy into his from a small Old Mr. Boston bottle. I kept shaking my head when he offered, kept slurping up the tea and sucking at the ice because I was always thirsty then.

He said, "Kennedy."

"Who?"

"You know, Bobby. Robert Kennedy? The First Brother? He's the one."

"What one?"

"He's the one the Chiefs are scared of."

"What chiefs?"

"Joint Chiefs of Staff chiefs. The admirals and generals. The princes at the Pentagon. They're scared that Kennedy will ride in on a wave of charisma via the McCarthy organization, eventually. They already have the infrastructure."

"Who does?"

"The McCarthy people."

"I didn't know Kennedy was running, too."

"You been away, son."

Pale, narrow face, looking as if it never needed shaving, and the big dark glasses, the narrow chin and jaw, the neck that didn't turn: he swiveled his shoulders to turn his head. He was in khakis with no insignias and a striped expansible civilian belt. His sleeves were rolled up. There were shrapnel scars on his arms. I said, "Where were you?"

"Near Chieu Hoi? We caught some shit. They blew me up pretty good. It was a routine kidnaping and information mission, and we had a little luck, was all."

"A little luck."

"It seems we weren't terribly coordinated that night. It seems our people were doing a little howitzer firing into the selfsame ville, and we didn't tell them we'd be there and they didn't tell us and there you are."

"There you are," I said, watching him turn his torso to follow an officer's wife with his eyes. "So Kennedy's considered soft?"

"It seems to have become convenient for him to hate the war, darn that ugly violence. And the Chiefs are worried McCarthy'll fold, his people will go to Kennedy, and then the Hubert people come on board. They love those Kennedys, the kids."

"The Chiefs want Nixon," I said.

"He's got a secret plan for us to win, the Chiefs say."

"The nuclear solution?"

"Fuck if I know. Meanwhile, the Democratic National Committee wants you."

"Will they get me?"

"They have people pressing us. We'd like to know, if you made, say, an Okinawa to San Francisco, San Fran to Chicago flight—what you'd do."

"Eat some barbecue, then some porterhouse, then maybe some kind of very sweet, really rich kind of dessert? Get as sick as I got last night, blow my dinner, sleep a while, and start again."

He raised his iced tea to his mouth and tilted his entire body to drink some off. "We'd like to know—"

"The Chiefs?"

"The people who get to know things. We'd like to know on their behalf whether you'd tell them war is hell, or if, you know, you'd say, Send us more airplanes and drivers and armament."

"You don't want me telling them the war isn't fun."

"Not unless you tell them we should *win* it."

"Fuckers shot me down with missiles that came from Russia down through the Trail. Somebody wants the C to win. Wouldn't it be nice if somebody wanted *us* to win? Is that what you mean?"

"You are aware of the political realities."

"Aren't I, though. Didn't I just get what you might call a crash course in the art of war?"

"We'll do a little more with the doctors, really make sure you're okay, your feet and your gut, the goddamned beriberi—they showed you a time."

"I learned a lot. My penmanship improved."

"So I hear. I hear you were a hard-ass during the interrogations. Debriefings, that is."

"You didn't hear me for yourself on the tapes?" I asked.

He smiled. His face was shaped like a wedge. It was like watching an ant try to smile. He said, "We'll heal you up. You're the color of old wall. You smell like piss." I sat up. "No," he said. "No offense. You've *been* through it. We want you back with the doctors for a good long stretch. This is, what, twenty May. You go home in, say, July. August. Right around there. You go home healthy, you go to their little convention in Chicago, you tell them what we need here."

"Do I say 'gosh' a lot?"

"It wouldn't hurt. All you really need, though, is you tell them the truth."

I said, "Which truth?"

"Our truth," he said, sounding the tiniest bit surprised.

They shipped me out in August. Goblin flew like freight. Cold on the aircraft, and even when the stew put blankets on me and smiled her big bucked American smile and then cried about her husband in I Corps, I was only cold. Chicago in August, the Whitehall Hotel where a man in a top hat bowed me into the lobby—English hunting scenes, leather chairs and sofas, politicians with motionless faces and mobile eyes.

This is the nice part of the best defense. Next day, walking in the city: breezy and warm, if you went by the way people dressed and moved and sweated. I was cold. The streets were wide, and there were more cops than I'd seen MPs in Saigon. For all the big streets and broad sidewalks, for all the hot, moving air, the city seemed rigid. Chicago was a city packed with something, tense with something. Goblin on the verge of spotting bogies. Off North Michigan Avenue, there was an air-conditioned place that served crabcakes and mussels and lobsters: red leather banquettes, funny waiters in tuxedos, a lot of wisecracking men, a few women, all of whom sounded like cops. Newsmen is what they were, and they were talking about hippies and yippies and the mayor's dragoons. A bunch of students were in a far corner, near the kitchen, of course, exiled by the maître d'. I saw this one woman, tall, long strong neck, very dark hair, light eyes, a handsome nose. She wasn't eating. The kids around her, maybe they weren't kids, maybe they were out of college, were putting away the chow, and she was drinking something, maybe soup I thought, from a cup, breaking flatbread and dipping it, but not eating much. Her lips were pursed unhappily, her face looked tight. When her head came up, I waited for her eyes to respond. They saw that I'd been waiting, and they did. Her smile. Schelle, your smile.

This part is true. This part—where you and your friends left and I followed and the crowd was outside the *Tribune*, and the cops thickened like something on a speeded-up film. And there was an asshole kid with wispy whiskers and an American flag over his shoulders like a blanket. Like Jack with Lee Beeton Palmer. Like me on the plane with the blanket that the stewardess gave me. You were telling something to the kid with the flag. You were arguing with him. You were shaking your head.

"Not this way," you said. Or: "Right this way." Or: "Fight *this* way," it could have been. You were giving him a bad time. I knew you were with the kids in Chicago. I knew you were *of* the kids. So did the cops. And finally they grew tired of watching someone who couldn't grow his whiskers right wear the flag like a blanket. Some big cop said a few words to another big cop, and I watched them getting ready. They were talking to each other. Men, when they talk like that and set their feet and backs, are getting ready to attack. That was when I went in, moved in across the wide street and got in behind you, and then the cops came. It was like water spilling over, it happened so fast. I went in and took hold of your shoulders and pulled you away. It was, as certain papers said in those days, a police riot. It became a protest in certain late editions, broken up by cops, a number of whom were hurt. But at the start it was a bad free-for-all, and by then I had you from the back, I got my arms around your waist. I had my arms around you in Chicago in 1968, and you know that's the truth, Schelle.

Fiat Justitia Ruat Caelum

THE TROMPE l'oeil facings of wood on the wall behind the judge, cornices, pediments, and four columns, outer two Corinthian, inner two Ionic, of the simulated temple front: Let there be justice and let the heavens fall, it said on the tympanum under the slope of the roof. It wasn't a roof at all, of course.

Dee was to cross on Guetterman. She was sleek this morning, her hair looked trimmer, its shape slightly changed, and she wore a sleeveless cotton sweater, bold figured skirt. Her royal blue linen blazer hung behind her chair. The courtroom was crowded, at last. The trial had grown important—entertaining, anyway. The bailiff turned people back. I heard them complain on the stairs, going down. Estella was in gray, a cotton twill the color of cigarette smoke, with stockings that were darker, and flat-heeled shoes. She wore garnets at her neck and wrist, and in a ring. Her lipstick was the depth of red of the garnets. My side ached where she had struck me, under the rib. Her nails were the color of her lipstick. She did not look innocent. She didn't wish to. I had told her to be colorless, shapeless, demure. She had chosen to look like the woman who last night bit and jabbed and snarled.

Dee walked to Guetterman. She smiled. Her cross-examination was polite, deferential. I had harpooned her shrink, now she would pinion mine. I read her face and smiled, and she saw me, reddened with an instant's anger, and I smiled again. Gotcha, Dee.

She crossed in different ways, each pass from a different angle.

First pass: "Good morning, Dr. Guetterman, and I wonder if we might discuss this matter of roughness in love." Guetterman nodded, opened his mouth to reply. Dee went on. "You have not used the term 'perversion,' and I wonder: what *is* perversion?"

On my feet: "Your Honor, does cross-examination entail the A.D.A.'s questioning Dr. Guetterman on *everything* he didn't say? He hasn't mentioned the football stadium referendum in Buffalo. Or the ice jams last winter in the St. Lawrence Seaway."

"Enough, Mr. Brennan. Thank you for the instruction. Ms. Tillim: he is tedious, but correct. I sustain. You knew I would. I am not a jury, Ms. Tillim. Do not *play* to me."

"Judge, if witness is an expert, and we accept that he is, then we stand to profit from his—"

"Yes, Ms. Tillim. Thank you. You must introduce the term via your own witness, or learned counsel for the defense must do so, before you can cross on it. Surely, Ms. Tillim, this is rudimentary."

"Sorry, Judge. Withdraw. Dr. Guetterman, shall we continue?" Second pass: "Are there many cases of child abuse in this country, in your experience?"

"We know of too many. And there are more, we fear, than we know."

"In your experience and study, Dr. Guetterman, do all the abused children grow up to murder people?"

"Of course not."

"Do many?"

This was when he would say, again, "Of course not," and Dee would point out that Estella Pritchett, the accused, was an aberration, and therefore, since singular, unprotected from general consideration, and therefore, when evaluated singly, a violent woman of perverse habits.

But the good, the wonderful, doctor said, "I would say that many if not most murderers—"

On my feet and shouting: "Objection! Counsel has led the

witness to describe those who may kill, for any variety of reasons, in terms commonly used to depict people convicted of intentionally causing death."

"I can protect myself, Mr. Brennan. Thank you. Dr. Guetterman, it is best, I think, to use a different term."

"Surely," the doctor said. "All I meant was that people who kill—outside soldiers and policemen, you understand—they would, I think, be found to have been somehow abused, abandoned, mistreated when young."

Dee didn't thank him. She dropped her line of questioning.

Third pass: "Are you saying, Doctor, that our world is made up of cruel adults who victimize children and children who are victimized and no one else? Doctor, *I* was never treated that way. I had a *happy* childhood."

Backus looked at me, waiting for me to rage a little. But I smiled in his face.

Guetterman said, "Of course. And I am pleased for you. Therapists do not have a wholly Hobbesian vision of the world. Children are still happy. Elders still are kind. There *is* goodness. I might point out that in her daily work Ms. Pritchett is very—"

"Yes, Doctor," Dee said. "Thank you. I want to return to the basic issue. Does everyone who has been mistreated as a child 'flash back,' I think the term is, to that mistreatment at certain, ah, difficult moments in their adult life?"

"Not consciously, I would say. I do think the past impinges on the present all of the time. But not consciously. No."

"Are you aware, Doctor, that you are threatening civilization?"

Guetterman smiled. Backus arched his brows. I called out my objection. He motioned Dee to proceed. "Be cautious," he said. "I will possibly stop you."

"Yes, Judge. Thank you. I'm simply indicating what Dr.

Guetterman has obviously read in Freud's *Civilization and Its Discontents.* Doctor, Freud's notion of civilization—"

"Ah," Guetterman said, smiling. "Yes. You mean that civilization is based on our renunciation of certain instinctual pleasures."

Dee looked at a paperbound book and then looked up. "So that if we do not renounce things we want, Doctor—"

"Lust for the mother," Guetterman so kindly supplied. "Murder."

"Exactly," Dee said. She smiled. She looked sexy. She looked victorious. "And, in your expert view, Doctor, does not punishment to some degree intervene in the commission of crimes? So that we feel compelled by the prospect of punishment to renounce our, ah, instinctual desires?"

"Your Honor," I said, "if it please the court. I was not aware that I had introduced this witness as a penological expert."

"Within his competence, I think, Mr. Brennan. I'll allow it."

Dee thanked him with warmth. She nodded to Guetterman, and he said, "I think opinions vary. But there are those, surely, who believe that strict penalties are useful. I suppose, then, that you could call them civilizing restraints."

"And, Doctor, if we remove them, we threaten the way we live?"

"Some would say. Yes."

"And if we agree to excuse those who kill, if they have had difficult childhoods, and if so many people in our troubled world have had them, do we not invent an excuse whereby people may kill and circumvent the penalties of our laws?"

"If so many people are so cruel in their behavior, Miss Tillim, I would say that the penalties don't do us so very much good!"

He grinned his little teeth like a professor winning an argument in class: good fun. Dee did not grin back. And the judge nodded ever so slightly, enjoying the fray. Then he frowned. He had just realized, I thought, that she'd wasted his time.

Not your fault, I wanted to tell her. I am older and meaner. And my witness is smart. In a world of logic, you'd win a few points. In the world of Backus, we had each built no more than the almost three dimensions of the putative building on the wall behind his back.

Birnbaum was in the spectator section again. Jack wasn't. And in spite of sophistries and psychiatrists, Dee Tillim, the assistant district attorney, had told the judge through the testimony of her witnesses how the defendant had undeniably killed the man she had fucked with so hard.

Tarsal

FUNNY FEELING of acid in the mouth, saliva too sharp for comfort, too plentiful: the juicy attorney-at-law. Pains in the chest again, but not what they call crushing, not what the disapproving doctor might call crushing. A pain in the chest, a little tingle down the arm, left arm, and of course a man of a certain age is thinking, in order, of angina, heart attack, death.

Smiling juicy attorney-at-law who in rainy weather, today's for example, feels the grating in the foot. Call it the war wound and bravely smile, limping so slightly, and walk ahead bravely in the body-temperature rain. Call it the foot your father caught in the door and see who pins a smile, a wince of sympathy, nod of approval, never mind the Navy Cross, on Goblin-gone-civilian, singing in the rain, though silently, about his wounds.

It was the way he slammed it with both hands when the foot was there on the floor where you'd fallen because of how he'd hit you in the neck just under the ear. It was the way he slammed it the second time because of the way you howled the first time he did it. The pain now in the center of the chest and down on the lower left side above the belt. Pain in the shoulder, down the arm. The foot breaking that way a good many years ago. But call it a war wound. Limp to your office in the early summer rain.

You know, a bone that never properly heals can keep you out of the Marines. It can keep you out of a plane. They can send you home. Your shoes would never fit right. They could never count on your body in emergencies. What if you flew? How would you operate the F-4 rudder pedals? What if you ejected? How would you take the stress on your foot, coming down?

And so on, Reader.

So is it one of the doctors? Luwein, my favorite? Is it more than one? And Birnbaum, by now? Because how can you live with a man who's a secret, who seems sealed away, and yet was the man coming up from behind you in Chicago, his hands on your waist, pulling you back to safety and into him and holding you like that? I see you, Schelle, in the bed at the former Holiday Inn that failed. This is the place about failure, and I see you here in a bed with a man. I hear you tell him, "Do that. Yes. Oh, *do* that." Then I hear the silence between you, and then I hear you weep. I fancy you weeping for me, about me, about the failure at last of what we were for twenty years. I hear that, and then I hear you on the telephone at home: commemoration, stone, the words about war to be chiseled, and how I must give the speech.

Am I sitting with your lover in the former Holiday Inn? Smiling to my witness after drinks, watching Guetterman shake Birnbaum's hand goodbye and row away on his metal sticks and then, alone with your ace reporter and possible lover, I drink my coffee and wince at the pain that comes back up my chest like an echo of the coffee.

"That was interesting," Birnbaum says, indicating with his thick dark hair what's behind us—the cross-examination in court. While Luwein's glasses make him threatening, Birnbaum's glasses give his eyes a boyish and surprised expression, and you have to be careful with him. In spite of the humidity, he wears a summer-weight tweed and chinos, polished brown loafers, no tie, and his notebook and pen are beside his cocktail napkin and his gin.

In front of the dark, uncrowded bar, a somber man on a hardbacked chair is playing an electric guitar with a slide. It's amplified too loudly and so is his voice. He sings that he's going to Carolina. The coffee looks oily on the edge of the cup.

"Dee's a good lawyer," I said. "She should have maybe gone in for research instead of litigation. But that's what all male lawyers are said to say these days about all female lawyers."

"It seemed to me," Birnbaum said, his young square face serious and innocent, his hand dancing on his cardboard-covered notebook, "that she was playing into your hands. She was talking matters of opinion, not law."

"You know the law, Mr. Birnbaum?"

"I know matters of opinion," he said.

"Well, that's expert witnesses for you. Especially psychologists. You can pick and whine and argue, but all you can do is listen to what they say and talk about it, and who are *you* to do that? It's how a jury's bound to think. Though they want to hate the experts. Always. It doesn't fail."

"And that's why there isn't a jury?"

"In part. I've got two more shrinks on call, just in case. I wanted the judge instead of the jury to think about expert testimony. He can afford to not resent it. He figures he's smarter than any experts. Smarter than God. This is off the record, of course. You aren't writing anything about the case, are you?"

He covered the notebook with his hand, like an ear he muffled. He shook his head, smiled his bitter, slightly wounded smile. "No," he said, "I'm here about the unveiling. It's so much about you. I thought I'd see you in action. You're impressive."

"Just a desperate lawyer, Mr. Birnbaum, scared shitless by a felony charge and doing whatever I can."

"I like country-lawyer talk," he said. "I used to love hearing Sam Ervin talk like that. But I don't think he was claiming to be a Marine vet, was he?"

"Sorry? No, I don't know about Senator Ervin. A great defender of the Constitution, I always thought. Brilliant man."

"But not a Marine." Birnbaum leaned forward, both hands on the edge of the table, and stared at me. "I was a PFC," he said. "I was on the ground. I hated it. I smoked a lot of dope and I did body lice one time. I mailed home small amounts of, you know, souvenir things I swiped and traded for: a Kabar, a bra off a Playboy bunny a guy I knew from Fond du Lac got me. Childish shit. I was a child. But I was, the thing is, Mr. Brennan, I was there."

He continued to lean that way and look that way, and his face seemed so concerned for me, so woeful, that I finally smiled.

He said, "You understand me?"

I said, "Yes."

"I mean, you know what it is that I'm saying?"

"Yes."

He looked at me. I smiled at him, and then the dark tastes came up and the sore throb at the top of my chest began. I leaned back and tried to smother the belch, then another one. "Excuse me," I said. Waited for him to crack wise: no excuses, et cetera. But he didn't. I liked him for that, for his worried, young-looking face. I said, "My wife?"

He shook his head, and I thought for a moment he would weep. Maybe I was thinking of you in the former Holiday Inn and in bed with someone, taking your pleasure, making your pleasure, then crying for our loss.

"You're a good researcher," I said.

"No," he said. "It's all very easy, this kind of thing, once you begin to look."

"Why did you begin? Why did you feel you had to look?"

"Forgive me," he said, "but how could you ever think people *wouldn't* look?"

"They never ever did," I said. "I refused to give interviews. I have some clout. I talked to the editors. I threatened, even."

"So nobody ever looked, huh?"

"Absolutely nobody."

"And your wife," he said.

"Schelle."

"Yes."

"She's a great, dear person, Mr. Birnbaum."

"Yes. I wouldn't want to hurt her."

"Nor my children?"

"No," he said. "Not them either."

"But something's going to happen."

He slowly nodded.

"Something has to happen," I said.

"You see, Mr. Brennan, I was there."

"Yes?"

"That's the whole thing," he said. "I was there."

Red Meat

ESTELLA WAS at her house, Sidney Birnbaum was in the former Holiday Inn, and Schelle and I dined out. She had dark brown circles at her eyes. She hadn't slept. Her cheekbones looked pointy, her face very pale. She didn't look worried, she looked ill. I drank tonic water over ice and she drank Scotch. The room was busy but quiet, no one came to gossip or shake hands or do business. It was a gentle weeknight in a second-rate steakhouse, and the beef was sizzling, the potatoes growing limp, the boiled vegetables softening.

"Jack's at the Y-league basketball game," I said. "He says."

"We're going to have to deal with that he-says part of it, aren't we," Schelle said.

Nodded. Sighed. I hadn't words about Jack. I didn't think I could protect him. "Tell me about Mickey, Schelle. Tell me she's all right."

She broke a breadstick and buttered it and put it on her plate. "I can't," she said. "I get sick when I eat."

"Don't be pregnant," I said.

"Don't be ridiculous."

"No. Tell me about Mickey."

"Well, I already did. All I knew. Remember, Mark? We've spoken? Hello, how are you, Mickey doesn't have the HIV virus, and she is still in love with this man who *might* have it. What do we know? And she doesn't admit sleeping with him—"

"I thought she did."

"She told me different this time. She told me they'd kissed, and she barely knew him, and she'd kissed his partner, his—you know."

"Lover."

"Oh, if that's what he is. Mickey's a baby, she really doesn't know. They'd, you know, been friends at work and kids kiss all the time these days. But she never slept with him, she said. She looked so cute, Mark. Little Miss Grown-Up in the City. And *young*. Scared out of her mind. And very sort of *distant* with me. Until I grabbed her and kissed her and we both started to cry. I don't think she knows AIDS from mononucleosis."

Schelle's eyes were full. I said, "You're a great mother, you know. You're a great wife and a great mother."

"I'm wonderful," she said, wiping her eyes with her napkin. "God."

"Well, you are. And Mickey's—did she give you any indication? About seeing this person?"

"Roy."

"Roy."

"Roy Algren. A clean-cut boy from Minnesota with a master's degree in theater arts who came to New York to change American drama. He works at a bookstore and in some Board of Education after-school thing about putting on plays. He's slender."

"Terrific. She'll be seeing him?"

"Yes."

I said to the tonic water, "And the sex part?"

Silence, and I looked to see Schelle shrug. "I don't know. The sex part's always so complicated, it seems, in our family."

I told the tonic, "Yes."

After a while, the kid brought our dinners. We had ordered carelessly and as if we were hungry. Thick, greasy steaks lay before us. I cut into mine and saw the rare flesh.

"I can't either," Schelle said. "We should have ordered a bottle of seltzer and some breadsticks. Yuck. I can't *eat.* What a waste. You shouldn't eat so much red meat, so much cholesterol. We should both be careful."

I pushed at what I'd cut.

"Mark? Do you remember the time we got looped on wine? In the kitchen? It was a little while back. I think I was sort of thinking about getting you in the sack. Don't be uncomfortable, I'm not talking now about the—"

"The sex part."

"Yes," she said. "I'm not. I was remembering. I was wondering. You never drink. You never, ever drink."

"You know why."

"Yes. So I was trying to figure out: why did you drink *that* time?"

"Maybe I was trying to get me into the sack too, Schelle."

"Were you? Do you think so?"

"Probably," I said.

"That's something, isn't it?"

"It is," I said. "It is."

Schelle said, "Mickey will be all right. She doesn't have it, and she'll be all right. It's—but to go all the way to New York and serve lunch to socialites so she could end up doing what *I* do."

"What you do?"

"Nurse people. Take care of people. You."

Ligature

THEN SCHELLE at home with Jack. The last sight of them through the kitchen door on my way to the car: Jack in his heft and wordlessness, his face the pallor of Schelle's, his arm on her shoulders in clumsy embrace. Schelle stood with her back against the kitchen counter, holding a tablespoon filled with antacid for her lurching gut. I saw the liquid spill as he hugged her. I saw her smile with pleasure. I saw them laugh at Jack's clumsiness. She would tell him of Mickey's dilemma. Jack would understand the part about her story. He knew the need to lie.

The rain had only retreated to invisibility above the ground. It was low in the air. Breathing was like sniffing in the spray above the ocean. The moon was hidden, the street lamps were balls of weak light in round bright clouds surrounded by darkness. With the front windows down and the mouth open, panting at the slipstream like a dog on a ride, and bearing his notes, his yellow legal pads, his pens, and other paraphernalia of the profession, there was the former Goblin, the present attorney for the defense, man of major untruths.

Estella was at the door, maybe had stood there for a while. She'd been watching for me, and she was not pleased.

"Do all your clients get this kind of treatment?"

"I'd have to answer no."

"No." She wore a long dark T-shirt cinched loosely with a braided leather belt, no shoes or jewelry. "By which you're telling me how specially I'm treated. But I've been here *alone* all night. You've been catting around with your wife."

"I've been not eating dinner in a restaurant with Rochelle, yes. Catting around?"

"*Fucking* around."

"Can we go in?"

"Are you sure you've time, Mark?"

It takes me a while. I'm slow, I'm stolid, and people might have called me steady except for what they'd learn. But it takes me a while. This wasn't Estella, of course. This was the jealous mistress she'd decided to play.

She pulled at the T-shirt, which hung below her buttocks, and she marched in. You might have said *flounced*, and other words which in the course of this testimony you will be asked to consider. She walked differently. She was dropping her weight hard on her heels, I saw. It made her head ride differently. She sat on her sofa in the dimly lighted living room and lit a cigarette—took it from a wooden box I hadn't seen before and dragged in hard. When she blew the smoke out, her small mouth and thin lips were shaped in a new way. It was as if they had shifted actresses during a film. I kept grinning at her because she did this so well. I said, "You're goddamned accomplished, you know?"

"I'm goddamned alone."

"Jesus," I said. "I don't know who—am I talking to my client, Estella Pritchett, or are you somebody else? It's like you're somebody else."

"Is it?"

"Wait a minute. I saw somebody do that, blowing the smoke up like that. It was in a movie, wasn't it? Jesus. Bette Davis? Isn't it—"

"Crawford."

"Joan Crawford?"

"My favorite bitch," she said.

"So now you're not being her?"

"Now I'm being me."

"I like you better."

"But you don't like me all that well, nevertheless," she said.

"That's not true. Look what, you know—" Waving my big hands around, unable to put them on the words. "Look at what I'm *doing*, will you?"

"You're having the best sex of your life," she said.

"I am?" Really. I said that, and all I can say to you is I never, ever, wanted to cause you pain. This is the most truth I've told: what she said, what I said, what we did. What really went on.

She stood. "I'll give you your choice, counselor. First we rehearse for court, or first we have the best sex of your life."

"And then go over the notes?"

"And then," she said. She didn't wait. She undid the belt and set it on the long coffee table, stubbed her cigarette out on a flat ashtray. She turned her back and walked toward her bedroom. I watched her pull the shirt up over her strong buttocks and her muscled back. She went in. I'm sorry. I went after her.

What else to say is I carried the briefcase: notes and legal pads, pens, citations, testimonies, ligatures. A boy outgrows sneakers every few months, it seems. He limps and winces to show you how tight they are, how worn. Given a new pair, he saves the unwearable former pair and wears them, saving the new ones for unidentifiable special occasions. Jack's closet was carpeted with outworn sneakers. I had the laces of five.

She kneeled on the bed. Watched me undress. When I opened the briefcase, she said, "Oh, Doctor." When I took the laces out, she smiled the sweetest smile. Her face was flushed. She held her hand out and I laid them on her palm. "All wrapped up in white lacing," she said.

"What's wrapped up?"

"You're wrapped up." She wound a lace on my penis and smiled. "You," she said.

What else to say is she tied my ankles first, not uncomfortably. She crawled up between my legs, kissing me. I was crazy with it, and still frightened, and I did, I swear it, I also did think not only about her. But then she was over me and on me. And while she was, she leaned forward like a jockey in the saddle, her *knees on his chest or, you know, the insides of his arms?* and she reached up while my mouth moved like a baby's, automatically, for her nipples, and she slowly tied each wrist to a bedpost.

Rocking, and saying, "All wrapped up," and leaning down and onto me, hovering over my face, and smiling the most innocent smile, Estella said, "Now you just have to let me get this one around—what size's your *neck*, Mark? God, you're big." Leaning back then, and driving me into her, biting her lip: "Big, uh-huh." But soon enough, after I'd bucked, and after she'd slid up on me a little, holding herself with her strong, thin legs in a kind of squat, she put her knees back on my ribs and smiled when I winced. Then she crawled forward on me, leaning on my chest, and pushed the lace under my neck and fiddled with it at my Adam's apple, and started to draw in tight.

"Just say no, Mark."

"No?"

"You know, if it scares you or hurts you. If it doesn't seem *right.* You remember what Mommy in the White House told us: just say no."

"All right."

"Not no?"

"All right."

And she lay on me. She adjusted her thighs and she lay on me and started to move. As she did, and as I moved beneath her, as my arms and legs pulled at the bed and the center of my body responded with motion, she rocked faster and pulled tighter. She said, licking my lips and talking to my mouth, "All right, still?"

"Yes." I'm sorry: yes.

"And now?"

"Jesus. Jesus. Yes."

I was crazy with it. But I was also waiting. I didn't know if either of us would last, but here it came, her face in my underwater vision, things swimming, then darting back and forth, my eyes showing me blurs and colors. Her mouth: suddenly hard, suddenly disgusted. The pressure on my neck now crushing at the larynx, and I started to panic, felt it happening as her hard mouth said, "Oh, yes. Oh, of *course.*"

Wanted to ask, "What?" It was a moan that came up.

"Of *course,*" she said. "Bastard. Weakling son of a bitch. *Now* you say—"

Tried to tell her no. But didn't I want this? Isn't it what I'd pursued? Tell the truth. And don't say no.

"Of *course,*" she said.

She said it from a distance, long distance, my legs were thrashing in place, I felt them, my arms pulled hard at the bed, and I was making noises in my throat. There was too much sensation in the center of my body. Then I thought I was oversleeping with a sore throat, my mother was waking me for school. I heard my name over and over from a distance.

Estella leaned over my face, tears in her eyes and on her cheeks. Mucus bulged from a nostril. Her eyes were enormous, her breath was phlegmy and rich. She was panting, pulling at the ligature I'd brought for her to wrap me in.

She wiped at her nose. "Oh, *excuse* me," she said. Her shoulders and throat and arms seemed flushed. Her hair was fastened with sweat to her temples. She giggled, propped on her arms above me. Then she leaned down, as if doing a push-up, and she nibbled and licked at my throat. She kissed me there and said, "You better wear a high-collared shirt all the time. Someone might be jealous otherwise, seeing what I gave you."

Safety off, and the weapon armed.

Sweating, breathing hard, she closed her eyes on her tears. She smiled.

I told her, "Thank you."

Rider on the Pony in the Air

THE RED she chose to wear when she sat on the stand had to be a joke about the spectators, or about what Dee would ask her on cross, or about the judge's efforts to see her as anything other than a Scarlet Woman. Of course, I had given him the fewest facts I could. Dee had showed him as many as there were. Estella was damned by the facts, already guilty, unless my non-facts, opinions of witnesses and exculpations by circumstance, on which I rested my flimsy case, could be seen by Backus as real. Estella was in a red dress, the blouse of which was large and military in cut, with epaulets of the same material and long sleeves. The skirt was very tight and very short. Before she stood to take the stand, I whispered, "A suicidal dress."

"How appropriate," she whispered back, then slowly walked to the stand. I looked at her face, to read her expression. Her lipstick was the same shade of crimson as the cloth of her dress. Her nails were uncolored and bitten. She often clenched her hands. I'd seen Jack, whose hands, I thought, would also be clenched. He sat among the spectators, pale and unsmiling.

She swore the truthfulness of her testimony. She smiled at Backus, who inclined his head. He looked alert and pleased to see her. Dee, in a tan blazer over a navy skirt and navy pumps, wrote on her legal pad as Estella took her seat. She pulled the microphone toward her and adjusted it. A jury would have hated her. Only a man in his middle age, with a dark hour or two kept secret, would feel something other than antagonism. That was my gamble: that this tough, bellicose woman with her obvious charities and equally obvious effronteries, might interest a man like the judge.

"Good morning, Ms. Pritchett."

"Good morning, Mr. Brennan."

"Ms. Pritchett, do you recall the assistant district attorney cross-examining Dr. Guetterman?"

"Yes, very well."

"Yes. And do you recall the assistant district attorney referring to herself, specifically?"

Estella of course told me that she remembered the reference.

Dee was by then on her feet, calling, "If we may, Judge?"

Backus beckoned us both forward. The stenographer cocked her shriveled head at him and he made a rolling gesture with his hand: keep taking it down.

Dee: "What in hell are you doing to me, Mark? Shit."

Backus leaned over the narrow bench to snarl at her, "Your language, counselor. I'll have decorum in here or I'll have *you* across the street overnight for contempt."

"I apologize, Judge Backus," she said, barely turning to him to say it. "I do. I'm very sorry." To me, she said, "How can you pull all these *tricks*? We're supposed to give him evidence."

"By *him* she means me, I think, Mr. Brennan." She apologized again, but he spoke through her words, "And it *would* be interesting if you remembered that I *am*, in this case, thanks to your strategy, the finder of fact."

"I am trying to present evidentiary material, Your Honor, I assure you. I apologize to the A.D.A., who seems to be taking this matter personally."

"Unlike you," Dee said.

"Both of you!" Backus warned.

"Yes, Your Honor," I said. "My apologies. But my client stands to do some hard time on the banks of the Hudson unless I get to lines of questioning I have in mind. I promise I'll abandon them promptly if you so instruct me—once I've demonstrated what it is. If it please the court."

Backus said to Dee, "If you can detach your personal feelings, Ms. Tillim, from the language in question—though there is this, Mr. Brennan: you were tricky once, with reference to testimony on the record. I will not appreciate seeing the same pony go jumping through the same small, burning hoop."

"No, sir," I said. "Different horse, different hoop, I promise."

Backus said, "You might consider trying the law, and leaving the hoops for circuses."

"No comment, Your Honor," I said. Dee raised her brows at my cheekiness. Backus turned his face down as if he were studying his notes. He looked up, motioned us back to our tables. We thanked him and left.

I resumed. "Ms. Pritchett, I will read, if I may, from the testimony in question. Your Honor, I took the liberty of copying these words from the transcript. If the A.D.A. wishes, however, we can ask the court stenographer to find the appropriate tape."

Dee said, "The People will stipulate that Mr. Brennan is not a crook or a cheat or a liar or a charlatan."

"Nobly stated, Ms. Tillim," Backus said, smiling an instant in spite of himself.

I read, " 'Are you saying, Doctor, that our world is made up of cruel adults who victimize children and children who are victimized and no one else? Doctor, *I* was never treated that way. I had a *happy* childhood.' "

Estella nodded. She licked her lips because, I thought, she was nervous. All she looked was sexy: women in a jury would have disapproved, and men would have resented her power to stimulate them.

"Are those the words you recall, Ms. Pritchett?" I asked.

"Yes," she said.

"Ms. Pritchett, did you, like the assistant district attorney, have a happy childhood?"

"No."

Dee stood. "Judge, I'm sorry, but do we have to go around the Cape of Good Hope in order to get from Utica to Syracuse? Is all of this about that? That she had an unhappy childhood? I didn't know that not being happy was considered an unimpeachable defense."

I said, "Your Honor, if Ms. Tillim believes that the state of her childhood can in any way affect testimony about childhood, and clearly she did, for she mentioned it to my witness, and if she then believes, further, that—we could look at the record, sir. It will show that Ms. Tillim was challenging my witness on the matter of flashbacks to childhood trauma. She leaned on that point, and I think I might therefore be allowed to do the same. I am simply building a foundation, Your Honor."

"I see the same horses jumping, Mr. Brennan. Same hoops."

"Acceptable horse, however, Your Honor. With permission."

"Go on, Mr. Brennan. Ms. Tillim, please don't pout."

"Thank you, sir. Ms. Pritchett, your childhood, unlike that of the A.D.A.—the assistant district attorney, that is—your childhood was, I believe you said, not happy."

"No."

"In what way, Ms. Pritchett? And we are not, I caution you, here to discuss allowances withheld, parties you weren't permitted to go to, things of that nature. I think you know what I mean."

"Yes. No, I'm talking about abuse. Dr. Guetterman talked about it."

"And you are something of an expert on child abuse, are you not? As a caseworker for the county's Department of Welfare, and as a social worker with a master's degree?" Dee was about to comment on my introduction of Estella as an expert witness on her own behalf, I thought. Backus raised his hand, and she sat back.

Estella said, "I know about abuse of children from an adult expert's point of view, and from that of my own childhood."

"Without analyzing the adults' motives, can you describe for the court what you are referring to?"

"Yes."

"Would you, then?"

"Yes." But she only licked her lips and stared into my eyes. I didn't know if she wanted to devour my flesh or take off my clothes or run away. She had a perfect mask of a face for an instant, and then it slipped, and I saw how uncomfortable she was—how embarrassed before the strangers in the courtroom. There was also something deeper, I thought.

"Ms. Pritchett? Would you like a moment to compose yourself? Is this too difficult for you?"

"No," she said. "It is difficult, I mean, but I'll say it. My mother—we had a pantry behind the downstairs bathroom. It was an old house, very old. The cellar was damp. You got down to the cellar by going through the bathroom, through a door at the back of the little bathroom, and there was a small landing before you went down the steps. It was very dark unless they turned on the cellar light. A little bulb is all it was, downstairs, out of sight. But you got a little light from it onto the landing. But she took out the bulb."

"Why?" I asked.

"So, I guess, you know, so when she locked me in the pantry, that little landing, I'd be more scared."

"And were you scared?"

"Very."

"What did you do?"

"Screamed and cried and, after a while, I would throw up. She made me sit in it. The mess. I didn't sit, I stood. She said, 'You sit in it,' but I couldn't. I was too afraid of spiders and snakes from the cellar."

"I meant, Ms. Pritchett, what did you do to earn such enmity, to warrant such punishment?"

"Well," she said, shaking her head, holding one hand clenched beside the other, "what do kids know at six or seven? I still don't know. I didn't know then."

"Were there other punishments—a moment, Ms. Pritchett: how long did these pantry jailings, if I may call them that, how long did they last?"

"Hours and hours and hours and hours."

"Thank you, Ms. Pritchett. I'm sorry. What else transpired?"

"We had one of those old-fashioned rug beaters. The curled metal on the wooden handle? She hit me with that."

"Hard?"

"She broke my wrist. I guess, strictly speaking, I broke it. You know, holding my hand up in front of me."

"To defend yourself."

"Yes."

"Was there more?"

"There was more," she said. She looked pale and exhausted. The lipstick stood out more boldly. She looked like a child who tried to look like a whore.

"And of what did it consist?" I asked.

"She pulled my hair. Out. She pulled out patches of it when I tried to give myself a haircut. She wouldn't send me to the beauty parlor, and I didn't have any money, so I used an issue of *Seventeen* and I tried to give myself a glamorous haircut and she found me doing it. She tore out pieces of hair. Some scalp came away with it."

"And?"

"Oh," she said, sighing it, raising her clenched hands and dropping them into her lap. "There was the time she got unusually angry. 'Disappointed,' she said. 'I'm very disappointed with this behavior,' she said. She had a screwdriver and screws, she was fixing something my father had forgotten to fix. She held a woodscrew between her fingers and she drew it back and forth on my arm and my back and my shoulder. I was coming out of the bath."

"And these depredations, if I may call them that, were frequent?"

"Constant."

"For how long?"

"Until I got too big for her to do it very easily."

"And then?"

"I made her stop. She would come at me and I would charge her, I would put my head down and swing my fists and kick and scratch and scream at her and she wouldn't do it anymore. She'd cry. She'd say—"

Her voice choked off. I said, lower, "These violent reactions to which you allude: did they happen unprovoked?"

"Excuse me?"

"What brought them on?"

"Her. Her violence."

"Did you ever charge, with your head down, as you described, and fight without provocation?"

Dee said, "With all due compassion for the defendant, Judge, Mr. Brennan is leading her through a recitation of purity and innocence that we need not accept as verifiable fact. With all respect."

"Defendant is being asked to recall a state of mind. She is best qualified to recall it. I'll overrule."

I said, "Did you do those things on your own, or did she stimulate them?"

"She," Estella said.

"Thank you. Have you had feelings similar to those you described as your adolescent or preadolescent feelings about self-defense?"

"I don't know. It's hard. There have been times when people have hurt me or tried to hurt me. Physically, I mean. You know, when it felt like I was being attacked. And I reacted with, apparently, violence."

"You don't remember?"

"No. I've been told, afterward, that I was violent and crazy and wild because people were doing things."

"What things, Ms. Pritchett?"

"Social, sexual things. A man danced with me once, years ago, a stranger at a party. He kept, you know, pulling at my waist with his arm, pulling me in against his leg and his—"

"Yes," I said. "And?"

"They pried me off him. He was on the floor and his face was bloody. I'd socked him in the nose." The spectators tittered, and somebody clapped.

"Never," boomed Backus. "*Never.*" They fell as silent as chastised schoolchildren.

"And you didn't remember what had transpired?"

"Not much, no. It's kind of a—it's a blackout."

"You recall Dr. Guetterman discussing and describing flashback episodes?"

"Yes."

"That sort of experience, then?"

"Yes."

"Judge," Dee said, "if she would just tell us she's innocent, we could all go home."

"I don't see this testimony as irrelevant, Ms. Tillim," he said. "And witness may, after all, be cross-examined."

I said, "So, Ms. Pritchett, you have had these flashbacks to trauma experienced earlier in your life—events similar to those described by Dr. Guetterman as common to those who have had experiences like yours?"

"Yes."

"Thank you—Ms. Tillim, it's on the record, it's been introduced, Dr. Guetterman described such flashbacks at length, and you yourself have in effect stipulated Ms. Pritchett's expertise. Surely, you admitted Dr. Guetterman's description of her expertise, from his own expert point of view, into testimony." I rushed on, before Backus could stop me. "Ms. Pritchett, you know these cases of which I speak?"

"Yes," she said.

"Are there recent such matters that are part of your professional knowledge?"

"A few weeks ago, a Marine, a former Marine, he'd been in Vietnam. He was arrested because he shot two men who were breaking into his car. He killed them," she said.

"Because of the flashback? Because war stays with you? Because even when you think it's over it isn't, am I right? That very often you can't end a war—or the stress of 'battles' in civilian life."

She recited, "Like war. Very much like war."

Dee was about to comment on my shameless leading of the witness. I shouted, "Life, ordinary life, can feel like combat, you're saying. And people *could* be affected by the civilian equivalent of post-traumatic stress."

"I suppose so," she said innocently.

Cardiac

DEE ON CROSS was in battle. She stood in front of the stand, a foot from Estella. She crossed her arms in front of her and clasped her own biceps. From the back, she looked like someone being hugged by a lover. No good morning, et cetera, no gestures of even insincere good will. "Ms. Pritchett, how did Lawrence Ziegler die?"

Brennan for the defense, laying down fire while the troops retreated: "If I may, Your Honor. Doesn't it seem that the A.D.A. is standing awfully close to the witness? Doesn't her posture and proximity strike Your Honor as belligerent and intimidating?"

Backus said, "Ms. Tillim, are you attempting to intimidate the defendant?"

"Yes, Judge, I am."

"Don't," he said.

"I am complying with reluctance," Dee said.

"How astonishing," Backus replied, smiling. Women were his favorite people, I thought.

"With your permission," she said to Backus, and then she went on. "How did your lover die, Ms. Pritchett?"

"I don't know the medical details," Estella said. She lifted her chin. Each of her hands was a fist. "But I think he had a, I don't know, heart attack?"

"Heart attack."

"Yes, apparently his heart stopped."

"Apparently it did," Dee said, talking to the judge, then looking back to Estella. "When you die, your heart stops. But the cause, Ms. Pritchett, according to the county coroner's office, was asphyxiation. Your lawyer didn't mention the coroner's report. An oversight, I assume."

"Objection," I said. Backus sustained. Dee bowed her apology, a quarter-inch nod.

She said, "Apparently, there were fibers of cotton in his nostrils."

"I wouldn't know about that," Estella said.

"You wouldn't. Why, Ms. Pritchett, I'd have assumed that you knew *all* about all of Mr. Ziegler's body."

I was on my feet, and the backs of my legs had shoved the chair back to the bar separating me from the spectators. I felt Jack's eyes. I'd seen Schelle's and Birnbaum's. But Backus had already begun to admonish Dee.

Dee said, "Yes, Judge." To Estella: "Can you think of any reason for Mr. Ziegler to have cotton fibers in his nose? During the course of your, ah, lovemaking, was it customary for one of you to put a pillow near your nose?"

The courtroom tinkled with embarrassed or titillated sounds. Backus stared the spectators into silence.

Estella said, in a monotone, "Ms. Tillim, in certain positions when men and women make love, it is not uncommon to lay your face down into a pillow."

Dee flushed.

"The *man*?" she asked.

"You'll have to, you know, consult your own experience on that, Ms. Tillim." Dee smiled. She looked at Backus, who stared back.

Dee said, "But you have no other ideas about how those fibers—"

"Your Honor, may I ask whether the A.D.A. must repeat the question yet again? It seems to me that Ms. Pritchett has answered it."

"Judge, she told the officers at the scene that things got rough and she thought maybe she did it. I'm trying to establish that at *that* time, anyway, the defendant was telling the truth."

Backus said, "Yes, Ms. Tillim, but apparently you aren't going to have much luck. I think you should move along."

No courtesy for the judge from Dee, only an angry shrug of the torso she held hard before Estella. She put her hands, then, on the desk of the recorder, who looked up. Dee moved a step backward, the recorder looked to her keyboard, and Dee said, "Are you a violent woman?"

"No."

"No fits of temper?"

"I have a temper. Doesn't everyone?"

"When do you lose your temper, Ms. Pritchett?"

"When I'm attacked, Ms. Tillim."

"Are you losing it now?"

"Oh, dear, no. I mean when, say, you know what I do, what my work is. When I go into some terrible unlighted apartment building or someplace, a trailer out in the woods, say. Some man is drunk and he's flailing around with a stick at his son, beating him. Or I find a baby, some pediatrician or the hospital ER calls me and I find a baby with cigarette scars up and down its little back and all over its thighs and buttocks. That's when I lose my temper."

"Very moving," Dee said. "You do a noble job well, I'm certain. You lose your temper, may I say, over injustice?"

"I don't—I can't tell you what the word is. Sure. Why not? Injustice."

"Would injustice include the case of a man"—she consulted the typed report she drew from the edge of the prosecution table—"weighing two hundred forty-four pounds who abuses or 'plays rough' with a woman of, oh, what do you weigh, Ms. Pritchett? Well, never mind. You're a petite woman. You're not two inches over five feet, are you? I can't imagine you weigh too very much. Would that be injustice? Would that cause you to lose your temper?"

"It did. All right?"

"It did," Dee said. "Thank you. What did you do when you lost your temper with your lover?"

"I said he should stop it."

"Stop what, Ms. Pritchett?"

"What he was doing to me."

"What was that, Ms. Pritchett?"

Estella looked at me. I said, "Your Honor, is this necessary?"

"Seems relevant to me, Mr. Brennan."

I shrugged my shoulders at Estella, as if to signal, What the hell.

She looked at me hard, then at Dee. Estella said, "He was pinching my nipples very hard. He was ripping at my breasts. Punching my breasts. He tore the skin off my back."

This time the courtroom stayed silent. This was what they'd come for.

"Did you ask him to stop it?"

"Yes."

"Several times?"

"Yes."

"And he didn't?"

"He did it harder. He did it more. He put my arms behind my back and he held them there and was on top of me. It felt like my arms were breaking. He leaned on me. And he pulled and pinched and yanked and punched at me. He smiled and laughed. He cursed at me."

"And what did you do, Ms. Pritchett?"

"I cried."

"Yes."

"I called him names."

"Yes."

"And he was panting. It was like he couldn't breathe. His eyes were rolling back in his head. It was frightening."

"Is this what your lawyer means by 'playing rough'?"

"I don't know."

"Isn't that what you said? The words you used?"

"Maybe. Yes. If I did, that isn't what I meant."

"How so?"

"When the two of you are agreeing to it and it's kind of exciting, that's one thing."

"But this was another?"

"I would say that. Yes."

"So what did you *do,* Ms. Pritchett?"

"I watched him get very pale. White, all of a sudden. His lips looked kind of blue. *Purple.* He couldn't breathe. Then he passed out or died, I don't know."

"On top of you?"

"Yes."

"Was it difficult to extricate yourself?"

"Yes."

"But you managed."

"Yes."

"And then?"

"I called the police and put some clothes on."

"Did you try to assist Mr. Ziegler? In case he wasn't dead?"

"That was what I did first. I tried mouth-to-mouth resuscitation. Oh!" She actually snapped her fingers and widened her eyes. "Maybe that's when the cotton, you know, from the bedding? Maybe it got into his mouth when I tried to make him breathe. Because I'd been face-down during the—earlier on."

"Ms. Pritchett, I said the fibers were in his nose. How did you know they were also in his mouth?"

"I thought that's what you said."

"No, it isn't, Ms. Pritchett."

"Well, it doesn't matter, Ms. Tillim. I was only trying to be helpful."

"Thank you very much, Ms. Pritchett. And did you tell the officers who arrived that you'd had rough sex and that maybe you killed him?"

"I meant the—you understand. I meant the physical exertions that led to his heart attack. I didn't mean specifically when he'd been hurting me."

"When you lost your temper over the injustice."

"Well, you said that's what it was."

"You agreed," Dee whipped back at her.

"Sure," Estella said, "whatever you say."

Dee was red again. Her arms were clasped across her chest again. "Your confession is on the record," she said. She sounded like someone daring someone else to fight.

Estella's eyes got wider again. She said in a gentle voice, "I never meant that to be a confession," she said. "Did I really sign a confession? I was just saying—*you've* done that over things that went bad. Hasn't everyone? I just meant that I thought if we hadn't begun making love, he wouldn't have died."

Dee said, "*That,* I'm certain, is a true statement, Ms. Pritchett. I think he wouldn't."

Redirect

I SAID, "May we redirect very briefly, Your Honor?"

He looked at me with puzzlement. By letting Dee take Estella through the events of the death, I had helped her to shake her own case. Anger your enemy's general and confuse him, says Sun Tzu. I knew that Backus thought I was threatening my gains. Silence ought to be my ally. He was right. But what I needed, now, was not for the sake of the case. It was for me.

I said, "I have only one more matter to trouble you with, Ms. Pritchett. Earlier, in your description of your childhood, you hardly touched on your father."

"My mother did those things I was recalling."

"Because, to use her word, she was 'disappointed.' "

"Yes."

"With you or your father?"

"We aren't talking about my father," she said. Her voice was low and hard. "We didn't agree to talk about my father. I said I wouldn't."

"Yes. But I am your attorney, Ms. Pritchett. And it is my responsibility to construct the best possible defense in your behalf."

"And I'm myself. And I won't answer another question."

"Ms. Pritchett, I have to ask you this. Is it because your father was raping you that your mother punished you? Because she couldn't punish him or didn't want to? Was afraid to?"

Estella sat without speaking or moving. Her head suddenly tilted to the left, as if her spine had lost its strength. Then she recovered her posture. The color of her face was closer to yellow than white. Her eyes looked bleak. She was biting her lips. I realized that, for the first time during the trial, Backus was pounding with his gavel on the rounded marble block to silence the spectators. He admonished them as their buzzing declined. Estella stared at me from the stand. Her color had grown slightly ruddier, but she looked as though she was going to be ill. Around her eyes were blue shadows. She was armed.

Backus said, "We're going to stop now, Mr. Brennan. I'm going to permit your client to rest. We're not going to follow this line of questioning unless you can demonstrate that your client is assisting in its formulation. I would suggest you speak with her so that I needn't do so."

After a while, I heard him. "Mr. Brennan?"

"Yes, sir. Sorry. Yes."

He said, "Ms. Pritchett," very gently. "You're excused."

She started, turned in her chair to look at him. I watched his face. He was going to let her off, I'd have bet. And then someone else would have to do it all over again.

Estella didn't leave. She turned from him to me. Dee paused beside me at the table's edge. She rested her stacks of folders next to my hand. I looked away from Estella's eyes at Dee's. She said, "Counselor, your client really looks pissed. Make sure she doesn't tuck your napkin around your neck too hard at lunch."

Summation

WE ATE TOGETHER. She didn't talk. I ordered for her and she pushed the food into arrangements on her plate. I didn't eat either. It was coming. It was coming. Jack and Schelle and Sidney Birnbaum had left the courtroom together. It was coming. Backus made us work to finish fast. Dee summarized before him with her hands in motion, not clutched across her body. Dates, times, deputies' reports, hard data: body, defendant's presence and involvement, over and out. "The People's case is solid. Its basis lies in fact. The defendant relies on fuzzy opinions. Did she or did she not cause decedent's death? She herself assays herself as guilty. You should, Judge, with respect, do no less."

I was ready, then, to strut the holes and assumptions and fallacies in Dee's thinking for Backus. But Dee wasn't done. Estella sat still beside me. Her fingers, under the table, shifted from the hem of her skirt to the filigreed edgework of the table's drawer to brush, once, at my leg.

"Finally, Judge, now that we've said what's simple and true—that he died and she caused him to—it seems fitting to point out, with no disrespect intended for anyone, that Mr. Brennan and, indeed, his client, her own expert witness I daresay, have given us cause to think of what is *not* the law. We have justifications for taking people's lives. We have war as peace and peace as war, and wouldn't George Orwell have enjoyed this echo of his *1984*? As if, because soldiers are afflicted, then civilians may be—*must* be—too. Because it suits the defendant's need to justify what is finally quite simple: killing another human being. Whether or not that person was big. Whether or not that person was cruel. Many men are large and cruel. They are supposed to be safe from being killed. But in this dubious reminder of a tormented past, in this presentation of cruelty and sorrow, we are asked to find not only a *reason* for wrongful death, but an *excuse*!

"Judge, do we deal in our courts with the law? Or must we tell our nightmares to each other? Laws are not to be broken. Anything else, outside of the law, is just words, just stories. Thank you."

Closing Argument

FIFTEEN YEARS AGO I wrote my will. You may remember. I wrote yours and you signed it at home, and I brought it back to the office for witnessing. Then I filed it in the vault. And then I started my own. It was to be a document as simple as the one I'd written for you. But sitting here, then as now, I began to talk to you. In my head, I was talking from the other side of my death. I started to tell you. I started to weep. I had to wait some time to finish the will. I did. It's filed in the vault, next to yours.

In the car after we had walked from the courthouse, across the green, past the monumental stone with its part-finished lettering, when we were driving away, I told Estella, "One more conference. At the Stone's Throw. All right?"

She didn't refer to the courtroom, the redirect, my treasonous guess about her father. She didn't object. She sat beside me, pale and silent, and I drove. When we were in the country, going slowly on the two-lane road, she put her stubby fingers with their chewed nails on my thigh. They rested there, exhausted obedient children, until I left her house.

She will be in the room at the Stone's Throw Motel. She'll know I've reserved the same room. She'll collect the key and go inside and wait for me. I don't know exactly what she will wear. Her clothing will be dark, I predict. There will be no lights on. She'll be there in maybe black silk pajamas, I think. Yes. Black silk pajamas, and no lights, and the ribbons she thought to buy. Maybe black silk ribbons this time. I will have the laces. They were coiled in my brief bag during the trial. They were there with my notes and the blank yellow pads with their line after line and the pen, the ink.

Goblin?

He is driving there directly. Wearing the summer-weight poplin navy blue suit with the button-down blue oxford shirt, the tie with its olive and navy rep design. The collar is open to ease the pressure on the bruised neck. I will drive there directly in these clothes and, in the room at the Stone's Throw, take them off and hang them in the closet, fold my socks and underwear and set my wingtip shoes, aligned, on the soiled carpet at the foot of the bed. In the dark I will do this, and then take the laces from the bag and we will not have spoken.

Her pale face will glow in the room. Or her body will, if she takes her pajamas off. I think that she will wait for me to take them off this time.

I think that she will bite at me more than kiss me. I think that she will slap open-handed and punch, she has done this, in wide clumsy swings of her small fists. I can hear her fists as they land on my chest and ribs and face. And then I think we will both be naked on the bed with its harsh sheets and thin blanket and flat pillows, and on our knees face to face, kissing, you would call it. She will chew at me and scratch. I'll defend myself by holding her, and she'll permit me that defense. We'll grapple while clutching each other, fight while making love.

Whatever we do, it will be extreme. It will be the lovemaking of loneliness. It will be noisy and liquid and wordless in the dark. We'll drive each other, and we'll be alone. Sooner or later, with her mouth and fingers working on me, it will happen. I will lie on my back with my arms and legs bound to the bed. She knows how to tie a man's arms to the metal frame beneath the motel mattress. She, moving on me, liquid and wordless, will draw me up and in and on.

Then: *"Bastard!"* she'll cry. Or anything else. But she will cry at me, she will lie on me or next to me, ride me, pummel me. She will state her grievances. And then, soon enough, not lie beside me or simply on me: she will be pierced by me, we'll be wounded together. And the terrible sensation, it is so lush, so *filling*, as the bites and scratches and jabs increase, as the nipples are torn and the flesh of the belly, the soft skin under the arms, is torn, as the pressure drives up and in, and the lace drawing tight on my throat, and the vision going, sound going, and then the long shudder, then death.

This time, she will do it.

There will be an unveiling. I'm a very good story. Sidney Birnbaum will say what he knows, but he will not say why. I'll be found in the shape of an X on the bed. And there are never reasons. There are pleadings, representations, and motions. There are grievances, there are awards. There are findings of fact and of law. But there are no reasons.

You should not linger in desolate ground, Sun Tzu instructs us. When I stop this, I will drive to the Stone's Throw Motel. You will soon enough read this. I'll be naked on the bed. She will not have cushioned my ankles or my wrists. She'll have left five laces on.

Vietnam, Schelle, and now you know I made it up. And then the dreams made me up, and then Rochelle Courbet Brennan, the girl of my dreams, was the wife of the Goblin, he lived in his dreams, his dreams dreamed *him.* I flew to them as aviators went to the war that really happened. And I lived there. And I do not want to live there anymore, or anyplace else.

Dear Schelle, who reads this: I would have saved you from it, you and Mickey and Jack, but I could not.

I apologize also for Estella. And if she fails to end me, I will do it by myself. I will do it, I am sorry, for myself.

Because what, now, could I ever do for you?

Dear Reader, dear Rochelle.

The innocent are not protected.

Closing Arguments

FREDERICK BUSCH

A Reader's Guide

A Conversation with Frederick Busch

Karen Novak *is a writer and teacher living in Mason, Ohio, with her husband and their two daughters. Her first novel,* Five Mile House, *was published in October 2000. She's currently at work on her second.*

KN: When you started down the path of this narrative, did you know where it was headed?

FB: I knew where I was going with this one. Sometimes I have to write my way into (and out of) a book. Sometimes I have to write it many times before I understand where it ought to go, how it ought to work. But this time I knew. I found a clipping, about two years before the publication of the novel that concerned a man—not a lawyer—who had constructed a story like Marcus's. He killed himself. His wife discovered his body, and a great pile of paper—a manuscript he left behind. I wanted so very much to read that manuscript! I couldn't, of course. So I wrote it. It's *Closing Arguments.*

KN: So, Marcus Brennan is lying—or is he?

FB: Marcus has been lying since the war he never served in. When he writes his closing argument, the summation of his "case," his brief on behalf of his client, in other words, he is telling the truth. The way to find out is to figure out the identity of his client: he, himself, whom he accuses, judges, finds wanting, but seeks to explain. In the place of a jury or judge, he places "the reader," "Dear Rochelle"—terms he uses interchangeably and even together. They are fused for him—or at least for me. Marcus directs, as do I, the pleading of his argument to Rochelle, whom he loves and whom he has crushed and exhausted and to whom he feels innumerable obligations and emotions. He calls her his "dear Reader," and the reader—the audience for this novel—might also feel as if Marcus is directing his history and commentary to them. I hope that happens.

This fiction is about the relationship of the author, who has lied, who does lie, but who also tries to shape the truth—that is, who creates a fiction—while, at the same time, it is about the loving, despairing, powerful, dangerous relationship between two characters who started out in love, who now are left with only the tatters of their love, and who cannot leave it behind them. They are connected to the end. Rochelle as well as the reader—she is Marcus's reader, just as you, the reader, are mine—will be the last person named in the book.

All fiction lies. All artful fiction lies in order to tell some truth. Marcus is both a liar and a man of decency. The novel is about decency and its loss, and it is about lying in order to get at the truth. So, is Marcus lying? Absolutely. And absolutely not.

KN: Concerns of telling and not telling, lying for protection and the lie of protection, wind as strong currents through much of your work. In *Closing Arguments*, however, you state it directly: "The best defense is a good story" but "The innocent are not protected." Pretty naked declarations.

FB: My "naked declarations" are about the two currents of concern that brought me to write the novel. One is the nature of the interaction between the reader, who seeks information, and the writer, who decides how it is dispensed, which I wished to examine without boring myself or my reader to death. That was a subconscious concern, apparently. For I set out, simply, to tell the story of Marcus and Estella and Rochelle, their family, their histories, their small-town world, and Marcus's remarkable misdeeds. When I reread some of the book, during the writing of my first draft, I understood the very simple shape of my book: a lawyer writes on his legal pad at night, alone in his office (just as Richard Nixon, one of the authors of the Vietnam madness, wrote on one in his), confessing to himself the reality of his acts and the truths of his being. But what struck me as not simple was the way in which the novel seemed to indirectly be commenting on the way stories are told, on how the reader reacts to the writer, whom he or she cannot quite trust but on whose every word the reader must rely. As Marcus addressed his wife, whom he loved and betrayed, to whom he had lied and to whom he now wished to address the truth, I heard the voice of the writer addressing the reader—whom he loved ardently and who maybe felt betrayed by the writer who is always talking, talking, talking. Is that meta-fiction? Postmodern fiction? Nah. It's the way it always has been: I love you; I am wooing you; I know that you don't thoroughly trust me, though I want you to.

KN: You use the horror of Vietnam on multiple levels to convey a sort of "ripple effect" in the tragedy of Marcus Brennan and his family. There's more than historical reference at work here?

FB: Equally important to me is the requirement of civilization that we must—if we are to think of ourselves as civilized—protect our young and those who cannot defend themselves. Life is a bully. Our contemporary life is so crowded—you are never alone: TV and the Internet see to that—and will not permit small or sick or scared or needy people to live without oppression. The Vietnam War not only oppressed the civilians of Southeast Asia; it killed a lot of, and it bent and perhaps even broke a generation. It changed the way we conduct our business as a government, and the way we respond to the actions of our government. It sent a generation of young black men to die or be maimed or changed horribly within their skulls. It blew up a generation of white men. In doing so, it tattered countless white and black and brown and yellow families.

I try, in my novels, to consider both the domestic and the larger, public, arenas of our interior and civic concerns. While I examined the big world of the Vietnam War, I wanted, as well, to examine the small—that of Marcus and Estella, that of Marcus's family. I wanted to think of individual children who are terrorized by adults, whose days are nightmares and whose nights are inconceivable. I hate bullies. I am drawn to the defense of littler people. It's probably some terrible adolescent self-pity of mine, but it has influenced a lot of my decisions. Since I am not built for the wearing of tights and a cape, I try, in my fiction, to do what I can about the defense of those I call the innocent.

KN: Do you consider Marcus one of the innocents?

FB: Marcus has been trying to protect what innocence is left in him, and in Estella, and, by extension, in the world. As corrupt as he is, he is also what is left of a good man—or, believe it or not, of a man trying to find out how to be good. My generation was blighted by the Vietnam War just as Marcus, the individual, was. In a time of cruelty of the large against the small—or a time when we are more aware of it, anyway—the novel is concerned with defending what innocence can be preserved. While Marcus behaves badly, he is also aware of the requirement that he try to be good.

KN: The character of Estella serves as the embodiment of huge and destructive forces in Marcus's life. In Dickens's *Great Expectations*, another Estella serves much the same role for

Pip in another story of falsified identities. What is the design behind the association?

FB: Yes, there was some design. I have always loved and feared Estella. During my youth—and I think I'm not the only man who can say this—I met an Estella or two. Oh, she wasn't necessarily corrupted by a parent or foster parent playing God, re-creating her so that she was an instrument of revenge, like the Estella whom Pip loved so desperately. But I knew girls and women whose sorrows and angers made them glow for me, drew me to them, and get burned because the glow was from some emotional fire. There is a sorrow in Dickens's Estella that is romantic and profound; it reverberates in male readers, who wish to possess her, and in female readers, who wish to wield that power. And that novel of education, acquisition, growth, and accretion is also one of the great novels of loss. Estella is about loss. Marcus loves and knows he must lose, and lose himself to, his Estella. And as she is the instrument of Miss Havisham's punishment of the world in *Great Expectations*, she is the instrument for Marcus of his own punishment in *Closing Arguments.* I named my character Estella as a salute to Dickens, whose work I revere, and as a salute to the women I knew who were creatures of sorrow and loss, and as an acknowledgment of loss itself as part of the experience of romantic love.

KN: **You obviously invested much time and care in pinpointing the accuracy of detail in the courtroom and in the jungle. How important is research to your fiction?**

FB: Research: I love it. It keeps me from having to do the tough work of writing the book. I live in the library, I wander along maps, I drive or fly with Judy—she has the family sense of direction—to look at places where I will locate certain events. Finally, I'm filled with facts—or filled with enough, anyway, to start. I then ventriloquize the characters in my book as they live on the landscape that is both actual and imagined. I believe in the physical actuality of my characters' worlds so that my reader will find them plausible. I visited a courthouse not unlike the one I describe in *Closing Arguments.* Judy took photographs of it so that I might see it as I wrote. I have always read a lot about Vietnam, but I wanted to know the airplane Marcus recalls flying in, and to know the countryside into which he plummeted when his plane was brought down. And I wanted to honor the physical truths of the war that was so cruel to so many; it was a way of honoring the wounded and distressed and dead of that conflict—to get its details right. Writers who are friends whom I admire, Toby Wolff and Tim O'Brien, served there; Ward Just, with his notebook and camera, lived under fire there. You honor the people who were there by at least observing with some accuracy the small physical truths of their service to us.

KN: Do you ever find that desire for accuracy to be an obstacle in terms of creating fiction?

FB: I try to get the physical detail and historical research right—whether I am writing about Melville in my native New York City, or about characters living in the landscape of upstate New York. But I find it important not to confuse physical accuracy—which is part homage, part a craftsman's desire to achieve plausibility—with psychological truth. I reserve to myself the right to make the characters in their place do what I need them to do. I have to trust my conscience—and it is a wrathful and merciless conscience—to see that I am not merely writing something self-aggrandizing because I like to play God (which is a role available to writers). I insist that I serve my characters and my readers. I want to honor them. I want to show them something entertaining, convincing, true-feeling. I cannot do any of this if I am cavorting about in praise of myself. The novels are for them, about them, in service of them.

KN: How do you feel about *Closing Arguments* in terms of your other work? Did you enjoy writing these characters, their stories?

FB: I think that *Closing Arguments* marks the beginning of a concentration by me on first-person narratives that have in common an increasing darkness of vision, and a craftsman's interest in seeing what I can do with aspects of first-person storytelling; yet the focus remains on Marcus's concern for "the innocent," or "the undefended." And while that concern, I've been told, runs through my work, it's my feeling that the heat and pitch and overall urgency of that concern comes to the fore, as maybe not in the past, with *Closing Arguments*, then *Girls*, then *The Night Inspector*. In the case of *Closing Arguments*, I did not "enjoy" the writing. I didn't like living inside of such conflict, and my characters' darknesses frightened me—for I knew that if I could invent them, then I had some, maybe much, of them inside myself. Still, I was drawn to write that novel, and I wanted to write it well. I also knew that if I gave myself an excuse, any kind of pause, I might well find ways of not returning to the cruel psychic countryside of the book. So, as I got close to being done, Judy—my dear enabler—and I drew up the moat: we visited no one from May through September of the year I turned the book in; we permitted none of our friends to visit with us, and that period was like being in a foreign country without its language. We spoke to ourselves, and I spoke with my characters, and the book made its way forward to the last page. I'm glad I worked that way, in that profound immersion, because I think I wrote it truly. I think the novel is as faithful to Marcus, to his children, to Rochelle, to Estella as I could make it. I brought such troubles down upon them; the very least I could do was give them all of my devotion.

Reading Group Questions and Topics for Discussion

1. In the entry entitled "The Braid," Marcus Brennan recounts watching his mother braid her hair. Do you see any significance between that memory and the way Brennan structures his narrative? What are the strands of narrative in the novel? By using this structure, what does Frederick Busch accomplish in terms of directing the reader's experience of Brennan's story?

2. The novel contains many scenes of characters being compelled to write "the truth" and then having their writing and the motives behind it questioned. How does this color your response to the novel, which is itself another truth-telling? Is this final version of Brennan's "truth" credible to you? Why?

3. Where do you place Brennan's captivity, his interrogation, and torture in the time frame of the narrative? Are these his manufactured memories or a metaphor for his current life? When exactly is Goblin shot down? Do the characters in the jungle scenes have counterparts in Brennan's exterior life?

4. When Marcus and Estella meet for the first time, he notices that she brightens, literally, after he rudely derides the disapproving prison guard: "I turned back to my client. She was beaming. Color came into her face, even her lips, which had been quite pale. Her eyes looked lively for an instant." What is being communicated between the two of them here? Discuss how the ebb and flow of Estella's association with certain colors translates into an emotional barometer over the course of the novel.

5. What does the violence of Estella and Marcus's relationship unlock for him?

6. The image of shoes is repeated with growing importance as the novel progresses. Discuss the way the image gains importance as the story unfolds. What do you make of Marcus stealing the laces from his *son*'s shoes to carry out his final plans?

7. Every member of the Brennan family seems isolated from the others, trapped in his or her own inescapable web of stories, and yet they try to touch one another through the context of their falsehoods. Identify those stories and the way they are used by each character to both reach out and stay safe simultaneously. What does it say about Marcus that he is so slow to comprehend that his daughter has been lying to him?

8. Which of Brennan's actions, if any, do you find defensible? Is he a sympathetic character? Empathetic? Is there any particular point in his confession at which you felt his character was beyond redemption? What of the other characters? Can you distinguish a single, overarching motive that unites these people?

9. War takes on an agency here that makes it more of a character than a setting. Consider where Brennan's references to war appear: the jungle and the courtroom. Consider also the moment in which he first sees and then "rescues" Rochelle at the antiwar demonstration. Why does Marcus, who never went to war, associate with it so intensely? Why do you think Marcus chose law as his profession?

10. In her closing argument for the prosecution, the assistant district attorney states, "Laws are not to be broken. Anything else, outside the law, is just words, just stories." Discuss this idea in terms of what you've learned about the idea of story through the novel.

11. In the end, do you think Marcus was more fearful of being found out a liar or having to own up to the abuse of his

childhood? Does this offer any clue as to his understanding of how to arm "the weapon" that is Estella? Which is the more dreadful admission: what we did or what we couldn't do?

12. You the reader are the "Dear Rochelle" to which the novel is ultimately addressed. Taking the intimacy of this shared perspective to its natural conclusion, how do you respond to Marcus and this novel? What is your closing argument?

THE ART AND IMAGINATION OF

LANGSTON HUGHES